all my
fault

BOOKS BY EMMA ROBINSON

The Undercover Mother

Happily Never After

One Way Ticket to Paris

My Silent Daughter

The Forgotten Wife

My Husband's Daughter

His First Wife's Secret

To Save My Child

Only for My Daughter

To Be a Mother

My Stepmother's Secret

Please Take My Baby

She Has My Child

all my fault

emma robinson

bookouture

Published by Bookouture in 2024

An imprint of Storyfire Ltd.
Carmelite House
50 Victoria Embankment
London EC4Y 0DZ

www.bookouture.com

ISBN: 978-1-83790-875-2
eBook ISBN: 978-1-83790-874-5

For Sarah
My lovely friend

ONE

In a garden full of roses, why is it always the most beautiful bloom that breaks its stem?

Joanna snipped the heavy yellow flower with slightly more aggression than was necessary and dropped it into the basket by her side. Even that made her think about Charlotte – her red-cheeked enthusiasm when she'd presented it as a Mother's Day gift a lifetime ago – and her anxiety about today dialled up a notch. She shifted her position further along the flower bed, knees wet and stained by the damp grass. As an act of distraction, this wasn't working.

It was already late afternoon, but Charlotte had said she would be here. She'd even reminded her last week. 'It's the fourteenth of April next Sunday.'

'I know, Mum. I wouldn't forget Dad's birthday. I'll be there. I promise.'

But that was before the conversation in the hall. Before she'd said those awful things. Asked her not to bring *him*. And now it had been a week and their only communication had been brief text messages. No kiss at the end.

'Ouch!' A thorn scraped her arm as she reached into the

rosebush. Blood bloomed through the torn skin. Dammit. Now she'd have to clean that off and get a plaster.

Leaving the basket by the back door, she flicked her muddy Crocs from her feet into the little covered shoe rack that Steve had made. She'd only had to complain once about not wanting her outdoor shoes to fill with water in the rain before he'd created a solution. Not before he – and Charlotte – had teased her mercilessly about the Crocs to begin with. 'What if someone sees you in them? The shame!' The image of them laughing together made her smile despite the sting in the memory's tail.

In the kitchen, the green plastic medical box in the corner cupboard contained an unopened box of plasters. One good thing about living alone was that everything was where you'd left it. Perhaps the only good thing. The arguments she'd had with Charlotte – and Steve – over the years about putting things away when you'd finished with them. What she'd give now to see Steve's car keys, spare change and random nails and screws dumped on the work surface. Or Charlotte's toys strewn across the sitting room like a parent death trap.

According to the kitchen clock it was 5 p.m.; later than she'd thought. Sundays were so quiet around here that hours could pass without her realising. The weekdays were fine – the house and garden kept her busy and then there was book club – but the weekends dragged. Even more so since Charlotte's visits had started to get shorter, always hurrying back to that ridiculous apartment. To him.

Cut cleaned and dressed, she filled the kettle, but when she opened the fridge there was no milk. As the only person drinking it, she rarely bought more than a two-pint carton these days. Steve's addiction to breakfast cereal meant that they used to get through pints of it, but not any longer. If she wanted tea, she'd have to change out of these gardening clothes and get to the shop before it closed.

On the hall table, her fiftieth birthday cards were still cheerfully stood to attention around the framed family photograph of their last foreign holiday together. How happy they looked. Steve – his deep tan from the Sorrento sunshine making his sandy hair blonder and his blue eyes more piercing. Charlotte, in her favourite coral bikini, her father's double in every way, eyes alive with her zest for life. And Joanna, chin-length hair lightened by the copper highlights Charlotte had persuaded her into that year, green eyes fixed on her daughter and husband. Was that the last time she'd felt that kind of pure happiness? The flush of gratitude for her life and the people she shared it with?

The birthday cards could come down now. She hadn't really wanted them up on display in the first place, but Charlotte had insisted. 'You have to celebrate, Mum. Birthdays are important. You can't just forget about it.'

Forgetting about it was exactly what she'd wanted to do. As she was gathering the cards into her hand, she caught sight of herself in the hallway mirror. It was a very different face to the one in the photograph. As well as a paler complexion, there was a stern crease between her eyes that hadn't been there back then. The wrinkles at the edges of her eyes had deepened too. The ones Steve used to call her laughter lines had a different role these days. And her hair needed attention. Along with the copper highlights, it had totally outgrown the sharp chin-length cut Charlotte had cleverly known would suit her roundish face. Now, her dark hair reached almost to her shoulders and the ends fell in waves that hadn't seen a straightening iron in months.

Cards in hand, she was halfway upstairs towards the shower when there was a knock on the front door, followed by an immediate ring of the doorbell. Someone was keen to get an answer.

When she opened it, her heart plummeted to her stomach

to see two police officers standing there. A man of her age and a young woman who could only have been a couple of years older than Charlotte. 'Hello?'

At least he didn't have his hat under his arm like they did on the police dramas Steve used to like. That had to be a good sign. 'Mrs Woodley?'

The tone of his voice made her heart thump in her chest. 'Yes?'

'Could we come inside?'

She stood back to let them into her hall. What was the form here? What was she supposed to do? Speak to them here? Take them through to the lounge?

Clearly, the police officer had done this a lot more than Joanna had. She was saved from her indecision by him taking the lead. 'I'm afraid there's been an incident. Your daughter, Charlotte, has been taken into hospital.'

The cards fluttered from Joanna's hands onto the floor. Wind rushed through her ears and she gripped the side of the table. 'Incident? What does that mean? Is she okay? How bad is it?'

Visions of disaster flashed through her mind. Car accident? A fall? What could it be? Why was he taking so long to answer?

The female police officer bent to collect the cards for her. 'There is evidence of an altercation. Charlotte hit her head.'

Altercation? A fight? That wasn't her daughter. Joanna pushed a fist into her stomach to stop the churning there, watched the officer stand and slide the cards back onto the hall table before she could form the words in her dry mouth. 'Are you saying that she was *attacked*?'

The older officer frowned at his colleague before addressing her again. 'At the moment we don't have all the facts. But if you'd like to come with us, we can take you to her at the hospital?'

'Yes, yes. Of course.' She turned around, dithering. Where

were her shoes? What did she need to take? What would Charlotte need her to bring? Her hand flew to her mouth to catch a sob. Her baby was in hospital. She was hurt. *Oh, please God, let her be okay.*

The female officer was gentle. 'Is this your coat on the hook? And your bag?'

Gratefully, she took them, found her shoes and followed them mutely to the car.

The first part of the journey to the hospital was a blur. All she could think about was getting to Charlotte. Imagining her in pain made every atom of Joanna ache to get to her. She needed to see her, hold her, soothe any hurt away with a cool palm and a soft word. When Charlotte was very little, she'd bring any graze or cut or sting straight to Joanna to be kissed better. Sometimes that was all it needed.

Watching the familiar streets pass them by, her mind raced through thoughts about what might have happened. Not having seen Charlotte for days, she had no idea where she might've been this afternoon. 'Where did it happen? Where was she attacked?'

The first police officer kept his eyes on the road ahead. 'We don't have the details of what happened yet, Mrs Woodley. But the ambulance was called to a flat on the new Westwood Estate. Around two hours ago.'

Two hours? Two hours that her baby girl was hurt and in pain and she wasn't there? And she was in that ridiculous flat of his with its gym and coffee shop and hard granite surfaces. 'Have you spoken to Freddie Knight-Crossley? That'll be his flat. Was he there when it happened? Is it his fault?'

The policeman's reply was measured, careful. 'Mr Knight-Crossley was the person who called the ambulance. He was very upset. He's speaking to some of our officers now.'

Upset? He'd be more than upset if she got anywhere near him. 'What did he say?'

'We're not in a position to discuss all the details yet. Let's just get you to your daughter and worry about everything else later.'

The young female officer smiled at her, her eyes betraying more than her experienced senior colleague was willing to reveal.

Joanna had known that when Charlotte started seeing Freddie Knight-Crossley it was going to end in something awful. Boys like him were bad news. Every part of her had sensed this wasn't going to end well. Why had no one listened to her?

Charlotte had always been a good girl – polite, kind, generous – but she was drawn to the wrong people like a moth to a flame. At school, the only time she got into trouble was when she was trying to stand up for another – usually naughtier – child. 'But Mummy,' she'd said when an exasperated Joanna had asked her why she'd told the teacher that she was the one who'd spilled the glue pot all over the class display work-in-progress on the desk, 'Lewis didn't mean to do it and he was already on the orange board and if he moved onto the red he would have to give up his breaktime and then he wouldn't be able to play football with his friends.'

It was difficult to be cross with her when her heart was so big, but Joanna couldn't help but worry who she chose to surround herself with. Joanna had wanted her to go to a grammar school when choosing a secondary school, but she'd flat-out refused and Steve had backed her up. 'She wants to go with her friends, Jo. It'll be okay.'

'And what if it isn't?' Her own memories of school days made her anxious for what Charlotte might encounter. 'What if she's miserable there, or she can't learn because the behaviour is so bad?'

'Then we'll move her. Let's worry about trouble when it happens, eh? Let's wait and see.'

Let's wait and see had been his mantra throughout life. She knew that he regarded her worries as overthinking. It was easy for him. When you'd had no shocking surprises in childhood, no moments that turned your whole world upside down, you didn't have to spend your life on high alert that it might happen again.

And now, she was arriving at the hospital to see what an awful price her daughter had had to pay.

Damp with cold sweat, her hands fumbled as she tried to open the locked door of the police car. Every muscle in her body was tight, ready to run. Heart beating out of her chest, hands gripped into fists to stop the trembling. The adrenaline of terror crashed through her, wave after icy wave. Why hadn't she fought harder to make Charlotte understand? *Please let her be okay.*

Like the scene from a nightmare, the hospital corridor seemed to get longer the faster Joanna walked; a clinical desert between her and her child. Echoing and sterile, the sound of her own footsteps bounced back at her. Doors stretched out in the distance. Where was she? Where was Charlotte? Wind rushed through her ears. All she wanted was to get to Charlotte. 'Where is she?'

The young constable was keeping pace. 'She's still with the medical team, I believe. We're taking you somewhere you can wait.'

Wait? Wait? They were going to keep her from seeing her? It was unbearable to think about Charlotte in there, hurt and alone. 'I need to see her now.'

'You will.' The older officer was behind, slightly out of breath. 'We can wait just over here.'

Behind the door he pushed open, the sight of the small room – its square chairs, garish posters, bin with empty coffee cups – made her want to throw up on the scratchy blue carpet. She'd been in rooms like this far too often in the last eighteen months. *Not again.* She thought. *Not again.*

Now the older police officer was speaking in hushed tones. There was something about the forced intimacy of rooms like this that made you lower your voice. He was whispering to his colleague. 'I'll stay with Mrs Woodley, you go and see if you can find someone to talk to her.'

The blood was freezing in her veins. Why weren't they taking her straight to her daughter? Charlotte would need her, might be asking for her. What was the hold-up? Somewhere in the back of her brain, dark thoughts threatened, but she refused to look at them. Instead, she focused on the door, with its peeling poster, willing it to open, desperate to be told that Charlotte was okay.

The police officer had his back against the wall to the side of the door, hands clasped in front of him. Unable to sit, Joanna paced back and forth in front of him, wringing her own hands, not taking her eyes off that door, each moment dragging like an hour. 'Do you know what's taking so long? Do you know if she's...' she forced herself to say it, 'if she's alive?'

She didn't breathe, waiting for his response. 'Mrs Woodley, I know that this must be frightening for you, but I only know what I've been told. That your daughter was brought here with life-threatening injuries.' He held up his hand at her gasp. 'Which means that she was alive when they brought her here. I know that the doctors will be doing everything they can and I'm sure we will hear something soon.'

Determined not to cry, Joanna wrapped her arms around herself and dug her fingers into her sides. The last year without Steve had been hard, but she'd never felt so alone as she did in that room. Joanna was all she had. Her clever, beautiful daughter. The last time she'd seen her, they'd had that stupid row. About *him*. It was always about him. Why had no one listened to her? Why hadn't she made them listen?

Finally, there was a firm knock on the door and the female constable appeared, followed by a doctor in a white coat. He looked young, too young to have such an important job, but he sounded confident and capable. 'Mrs Woodley? I'm Dr Doherty, I've been looking after your daughter. Please, can we sit for a moment?'

She didn't want to sit, she wanted to go to Charlotte. But she took the miserable chair he indicated and gripped its wooden arms. 'Is she going to be okay? Can I go to her now?'

Dr Doherty perched on the arm of the chair opposite. His white coat opened on pale-blue scrubs. Had Charlotte been in surgery? How bad was it? 'I'll take you through to your daughter very shortly. But you need to prepare yourself.'

Another wave of fear engulfed Joanna. How bad was it going to be? Had that monster damaged her beautiful daughter? 'What do you mean? How badly is she hurt?'

He pressed his lips together before he spoke. 'Most of Charlotte's wounds are superficial. Scratches, bruises. The main issue is the wound on the back of her head. We've managed to stop the bleeding, but when you see her, her head is bandaged.'

There was clearly something else. Why was he taking so long to get to the point. *Just tell me.* 'What is it, then? What do I need to prepare myself for?'

Holding fast to the arms of the chair, fear clutched at Joanna's stomach, She'd seen this kind but professional expression before. *I'm afraid it's not good news.* But not Charlotte. Not her baby girl. 'I'm afraid Charlotte hasn't regained consciousness. We are running some tests on brain activity and I'll be able to tell you more soon. But I assume you'll want to see her straight away.'

Joanna stood too quickly, her legs – jelly beneath her – gave way and she had to sit down again. Unconscious? Brain activity? What did all this mean? 'Please can you take me to her? I just need to see her.'

TWO

The thick smell of disinfectant hit Joanna as soon as the doctor used his pass to bleep them onto the ward. He nodded hello to the nurses at their station. 'This is Mrs Woodley. Can you take her in to see her daughter?'

A woman in a darker uniform than the others smiled. 'Of course. Come with me, Mrs Woodley.'

Following the nurse, Joanna tried not to look left or right at the other patients. The smell of tinned soup and liniment curdled in the air. With each step, a sense of dread descended on her. Joanna had spent more time around a hospital bed than she'd care to remember, but she wasn't prepared to see her only daughter laying in one. The nurse led her into a side room at the end of the corridor and there she was. 'Oh, Charlotte. My darling.'

Charlotte's bed was in the middle of the room and she lay still, eyes closed, her arms on top of the sheet that was tucked up to her chest. As Dr Doherty had described, the top of her head was bandaged but, other than that, she looked as if she was asleep. 'Can I touch her?'

The nurse's smile hadn't moved from her face. Maybe for

her, this was an everyday scene. 'Of course. You can see where the wires are, so obviously you need to keep an eye on those. But I'll leave you alone for a while. If you need anything, the nurses' station is outside on the right.'

What she needed was to hold her daughter close. As soon as the nurse was gone, Joanna leaned to kiss Charlotte's soft cheek; she was warm. 'I'm here now, sweetheart. Mummy's here. We're going to get you better and I'm going to look after you.'

From underneath the bandage, Charlotte's hair curled towards her closed eyelids. Taking care not to dislodge the elastic of her oxygen mask, Joanna moved it away. 'That's better. You always hated your hair in your eyes, didn't you?'

Charlotte's skin was pale, but that only made her more beautiful. Everyone believes their child is attractive – it's biology – but she knew that Charlotte was stunning; everyone said it. Faces would turn towards the bounce of her wavy long blonde hair and smile at the large blue eyes that glittered in their search for her next adventure. Whatever was good in her and Steve, Charlotte had inherited it. 'She got the best of us,' he used to say. Even so, they would sometimes marvel at how she came from the two of them. How could they have made something so perfect?

Joanna pulled a plastic chair in close to the bed so that she could hold Charlotte's hand. She brought it up to her lips and kissed it. 'You need to wake up soon, my love. I know it probably hurts, but you need to wake up so that the doctors can make you better. And then I'll take you home and get you back to normal.'

There were so many tubes going in and out of Charlotte. What did they all do? Were they just giving her medication or actually keeping her alive? 'I don't know if you can hear me, sweetheart, but I'm here and I'm not going anywhere until you wake up and talk to me.'

She rubbed at Charlotte's arm. Beneath a light suntan and freckles, it was so slim and fragile. Pale and vulnerable on the underside, the bruises were still there, the ones that had caused their argument last week. If only she'd known what was going to happen, she'd never have let her leave the house. She would've held on to her, begged her to stay. Remembering her last words as Charlotte left – *You'll realise I'm right* – made her wince. She hadn't even said goodbye. No *I love you* or *drive safely* or *see you soon*. Why had she left those words hanging in the air before she left?

More than anything, she wanted to lay down next to Charlotte on the bed and take her in her arms. When Charlotte was small, she hated sleeping on her own. *Stay with me, Mummy. One more story.* Sometimes, Joanna would fall asleep next to her, wake up two hours later and then stumble off to bed. Friends would tell her she was crazy. *Just let her cry.* But she couldn't. And neither could Steve.

Above the bed, monitors displayed digital numbers in various colours. What did it all mean? Were they good or bad? She'd never been good with numbers. It was Steve who would sit at the table with Charlotte night after night, trying to get her to understand her maths homework. Sometimes she would cry with frustration and he would tell her they could leave it for another time. But Charlotte would shake her head. 'It's not going to beat me.' Steve would smile over her head at Joanna, proud of their daughter's strong spirit. The flip side to that spirit wasn't quite so easy to manage. Even then he'd shrug, 'She knows what she wants,' before kissing Joanna. 'Like her mother.'

That was possibly the only way she was like Joanna. Looking at her now, her long hair falling beneath the bandages threaded with bright highlights, she was the image of her father. It was his long eyelashes that rested on her lightly freckled cheeks and if she – *when* she – opened them, it would be his blue eyes that would look at her. How often had she been at the receiving end of a joke from two sets of eyes like that as they'd mocked her for something she'd said or done? What would she give to see that again. Her heart burned with the pain of it. 'What are you thinking about in there, sweetheart? You take your time. I'll be here whenever you wake up.'

A gentle knock on the door heralded the entrance of a nurse. 'Hello. I've come to do Charlotte's obs. I'll be as quick as I can.'

The nurse was young. Maybe only a few years older than Charlotte. Neat and pretty, Joanna welcomed her calm efficiency as a sign that no one was giving up on Charlotte yet. Maybe she had some words of encouragement to offer. 'Do you always work on this ward?'

Her cheeks squeezed into apples when she smiled. 'Actually, it's my first day back today. I've been on maternity leave.'

Joanna's heart ached. She forced herself to focus on the nurse. 'Congratulations. Boy or girl?'

The pride in her voice was unmistakable. 'Little boy. Ben.'

She returned her focus to the monitor above Charlotte's bed, but Joanna could still see the tears in her eyes. 'First day back, isn't easy, is it?'

Her smile was grateful and she wiped away the tear that escaped. 'No. I love my job, but it was tough to leave him with my mum this morning.'

Joanna remembered that feeling well. Tearing yourself in two directions and never feeling you were fully present in either. 'It gets easier. I promise.'

'Thank you. That's what my mum said. And she said you always worry about them however big they get. Even when they're twenty-six and having their own babies.'

Joanna looked down at Charlotte. 'Your mum is right. You will always worry.'

With her thumb, she stroked Charlotte's hand, and her eyes blurred with tears. It had been worry that made her try to get Charlotte to see sense last week. She hadn't wanted to start an argument. She just needed her to understand. It'd been a tough year for both of them, but they'd promised to get through it together.

The nurse smiled. 'All done, I'll be back in an hour to check again.'

Joanna was desperate for information. 'Does it all look okay? I mean the checks you've done. Is she going to be okay?'

The nurse was kind but professional. 'I'm just checking that she's stable. The doctor will be round soon and he'll be able to tell you more about her condition.'

Joanna swallowed, tried to smile. 'Of course. I understand. Thank you.'

But she didn't understand. If Charlotte was still unconscious, what did that mean? Stable meant nothing. You could be stable but still critical. Hours of watching *Grey's Anatomy* had taught her that much. In the silence of the room, the hiss of the oxygen machine had a sinister tone. How bad was this? Would Charlotte ever be that same headstrong girl who'd, politely – but firmly – informed her that she was going to 'live my life the way I want to'?

When Charlotte had first mentioned Freddie Knight-Crossley, it'd been in such an offhand way that Joanna hadn't realised the full extent of the danger.

She'd been dropping her off at the venue for her latest gig. She never enjoyed doing that. It wasn't the driving – she'd been running Charlotte here, there and everywhere her whole life – it was the kind of places she was playing. Rough-looking pubs, or clubs where the door was made of metal, covered in torn flyers and paint, which opened onto stairs down into a cavern of darkness.

Charlotte would laugh at her. 'You can bring your nose down a few inches, Mother,' she'd said. 'I know where you're from, remember? I did say that you should drop me round the corner. Then you won't risk anyone seeing you.'

'It's not that, Charlotte,' she'd half-lied. 'It's the worry of you being in a place like that. It looks dangerous.'

She could see Charlotte roll her eyes in the rear-view mirror as she'd pulled her keyboard from the back of the car. 'Well, you might not have to do it much longer. We've got ourselves a roadie. And he's got his own van for all our kit.'

That was the first she'd heard of it. 'Really? Can you afford to pay someone to do that?'

Charlotte had been at her window now, leaning in to give her a kiss goodbye. She'd shrugged. 'He doesn't want paying. He said he enjoys it. He likes our music.'

Suspicion had made her sarcastic. 'And you believed him? Who is he? What's his name?'

'Why do you need to know his name?'

Always this pushback. When would she understand that Joanna needed to know everything – and everyone – that affected her daughter. Knowledge kept you safe. 'Why don't you want to tell me?'

Charlotte had sighed. 'Not that it matters, but his name is Freddie Knight-Crossley. He went to school somewhere frightfully posh in Surrey and he has just graduated and is about to start some kind of MA in business in September. His family has a house the size of a small school on Hutton Mount and the van he drives is blue, I think, some flavour of Renault. Does that make you feel better? I'm going in, Mum. I'll see you later.'

That had not made her feel better. Not at all. What was a boy from a family like that doing driving Charlotte and her band – another two young girls – to their tiny gigs in pubs? For free? After watching her disappear into the dark hole of the door, Joanna had driven home with another worry to add to her portfolio.

A sharp ring cut through her memory. Joanna jumped. She grabbed her bag from the floor beside her chair. The damn phone was so loud. Were they allowed to have them on in here? Heart racing, she scooped the contents of her bag – mints, tissues, lipstick, comb, mirror, receipts, receipts, receipts – onto her lap to try and find the phone to stop its shrill insistence. 'Where are you?'

At last she found it, just as the call rang off. At least it wasn't making a noise anymore. The number wasn't one she recognised. She swiped the screen to silent in case they called again and slid it on the cabinet by the side of Charlotte's bed.

Bag back on the floor, contents safely inside again, she pulled her chair even closer to Charlotte and picked up her hand. Inside her wrist, the butterfly tattoo that Joanna hated. That'd been another argument. Another time when she'd told Joanna it was 'her life' and Steve – as always – had failed to back her up. 'It's just a little tattoo. She's a good kid. Why does it matter what people think? It's not really important, is it?'

How many times had he said that to her over the years? How many times had she replied with 'but it's important to me'?

Her phone vibrated. Whoever had called must've left a voicemail. When she picked up her phone, she was assailed by the photo on the home screen. Her, Charlotte and Steve on holiday in Cape Verde three years' ago. When life was good and the worst thing she'd had to worry about was the size of Charlotte's bikini.

She clicked onto the voicemail, but as soon as the message started – *Hello Mrs Woodley, this is Lloyds Bank. We've been trying to call you urgently about* – she clicked it off. Money problems could definitely wait.

She stared at the family photo on the home screen until her eyes blurred. That had been a wonderful holiday. Charlotte had just finished her A levels and they'd taken her away as a surprise. She had a holiday booked with her girlfriends for after their prom but was thrilled to have the opportunity to get a tan before wearing the expensive full-length dress they'd bought for her. Unlike Joanna's friends' daughters, she'd agreed with her dad that buying second-hand from a charity shop or eBay was the way to go for something she would only wear once. But Joanna had insisted. 'I want you to find something you really want. And I'm looking forward to seeing you try them all on.'

'But it's so much money, Mum.'

'That's okay, I've got the money saved already.'

Charlotte had given a little shrug. 'Okay, that'll be fun. When shall we go?'

That afternoon, watching her beautiful daughter twirl around the dress shop in ballgowns of every colour, had been one of the loveliest days they'd had together. They could have had so many more days like that if she'd stayed home with Joanna instead of moving into that sterile executive apartment in Stock with Freddie bloody Knight-Crossley.

There was a soft knock on the door and another nurse stepped into the room. 'Mrs Woodley? There's a police officer here and they'd like to talk to you about what happened to your daughter.'

THREE

For the first time, Joanna realised how scruffy she must look to the police officer. Still in her gardening clothes – torn t-shirt and grubby combat trousers, the legs baggy with age – she must look an absolute sight. Pulling at the bottom of her t-shirt, she followed the nurse out of the ward, where she pointed at the same small room Joanna had waited in when she first arrived. A tidy-looking woman in a navy suit with short dark hair and a professional smile waited for her in the doorway.

Though she looked terribly young, the officer's voice was surprisingly confident and assured. 'I'm Detective Constable Abbie Lineham. I've been assigned to your daughter's case. How is she?'

What was she thinking behind that professional exterior? What did she already know about what'd happened? Of course, she must see incidents like this all the time. For her, Joanna thought bitterly, Charlotte would probably just be another problem to solve. 'We don't know. Her doctor said something about running lots of tests. She hasn't come round yet so we're waiting on that. Do you know what happened?'

She looked very tired as she nodded. Did it get you down?

Having to deal with incidents like this all the time?' 'There was a nine nine nine call from Apartment 2a Coleridge Place this afternoon. The ambulance attended the scene and then brought your daughter straight here.'

2a Coleridge Place was Freddie's apartment. They'd told her that he'd called from there, but not where it'd happened. 'Was she hurt inside the apartment?'

The detective nodded. 'Your daughter had a head injury and quite a loss of blood. Forensics are on the scene and it appears she hit her head on the edge of a metal cabinet.'

Hot violent fury flashed through Joanna. Her hands shook and it was all she could do not to grab hold of the detective and shake the information from her. 'So she was attacked. You know that for definite now? You *know* it wasn't an accident?'

As if deciding which colour wire to cut to avoid setting off a bomb, the detective watched Joanna carefully, her dark eyes betraying nothing, but she nodded. 'From the angle of the wound, it would appear that your daughter may have been pushed.'

May have been pushed? *May?* Joanna wanted to scream and shout and strike out at the world. 'She was attacked in her own home. No one falls backwards on their own. Of course she was pushed. And you know who did it, don't you? You know it was him?'

Her hands in front of her, palms down to encourage restraint, DC Lineham spoke slowly and carefully. 'Like I said, forensics are at the residence now gathering evidence.'

Evidence? She could give them plenty of evidence. How he'd broken her daughter, left Joanna to pick up the pieces and then come back to hurt Charlotte all over again. That entitled, arrogant... 'What has he said? Freddie Knight-Crossley. Have you asked him what happened?'

'Mr Knight-Crossley is helping us with our enquiries, yes.

He made the call to emergency services. We believe he is the partner of your daughter?'

In these grubby clothes she felt vulnerable somehow. How she wished they were having this conversation at home so that she could see where Charlotte had come from. That they were just as good as him. That boy and his family. She swallowed. 'Yes. They're together.'

Charlotte had first started seeing Freddie three years before. The summer between her second and third year at university. Despite insisting he was just a friend, the extra care she took with her make-up, the length of time it took to choose what top to wear with her jeans, on the days she would be seeing him, told a different story.

A few times, he'd picked her up from the house. To give him credit, he always parked the van and came to the door – Steve liked that about him – but Charlotte would thunder down the stairs to be there and gone before Joanna had even got out of her seat. She'd watch them drive away from the sitting room window. 'I'm sure she's seeing him.'

Steve had looked up from whatever nonsense he was watching on his phone – how to unblock a drain with a coat hanger, probably – a frown of concentration still on his face. 'Does it matter? She *is* twenty. And he seems like a decent boy.'

'You've only spoken to him once.' The week before, Steve had been in the garden on the Saturday afternoon when Freddie had pulled up.

'I know. But he was very complimentary about my oleander tree and you know that's all it takes.'

He'd winked, but she'd wanted him to take it seriously. 'Well, of course he knows how to charm someone's father. They're brought up like that. It's the expensive schooling and the money. All the niceness is on the outside. It's a veneer.'

'It's not fair to judge him on that, is it? Charlotte likes him.

We have to trust her. Come away from that window and give me a cuddle. Let's wait and see before we write him off.'

She'd dropped the vertical blind she'd pushed up and moved towards his outstretched arm. 'I'm going to write "let's wait and see" on your gravestone, Steve Woodley.'

Detective Constable Lineham checked her notes then looked up at Joanna. 'And they were living together at the flat where your daughter was hurt? There were bills in both their names.'

Her cheeks warmed. She hated to think of the two of them living there together. She'd only been there once, when Charlotte had first moved in. It was part of a large modern block with Juliet balconies and carpeted hallways. Charlotte – a caffeine addict – had been particularly excited by the coffee shop on the ground floor with its expensive oat milk flat whites and USB charging points. With her waitressing job and the pittance she made from gigs, she'd never have been able to afford somewhere like that to live. Joanna had tried to persuade her to stay at home, save up for a place of her own, offered to help her as much as she could. But she'd wanted to move in with him and, when Charlotte made up her mind about something, there was no stopping her. 'Yes. They've been living there together for almost a year.'

The police officer's eyes searched hers for everything she wasn't saying. 'I'm sorry to ask this, but were there any issues between them? Did you have any concerns?'

She almost laughed at that. It would be quicker to tell her what she wasn't concerned about. 'Yes, I have a lot of concerns. He comes from a very privileged background and he thinks he can have whatever he wants. He's already broken her heart by making her think she was his world and then playing around behind her back. Charlotte isn't like him. She's a good girl. A kind girl. I knew that he wouldn't make her happy. But I never thought...'

A sob escaped from her throat. It was all starting to filter down into her shocked brain. Freddie had pushed Charlotte. He'd pushed her so hard that she'd hit her head and now she was lying unconscious in that room with who knew what damage to her brain.

'Mrs Woodley. At the moment, we don't know what happened. There is still the possibility that this was an accident.'

Surely she knew as well as Joanna did that this wasn't the case. 'What did he say? When you spoke to him. Did he admit what he'd done?'

The officer sighed. 'We can't divulge any details at the moment, I'm afraid. But anything you can tell us that might shed some light on their relationship would help.'

Most definitely she had something to tell. 'There are bruises. On her arm. I saw them there, last week. They look as if someone had pressed their fingers into her skin. Like they've grabbed hold of her arms.'

DC Lineham was noting down her words as she spoke. 'We'd like to examine those if that's okay with you?'

Charlotte had been so flippant about them when she'd asked her. She'd been over for a flying visit – every visit was short lately, prefaced with an 'I've only got fifteen minutes' – and she'd asked her to help straighten the family photo on the sitting room wall. The frame was so heavy, she was worried about doing it on her own in case she dropped it and smashed the glass. When Charlotte reached up, Joanna saw the five round bruises on her arm – four in a row and one for a thumb – and had asked her immediately. 'What are they?'

She'd flipped her arm back over immediately. 'What? Oh, nothing, just bruises from picking up the equipment the other night.'

She'd known that was a lie immediately. Charlotte had been moving amps and instruments around ever since she started the band at seventeen. Before that, even. And she'd never seen such specific bruising on her arms before. 'It can't be that. It looks as if someone has grabbed you.'

Perhaps she could have worded it better, but she still hadn't expected Charlotte to fly off the handle like she had. 'So now you're going to accuse Freddie of grabbing me, Mum?'

She'd tried to keep her voice level. 'I didn't say anything about Freddie. You brought his name into this.'

'Mum! When are you going to get it? Freddie is a really nice guy. You cannot keep judging him because he reminds you of some boy you used to know. You just won't give him a chance.'

That had stung. It had taken a lot for her to tell Charlotte about that. But now Joanna was far more concerned about those bruises. 'Tell me the truth, Charlotte. What happened to your arm?'

At that, she'd flown off the handle. 'Okay, I'm done. Call me when you're ready to treat my boyfriend with just a tiny bit of respect.'

She'd grabbed her keys and stormed out of the front door. And Joanna – like a fool – had just watched her go.

DC Lineham closed her notebook. 'I think that's all we have to discuss at the moment. We'll keep you informed, of course. Is there anyone else we need to tell for you? Charlotte's father? Siblings?'

She wasn't to know that each of those questions was a bullet to her heart. She focused on the tissue in her hands as she shook her head. 'No. There's no one else I need to call.'

The sympathy in the detective's voice was genuine. *Poor woman. All on her own.* That's what she'd be telling her partner tonight as they sat down to dinner together. 'Okay, well, I'll be in touch tomorrow.'

If Joanna was on her own, she had only herself to blame. What had Sally's words been to her? 'You'll drive her away. The more you try and keep her from him, the faster she will run.' If she'd listened, maybe she wouldn't have driven her out of the house to live in that apartment. Was this all her fault?

If only she could call Sally now. But how could she ask for help after what she'd said to her? The hurt in her best friend's voice at her cruel words. What a mess she'd made of everything.

DC Lineham was standing to leave when there was another knock on the door. As it opened, Dr Doherty's head appeared. 'Sorry to interrupt. I was hoping to catch up with Mrs Woodley about Charlotte.'

Within a fraction of a second she was out of her seat. 'Has she woken up?'

He shook his head. 'Sorry. No. But I wanted to update you on our initial test results.'

The wave of disappointment receded, leaving her heart thumping in her chest. She tried to read his face; was this news good or bad? 'What is it? What do they say?'

Dr Doherty stood to the side to give the detective room to leave and then turned back to face her. 'Shall we sit down?'

Nothing good ever came from those words. 'I'd rather stand. What is it?'

Dr Doherty took a deep breath. 'I really think you should sit down.'

An icy cold rose through Joanna's body. She lowered herself onto the seat, her throat almost too dry to speak. 'What is it?'

Dr Doherty sat opposite; his professional calm made her want to scream. 'Firstly, I wanted to talk you through the tests we've done. Obviously, we've also had to be extremely mindful of your daughter's condition.'

He wasn't making any sense. For a moment, a wisp of hope rose that he was talking about the wrong patient. She frowned. Her *condition*? 'What do you mean?'

He looked up from his notes and tilted his head in shock. 'I'm so sorry. Did you not know?'

FOUR

FREDDIE

The first time Freddie met Charlotte, he made a total idiot of himself.

It was only chance that had found him and Dominic in the bar where she was playing. Dom's old man had flatly refused to buy him another car after he'd burnt the gear box out again, and the poor old Fiat had smoked so badly on their way out of Suffolk that he'd made him pull over at the first bar they came across.

Set back from the main road, the bar was one of those old places with thick beams and brick fireplaces that was ripe for someone to buy it and turn it into a gastro pub. The current clientele were more ASBO than gastro, though, and he and Dominic looked like they'd been marooned on a particularly inhospitable island. He wanted to leave immediately.

Dominic, his voice raised above the sound of the music, was blithely unaware of the looks they were getting. 'You must be joking. I need a drink. We'll get some shots in and then I'll call us an Uber.'

It wasn't worth the energy to argue. 'What about your car?'

He shrugged. 'She's dead, mate. We can raise a glass to her.

Find us a seat, will you?' In three strides, he was at the bar, squinting at the whiskey on offer behind the stroppy barmaid wiping a glass as if she'd quite like to put it in his face.

After a quick scan of the bar, Freddie spotted a table that was out of the way. Once he was seated, back against the splintered wooden panelled wall, he avoided eye contact with anyone nearby by scrolling on his phone. Places like this made him nervous. Back in sixth form, they used to go out in the local town and there was always trouble. Some local lad who wanted to pick a fight with the 'posh knobs' from the school. Dominic was his mate, but he didn't help matters with his loud voice and a laugh that brayed louder than a donkey.

Which was why, when the people around him started shifting in their seats to face in the same direction, his heart sank. But it wasn't in the direction of the bar, from which Dominic was wobbling towards him with a tray of vicious shots. No, everyone was turning towards a raised platform at the far end where three girls around his age were slotting themselves behind a keyboard, guitar and microphone respectively. A small cheer greeted the dark-haired singer in a tartan dress as she held up a hand and introduced the first song, looking as if she could hold her own in this room full of men with a sprinkle of their girlfriends.

But it wasn't the singer who stole his attention away from whatever joke Dominic was telling. It was the girl behind the keyboard. Long blonde hair swayed as she moved to the music coming from her fingertips. Open-necked shirt, which was unbuttoned just enough to make you want more. Slim hips in jeans stretched tightly across her thighs.

From that moment, he was lost.

The set lasted for about an hour, but he couldn't stop watching her. The ease at which she played and moved, the red of her beautiful mouth as she added backing vocals to covers of Alanis Morissette, Amy Winehouse, and a rock version of something he was pretty sure might be Madonna. It was the kind of music his mother would ask Alexa to play when she'd had more than two glasses of wine, but they made it sound edgy and different. Two or three times, Dominic jabbed him in the arm, before giving up trying to talk to him and just sliding one drink after another in front of him. Who knew how much he'd had? Enough to make him sound like a total and utter prick the first time he spoke to Charlotte.

Almost the minute she came off stage, Dominic announced that their Uber was outside.

Freddie panicked. 'You didn't tell me you were booking an Uber?'

Dom drained the final shot glass on the table. 'What's the problem? You didn't even want to stay here.'

He didn't have time to explain. He had to speak to her before he lost his nerve.

In his defence, Freddie hadn't realised just how drunk he was and his legs almost betrayed him as he launched himself in her direction. Her head turned at the jeering cheers as he knocked into a table. She rolled her eyes and turned to say something that made her friends laugh. Making his way towards her, he was sure one of those friends was warning her of his approach. She didn't turn around.

Freddie knew that he was a good-looking boy. It wasn't arrogance. Just fact. His mother would say it was her Irish heritage that gave him his thick dark hair and translucent blue eyes, but his height and swimmer's shoulders came directly from his father. Among his friends, he was always the one who'd start a conversation with a group of girls. He was good at putting on the charm. At the very least, he always got a smile for his trouble.

Except, this time, he didn't.

His opening gambit made him sound like an extra from an American teen-flick. 'Hey. You were great up there.'

Her glance was so fleeting it almost cut him. 'Thanks.'

Why wouldn't his brain feed him the right words? It had never let him down before. 'Can I buy you a drink?'

She lifted a pint glass. 'Already have one. But thanks.'

'What about a shot?' He held out his hand to include her bandmates. 'For all of you.'

'We're good, thanks.'

She turned back to the bar. He couldn't ask again without looking like a total creep. And, to make matters worse, Dominic appeared at his elbow. 'Have you worked your magic yet?'

Freddie wanted the ground to open up beneath him. 'Let's just go.'

If Freddie was drunk, Dominic was absolutely smashed. Way beyond the ability to read a social cue. He raised his voice. 'We're going on to a club. Why don't you girls come with us? You won't need to buy a drink. My uncle owns the place.'

Charlotte's eyes narrowed. 'Of course he does.'

In his inebriated state, Freddie misunderstood her sarcasm. 'He's not lying. His uncle is—'

Charlotte held up a bored hand to stop his explanation. 'I'm sorry if I looked interested. I'm really not. We just want a quiet pint after our set. Have a good night.'

She picked up the jacket on the stool beside her and the three of them disappeared to the corner of the bar.

Dominic shrugged. 'You're losing your touch, mate. Come on, let's go.'

All the way to the club in the Uber, he wanted to punch himself in the face. Why had he made such a mess of that?

For the next two weeks he couldn't get her out of his mind. When he saw a flyer for her band playing in another bar near Colchester, it felt like fate. He was going to talk to her and, this time, he'd do it sober.

FIVE

Time seemed to stop in the silence between Joanna and the doctor. 'Did I not know what? Her condition? What do you mean?'

Dr Doherty stared at her. He was young, she realised. There was something about a white coat that made you assume that the person you were speaking to had seen and done everything before. Like a cloak of experience. For all she knew, this might be the first time he'd had to talk to a relative like this. Everyone had to learn somewhere.

Dr Doherty swallowed. 'Well, as you're next of kin, I just assumed that you'd know. Charlotte is twenty-eight weeks' pregnant.'

Even sitting down, Joanna felt as if she might keel over. She gripped on to the arm of the chair to keep herself upright. Pregnant? That wasn't possible. 'Are you sure? Could there have been a mistake?'

He coughed into his fist again, shuffled his feet. 'Quite sure. The gentleman that called the ambulance informed them of the pregnancy and we've done an ultrasound to check.'

Air rushed in her ears. She felt hot. Then cold. Then hot again. This wasn't happening. It couldn't be. Pregnancy? A coma? Numb with shock, she shook her head at the doctor; her voice seemed to come from somewhere outside her. 'No, I didn't know that she was pregnant.'

He sat up and looked at her differently now and who could blame him? What kind of mother wouldn't know that her daughter was pregnant? Why hadn't Charlotte told her?

She bent forwards in her chair, the pain in her chest becoming too much to bear; she couldn't breathe. Dr Doherty crouched down beside her. 'Are you okay? Just breathe slowly. I'm sorry; it's been quite a shock, I'd imagine.'

Pregnant? Twenty-eight weeks, he'd said. How had Charlotte kept a pregnancy secret for so long? All she could think about was the last time they'd seen each other. The argument in the hallway. How had she not noticed that she was that far pregnant? What had she been wearing? Hadn't they hugged when she'd arrived?

She couldn't remember. When someone is in your life all the time, you don't notice those tiny details, do you? It all merges into one. Unless there's something dramatically different about them – a new haircut, weight loss, different clothes – then you don't really see them at all. They are just them: your daughter, your parents, your husband. 'How would she have hidden that from me? I see her every week.'

Seeing she wasn't about to black out, Dr Doherty stood and took a step back into professional mode. 'It's more than possible to hide a pregnancy at six months. Especially a first pregnancy. Even in someone as slim as your daughter.'

She knew that. She herself had taken a long time to develop a noticeable bump when she was pregnant with Charlotte. She'd been desperate for it to be there. It didn't matter how much Steve would tell her that he could see a beautiful round bump, she used to worry that people would just think she'd put on weight. But that didn't explain *why*. Why would Charlotte not have told her she was pregnant? Were things that bad between them that she didn't want Joanna to know?

She pushed those thoughts away and tried to focus, raising herself back into a sitting position. The pregnancy wasn't what the doctor had actually come to tell her about. She wrapped her arms around herself, cleared her throat, chewed her lip. Wanting to know everything at once, but terrified of the answers. What should she even be asking? 'When is Charlotte likely to come round? Will she need to be in hospital for a long time?'

Again he pressed his lips together before he spoke. 'The wound to the back of Charlotte's skull was very deep. We have managed to stop the bleeding, but there is a considerable amount of swelling. We are running a series of tests to ascertain the level of brain function. At the moment, there is very little brain activity, but this is still early days. We need to monitor her closely to watch for any further bleeds on the brain. These first hours are the most important.' He paused, then: 'You need to prepare yourself that she may not recover.'

Inside the room, the clock ticked. One. Two. Three. Outside, she could hear the rattle of a trolley, voices calling. Dr Doherty was looking at her, waiting for a response. But she didn't understand what he was saying. 'What do you mean?'

His mouth was a straight line: not smiling, not frowning. 'Your daughter hit her head at a particularly vulnerable angle. Her injury is extremely dangerous. We can hope that she'll recover, but the chances are quite slim. I just want you to be clear on that.'

This couldn't be right. She was in hospital, she was breathing. Surely they could help her? She squeezed her fists to stop them from trembling. 'Is there anything else?'

He shook his head. 'No. At the moment, we just have to wait and give it time for the swelling to go down and monitor how her brain reacts.'

It felt like she was living an episode from a TV hospital drama. He wasn't talking about Charlotte. He couldn't be talking about Charlotte. In a minute, someone was going to shake her awake and this would all be a terrible, terrible dream. 'Can I stay with her?'

He frowned. 'It isn't usual for someone to stay on a ward overnight. But you can rest assured that we'll have a nurse one on one with her for as long as it's needed. So you can go home and rest and know that she's being looked after.'

He clearly had no idea what it was like to be a mother. Where else would she be but right by her side? 'I want to stay with her. I can't leave.'

He looked uncertain. 'I'll see what the matron thinks. Charlotte is in a private room so it might be that she can ask one of the nurses to set up a bed for you beside her just for tonight if need be.'

If need be? Did he think this was going to end before tonight? Ice in her spine made Joanna shiver, but her face was on fire. 'Thank you. Can I go to her now?'

'Of course.' He stood aside to let her pass. 'We'll keep you informed of any changes.'

Never before had she had to exert so much effort into putting one foot in front of the other to get back to Charlotte's room. The nurse by the side of Charlotte's bed had changed and Joanna could tell by the sympathy on her face that she already knew what she'd been told.

Laying there, slightly raised – face relaxed, no make-up – Charlotte looked far younger than her twenty-two years. Was there ever a point where you really, truly, understood that your child was an adult? What did it take? Starting work? Moving out? Having a child of their own?

Her eyes wandered to the section of the sheet that covered Charlotte's body; her hand fluttered to her own chest. She still couldn't get her head around the idea that she was pregnant and hadn't told her. More than anything, she'd wanted their relationship to be open and honest: had thought it was. Why had Charlotte not told her?

It all came back to him: Freddie. Once Charlotte had started seeing him, the ties that bound their family together had been stretched, loosened. She'd been right about him from the start. Why had no one listened to her? Why hadn't she made them understand? All it seemed to achieve was pushing Charlotte further away. Was this all her fault?

When it had become more obvious that they were properly dating, Joanna had been terrified. Steve had, as usual, sided with their daughter. 'You just need to trust her, Jo.'

She'd turned from the dishes in the sink to look at him, blithely repairing an old alarm clock at the kitchen table. 'But he's not good enough for her.'

Twisting two of the wires spilling out of their casing, he'd smiled at her. 'We don't even know him, Jo. Charlotte says he's nice.'

Sometimes she'd loved his trusting outlook, others it had been exasperating. 'Of course he seems nice now, he's trying to get her to go out with him. But he's not right for her. She says he's still studying, but it sounds to me like he's living the high life off his family's money while he's playing at being a roadie for the girls' band.'

Steve had waved his screwdriver at her. 'He's young. When you met me, I was still living with my mum. You don't hold that against me.'

'That's different.'

'How is it different?'

She'd turned back to the washing-up and had attacked a stubborn flake of breakfast cereal with the sponge. 'Because you were working every hour you could to help your mum out as well as save up the deposit for a house. No one gave you life on a silver platter like they do to boys like that.'

She'd heard the scrape of his chair on the floor tiles as he'd come to stand behind her. 'We don't know that he's like that.'

He'd wrapped his arms around her and kissed the top of her head. How could he be so calm? That boy – she knew his type all too well – had no business being anywhere near their precious daughter. Steve might not have seen the danger, but she'd known first hand where this was going. 'I just know it's going to end in tears.'

He'd nuzzled his nose into the side of her neck. 'Well, then it's good that she's got us to wipe her face and make it okay again if it does, isn't it?'

Against Steve's advice, she'd tried to make Charlotte see that she shouldn't be spending so much time with him. But she hadn't wanted to hear it. Not even Sally had wanted to listen when, just last week, she'd told her what was happening. And now Joanna was here. Having to wait and see if her precious only child would even live through this.

The nurse finished checking the monitors and slid the file back onto the end of Charlotte's bed. 'I'm just going to check on the patient next door. Shout if you need me.'

Joanna smiled her thanks. 'I will.'

Sitting here on her own was awful. She didn't want to call any of her local friends. There was someone she could call. Who cared about Charlotte almost as much as she did. Sally. But would she want to come after the last time they'd spoken?

She reached for Charlotte's hand, holding it in her own, stroking it with her thumb, just as she used to when Charlotte was small. What a mess this all was. Freddie had destroyed their family, destroyed her relationship with her daughter, but she had let it happen. Worse, her attempts to save her daughter had merely pushed her further away.

The last year had been so tough; she'd been so centred on her own grief that she'd handled all of this the wrong way. She closed her eyes and brought her head down so that her forehead rested on the back of Charlotte's hand. 'My darling girl.' Her voice was just a whisper. 'Is this all my fault?'

SIX

FREDDIE

The second time Freddie met Charlotte, he was stone cold sober.

The pub her band were playing in was slightly more upmarket than the last one and he'd managed to get a stool by the bar with an uninterrupted view of the stage.

There was something about the way she played that made it clear how much she loved the music. How must it feel to be doing something that you loved that much? He'd lost interest in his Physics degree by the end of the first year and actively hated it by the time he'd graduated. Now he was about to start a Business MA at UCL followed by a future working for the family business, neither of which filled him with excitement.

When they finished their set, the three of them headed straight to the bar and Charlotte ended up standing right beside him. He took a deep breath. 'That was great.'

She turned to him with a smile and then narrowed her eyes. 'Have I met you before?'

For a split second, he'd wanted to lie. But if this was going the way he wanted it to, that wouldn't be a great place to start. 'I offered you a drink a couple of weeks ago. In the Dog and Partridge. I was drunk.'

Recognition widened her eyes. 'Oh, yes. The rich boys. No awful mate with you tonight?'

He shook his head. 'No. Flying solo. I'm Freddie.'

She raised an eyebrow at the hand he held out but took it anyway. Hers was cool and soft, but her shake was firm. 'I'm Charlotte.'

The red-haired drummer slid her wallet across the bar. 'It's my round, but I need to go to the toilet.'

'I'll come with you, Lucy.' The singer nudged Charlotte as she stood. 'Give him a chance, Mother Teresa. Lift the ban for one night.'

They passed a knowing look between them, so Freddie had to ask. 'What does that mean? What's the ban?'

Charlotte sighed. 'Ignore Rachael, there's not a ban. I'm just focused on getting my degree finished this coming year and then saving up some money to go travelling with my so-called friends.'

She directed the last three words towards Rachael who stuck out her tongue and laughed, before following Lucy to the toilet.

Freddie twisted his pint glass in his hands. 'I get it. I'm about to start an MBA this year, too. I've just graduated from Bristol. Where are you going travelling?'

'South America. We think. Lucy is doing a *lot* of research.' She rolled her eyes. 'What will you do after the MBA?'

He frowned into his pint. 'We have a family firm. Business consultancy. I'll start an apprenticeship there next summer.'

She dipped her head to look up at him. She was so beautiful. 'That doesn't sound like it fills you with joy?'

He didn't want to think about it, much less waste his precious minutes with Charlotte talking about it. He turned his smile into a brief grimace. 'No, it doesn't. But it is what it is.'

Charlotte tilted her head to the side; it was taking every gram of self-restraint he had not to lean in to kiss her. 'It's your life though. If you don't want to do it, you should do what you want.'

He could see her bandmates coming towards them from the toilet. It was now or never. 'Speaking of doing what I want. It wasn't actually an accident that I was in here tonight. I'm not a stalker, I promise. But I did want to see you again. I made a complete fool of myself last time. And I wanted to ask you out for a drink.'

The two girls were back in time to hear the last sentence and they froze in place, staring at Charlotte. Without turning, she threw a beer mat at them. 'I'm sorry for my friends doing some kind of tableau thing behind us. That would be great. Yes. I'll give you my number.'

The girls cheered and Charlotte laughed, her humour lighting up her eyes. He'd never felt like this about a girl before. He smiled at the chorus behind her. 'You're a really great band. That was a pretty professional performance.'

The drummer with the short red hair pulled out a chair next to Charlotte. 'Well, I hope you enjoyed it, because I think it'll be our last for a while.'

He looked to Charlotte for confirmation and she nodded. 'Lucy's right. Rachael here has decided to break up with the guy who drives our van. Well, his van technically. Hence the problem.'

Rachael stirred the ice cubes at the bottom of her glass. 'I'm sorry that I don't want to carry on dating a cheating loser just because he has his own transport.'

Charlotte raised an eyebrow and twisted the side of her mouth into a smile. 'Lack of commitment, I call it.'

It can only have been the desire to please that made the words circumvent his brain and come straight out of his mouth. 'I can get hold of a van. I could take you to gigs.'

Rachael raised an eyebrow. 'Really? That would be brilliant. We have one booked for next week at the Red Lion.'

Charlotte frowned in suspicion. 'Hang on a minute. Why would someone like you be driving a van? Don't you have the keys to Daddy's Porsche or something?'

He wasn't about to make her feel bad by telling her that his father had passed away a decade before so he didn't have a daddy, much less a Porsche. He held out his hands. 'Well, I'm a man of surprises. What can I say?'

A couple of days later, there was definitely a look of surprise on Dominic's face when he told him he was buying a second-hand Ford Transit he'd seen advertised on Facebook Marketplace. 'What are you doing? Buying a van? I'm assuming you're hoping to get her in the back of it.'

Freddie didn't want him speaking about Charlotte in that way. 'It's not like that. I'm just doing her a favour.'

'Yeah, right.' Dominic laughed, then his jaw dropped. 'You've got it bad, mate. I can't wait to see the look on your mother's face when you take that van home.'

He had a good point. 'Maybe I can leave it at yours? Your dad won't even notice it behind the barn.'

Dominic's father owned acres of farmland beyond the A12. They'd spent a lot of time there as younger lads, camping out and getting drunk. Dominic laughed at him and raised his hands. 'Whatever you want, mate.'

He was a good friend. But Freddie would live to regret accepting a FaceTime call from Dominic as he walked up the path to collect Charlotte the first time.

'So, did you pick up the passion wagon? What's it like?'

He turned his back on Charlotte's house and reversed the camera on his phone to show Dom the van across the street. 'There she is.'

Dominic gave some kind of cowboy yahoo. 'Looks good, mate. How long before you're going to have her in the back of it?'

'Excuse me?'

He almost dropped his phone as he turned to see a woman who must be Charlotte's mother in the open doorway. 'Sorry, I'm... er... I'm Freddie. I'm here to collect Charlotte for her gig.'

She folded her arms. 'Are you, indeed?'

SEVEN

Dr Doherty spoke to the matron and she reluctantly agreed to let Joanna stay for just one night. She slept fitfully beside her daughter's bed, the hiss of the breathing tube receding into the background like wind through a window. Her bed for the night, a low fold-out metal contraption with a thin mattress, never seemed to warm. Every time she turned, it creaked and whined in complaint. In the half-light, she'd imagined movement from Charlotte's bed and risen to check on her, willing there to be something to give her hope. Several times, the nurse came in to check on Charlotte, the hush of her shoes on the floor reassuring. But then, Joanna would be awake again, scrolling on her phone, looking for stories that would comfort her that people survived this, that Charlotte would survive this.

When sleep did claim her, dreams assailed her rest. In one, Steve and Charlotte were just ahead, climbing a soft slope. Trying to catch them, she called out, 'Wait!' Her voice was taken by the breeze; it returned their laughter to her. The sun deepened the blue of the sky and the green of the grass, but they got further away. Steve picked up Charlotte and turned her around and around, her head thrown back in joy. From somewhere beyond the sky a beep persisted. Joanna tried to ignore it as she called to them, 'Wait for me!' It got louder and louder.

The hospital room came into focus. An alarm from the machine above Charlotte's bed ended with the push of a button from the nurse from the night before. She smiled at Joanna. 'Everything's fine. You can go back to sleep.'

At eight o'clock the next morning, the electric light through the door was almost as loud as the tea trolley that rattled past. After a soft knock, a kind face appeared around the door. 'Can I get you a cup of tea, love? How do you take it?'

For a moment, Joanna didn't know where she was. The memory of the day before came crashing in like a wave that threatened to pull her under. It was all she could to do to nod and whisper, 'Yes, please. With milk. No sugar.'

The heavy green cup wobbled on its saucer as the tea lady slipped it onto the cupboard next to Charlotte's bed. 'I'll leave it there for you.'

Pushing herself up and out from under the thin hospital blanket – when did her body get so creaky? – she leaned over to find Charlotte remained still as a statue. 'Good morning, sweet-heart.' She searched her face for any movement. There was none. But it was still early days. Far too early to be sure about anything.

Her eyes swept the length of her daughter. In that body was another little baby. When she and Sally were pregnant together, they'd learned that – if their babies were girls – they were already carrying the eggs that could bear their own children. Effectively, they were carrying their own grandchildren. It was such a strangely beautiful thought. If Charlotte's baby was a girl, then she would have the eggs that could make her great grandchildren. Hers and Steve's.

Rubbing at her face, she tried not to think about any of that. Most important thing was to get Charlotte well. She took her hand and laid it on her stomach. 'Your baby is in there, Charlotte. You need to wake up. She's going to need you.'

She'd had so many hopes and dreams for Charlotte. Clever, funny, beautiful and kind: the world should've been her oyster. But the most normal life would be a gift right now. It didn't matter that she hadn't gone to Durham University as they'd planned, choosing Colchester instead so that she could stay closer to home and her friends. It didn't matter that Charlotte had spent the last year picking up temporary waitressing work rather than getting a 'proper' job so that she could focus on her band. Whatever she wanted would be fine. As long as she woke up.

In her handbag was the comb Joanna always carried. When Charlotte was little, she hated having her hair brushed and would ask again and again if she could have it all cut off. Steve couldn't understand why she wouldn't let her. 'It'll grow back, Jo. What does it matter if she wants it short?'

But she looked so beautiful with long hair. 'She'll regret it if she cuts it short. I know she will.' Eventually the decision had been taken for her when Charlotte had attacked the sides of her hair with the kitchen scissors. She looked like an extra in a sci-fi film. Joanna had cried when the hairdresser had to cut it to chin length to even it out. Charlotte had been ecstatic. How ironic that now her long hair was one of her favourite things about herself. Unable to bear thinking about what the back of her head might look like, Joanna gently combed her fringe until it was smooth, then arranged the front of her hair on either shoulder. 'There you go, my love. Back to yourself again.'

Watching over her like this reminded Joanna of the nights she'd tried to get her to sleep as a toddler. Lying beside her in bed, reading story after story. At every *Happily Ever After* she would hold up her index finger at Joanna and say, 'Just one more, Mummy. Just one more.'

The lunch trolley had just rattled its way down the corridor when there was a soft knock on the door. When she saw who it was, relief washed through Joanna's body like a warm bath. Sally was here.

'You came.'

'Of course I came. Where else would I be?' Sally reached out her arms and pulled Joanna into a tight warm embrace.

Everything about Sally – short stylish hair, well-cut navy suit, creaseless pale-pink shirt, Jo Malone Blackberry and Bay perfume – emphasised her efficient, confident ease with the world. Just for a few seconds, Joanna's shoulders dropped and she let herself breathe. With Sally holding her up, everything she'd been pushing down since yesterday bubbled to the surface and she released heaving, painful sobs into her dear friend's shoulder.

Sally stayed strong, held her tight, waited for the storm to pass. When the tears subsided, she stayed there, still. From inside Sally's embrace, Joanna's voice was muffled. 'I'm so glad you're here.'

With a final squeeze, Sally released her and turned to Charlotte. The shock on her face showed how unprepared she must've been by Joanna's brief text message. 'Has she still not woken up?'

Those words transported Joanna to the many mornings when a teenage Charlotte would still be in bed near lunchtime. They didn't correspond at all to the reality of the situation. 'The doctor said that the next couple of days will be critical. If she's going to regain consciousness—'

'If?' Sally's head snapped around towards her. 'Of course she's going to regain consciousness. This is Charlotte we're talking about. When have you ever known her to miss out on anything that's going on?'

Joanna smiled. It was true. Even as a little baby, Charlotte would want to go everywhere and do everything. 'Yes, you're right. *When* she regains consciousness.'

Sally pulled a chair close to the bed where she reached out for Charlotte's hand. 'Hello, sweetheart. It's Auntie Sally. I've come for a visit. And there you are sleeping through it. We need you to wake up now, love. Me and your mum. We need you to wake up and tell us who did this to you so that we can do something about it.'

Joanna swallowed. She was pretty sure she knew who'd done this but she didn't want to bring that up now. Who knew what Charlotte could hear? 'Listen to your Auntie Sally, Charlotte. You know how bossy she gets if you don't.'

She looked at her best friend, checking that – after their last conversation – that joke had landed okay. Sally kept hold of Charlotte's hand as she looked to Joanna. 'Have they said anything else?'

There was something in her tone that made Joanna suspicious. Did she know? 'The doctor told me that she's pregnant. Twenty-eight weeks.'

Sally's face didn't change. 'I see.'

Why wasn't she as shocked as Joanna? There was only one explanation, but she couldn't believe it. 'You knew?'

Sally shook her head. 'No. Not for sure. She didn't say anything. I just had a feeling. That last time I met her for lunch, about six weeks ago, there was something about her. And she didn't want a drink. Said she had a hangover from the night before. But she always has a glass of champagne when we meet for lunch, it's tradition.'

Sally had always taken her godmother duties seriously, taking Charlotte out for ice cream as a child and a glass of wine as an adult, for regular 'dates' as they used to call it. Though Joanna loved their relationship, she'd often been a tiny bit jealous. 'Did you not think to say something?'

Sally had the decency to look a little sheepish. 'I didn't know for sure and it wasn't my news to tell if she was. I did try and get you to talk to her. On Saturday. The last time we spoke.'

The word *spoke* hung in the air between them. Yelled might have been more accurate. Joanna felt wretched as she remembered her words. 'Sally, I'm so sorry I...'

But Sally shook her head and reached out for Joanna's hand with the one that wasn't holding Charlotte's. 'There's no need for that. I totally overreacted. I've got some... stuff going on. I'll tell you about it later. Not now. Let's focus on getting Charlotte better. You and I are fine. We'll always be fine.'

A fountain of emotion threatened to overwhelm Joanna again. She tried to head it off at the pass. 'Who's looking after Harry?'

Harry was Sally's son. The same age as Charlotte, he'd been diagnosed with autism when he was four. He lived at home with Sally and Graham, but it was getting more and more difficult to manage his needs. 'Graham's not working today, so I've left them to have a boys' day. If he has to, he can go into work late tomorrow after he's dropped Harry at his day club so that I can stay with you.'

Her friend's love was so fierce it almost hurt. She didn't deserve this after the way she'd spoken to her. Tears filled Joanna's eyes. 'Thank you for being here. It means so much to me.'

'Don't be silly. Of course I'm here. You and this girl are my family.' Sally wasn't given to tears – Steve used to call her *No-Stuff-And-Nonsense-Sally* – but Joanna could tell her throat was thick with feeling as she spoke.

Joanna was so lucky to have her. Without Sally at the other end of a phone, she wouldn't have got through the last year. And just think how she'd repaid her the last time they spoke. Her eyes welled up again and she brushed the tears away with the back of her hand. 'How was your drive here? Do you want me to hunt you down a coffee or something?'

Sally lived about ninety minutes away and normally didn't function for more than an hour without caffeine, but she shook her head. 'No. I'm fine. Do you want me to go home and get you anything? Or shall I stay here while you go home and take a shower?'

She didn't want to leave Charlotte's side, but really needed to wash her hair and clean her teeth. 'I definitely need to do something. Look at the state of me. I had to talk to the doctor looking like this. And the police. I don't know what they thought of me.'

Sally shook her head. 'You need to stop worrying what people think of you.'

Like godmother, like goddaughter. Hadn't Charlotte said the exact same thing? During one of the many rows they'd had about Freddie over the last year. 'You don't like him because you've written him off as arrogant because his family have money and he went to a posh school.'

She was right, but that wasn't the reason she didn't want him in her daughter's life. 'It's not that, Charlotte. It's about him not being right for you. Not being good enough for you.'

'Good enough? Who decides who's good and who's not? Freddie is one of the kindest, most thoughtful and caring men I've ever met. Isn't that good enough?'

She didn't want to hurt Charlotte, but she had to make her see the truth. How else could she protect her from having her heart trampled on all over again? 'How thoughtful and caring was he when you broke up? And what about his family? The way his mother was with you that day? What does she think about the two of you being together? How does she treat you now?'

Charlotte was sharp: she'd known exactly what Joanna was getting at. As if she were the parent, she'd shaken her head like Sally had just done. 'Do you know what, Mum? You'd be a lot happier if you stopped worrying what everyone else thinks.'

And then they'd had the argument about the bruises and she'd left. And Joanna had let her. If only she'd known that it would be the last time she'd see her before this happened. It was all such a terrible mess. She couldn't lose her daughter. Charlotte was all she had in the world. Just the thought of that took her straight back to the last time she was in here. The day when her world imploded.

EIGHT

It had all happened so quickly. No warning. In the October, Steve had collapsed at work and been rushed to hospital. Within days they were dealt the devastating blow. Inoperable brain tumour. He had two years. The only part they were thankful for was that Charlotte was away at university, giving them time to try to process the terrible prognosis.

Before that earth-shattering news, they'd been planning how to celebrate their fiftieth birthdays. She'd wanted a party; he'd preferred the idea of a holiday, just the two of them. In the end, they'd booked both. After that awful day, they knew that he was unlikely to reach the date of either of them.

After he'd recovered from the collapse, Steve seemed to rally. For three months, she'd dared to hope that he would defy what the doctors had said. They'd put off telling Charlotte at Christmas. She was in her final year at university and they didn't want her to be distracted. Then Steve wanted to wait until she'd finished her final exams the following July. Joanna didn't agree with keeping it from her, but Steve was impossible to refuse. She knew why. When they told Charlotte, it would become real. He'd have to look his daughter in the eye and see her pain. Would have to acknowledge to himself that he wouldn't see her grow up, get married, have children. All the while they kept it between themselves, a horrible secret, life could continue as normal.

By July, Steve had taken a turn for the worse and their subterfuge became impossible. When Charlotte returned home from her last exam – before she'd even had her graduation ball – she could see for herself that something was badly wrong. When they told her, it felt as if they were giving her a death sentence too.

She'd shaken her head furiously. 'No. No, Dad. This isn't happening.'

Steve's eyes had shone with the tears he was trying to keep back. 'It is, baby girl. I'm so sorry.'

She'd looked at Joanna then. 'They have to be able to do something. They have to be able to operate. Or radiotherapy. Or chemo. Why aren't they doing anything?'

Joanna had tried to explain why it wasn't possible to operate on the tumour because of where it was, but her own words were drowned in tears. 'We have to be strong for your dad now, love. Like he's always been strong for us.'

But Charlotte had just repeated over and over, 'I don't want to be strong. I don't want to be strong.' Until Steve had pulled her to him and held her close while her slim body had jacked up and down with her sobs. Over her shoulder, he'd looked at Joanna and mouthed, 'It'll be okay.'

But it was never okay again.

The day after they told her, unable to be angry with the father she was going to lose, it was Joanna who'd had a thousand difficult conversations. 'Why didn't you tell me? I wouldn't have booked all those gigs for the weekends I was home. I would've been here.'

'That's what your dad didn't want, love. He wanted you to enjoy being with your friends.'

'But I can see them anytime. I only have a few months with Dad. That should've been my choice. I've just been deprived of that time with him.'

How could Joanna argue when that was the exact same case she'd made to Steve when he'd put it off. Now all she could do was try to ease the pain as much as she could. 'We just need to make the most of this time, love.'

She'd taken Charlotte into her arms and rocked her like a baby, kissing the side of her head and wishing, so much, that she could take this agony away.

And then, Freddie Knight-Crossley made her daughter's pain even worse.

She still didn't know the details of what had happened that day. All she knew was that, after leaving to speak to him, to seek comfort, Charlotte had come home even more broken than when she'd left. It was all over between them. She didn't want to talk about it. She just wanted to focus on spending time with her dad.

Joanna hadn't pushed her to confide what had gone on, but all the anger she had about the tumour, the impending loss of her husband, of Charlotte being denied her father, now had somewhere else to focus. Whoever said hell hath no fury like a woman scorned had it wrong; the fury of a mother whose child has been hurt is incendiary. If it wouldn't have made Charlotte feel even worse, she would've hunted that boy down and made him know what he'd done to her precious girl at the worst time in her life; the worst time in all of their lives. She would never forgive him.

By that Christmas, Steve had barely been able to lift his head from the pillow. 'I'm sorry, love. I'm sorry that I'm leaving you.'

She'd shaken her head, trying to avoid his words. 'No, you're not leaving. You're not going anywhere.'

He'd taken her hand then and she'd felt the weakness in

him. Her husband, who'd always been their foundation, always protected them, kept them safe. 'You and Charlotte need to look after one another.'

It had been difficult between her and Charlotte. She'd tried to be patient. Tried not to tell her that she was well rid of that selfish, entitled boy. But they were both at the end of their rope, both trying to keep their brightest faces for Steve, which meant they saved their short tempers and frustrations for each other. Even though they would flip from biting at one another one moment, then back to tears and apologies at the turn of a switch. At Steve's words, she'd fought to keep the tears back, knowing if she started that she might never stop. 'Of course, I'll look after her. I'm her mum. But you'll be there, too. You can't give up, Steve. We need you.'

His smile had barely moved his tired face. 'Okay, love. I'll stay.'

But he hadn't been able to stay and she hadn't looked after Charlotte, had she? If she had, she would've realised that she and Freddie were back in touch. Stopped her from allowing him back into her life. If she'd done that, they wouldn't be in this position now. Back here in this place, where the scraps of her life that she'd tried to pull back together had been ripped apart anew.

Sally came in the door backwards with two takeaway cups of coffee in her hands. 'It's very kind of Pamela the tea lady to make us something, but I can't drink that slop. Thank goodness the hospital has a Costa now. That's an upgrade from the last time I was here.'

It was no surprise that Sally knew the name of the tea lady already. She'd probably made best friends with half the ward on her way back with the coffee. Joanna accepted the offered cup, its warmth comforting in her hands. 'Yes, there's an M&S Food, too.'

Sally took the lid from her coffee and blew on it. 'I clocked that. I'll pick us up a sandwich later. The hospital is going upmarket.'

It was so good to have her here. 'How long can you stay? Will you need to get back to Harry and Graham tonight?'

'No. I think it'll do them some good to be without me.'

Sally's tone had changed. She sounded tense or irritated. Joanna was surprised. 'Why's that?'

But Sally just shook her head. 'Oh nothing. Just ignore me. Maybe it's me who needs a bit of a break. I'm sorry that I snapped at you on Saturday.'

Though they'd been friends since school, Joanna and Sally had rarely had a cross word. Their personalities interweaved so seamlessly that there was no need for conflict. But Joanna's thoughtlessness over the phone on Saturday had provoked a strong reaction in her best friend.

They'd been talking about Charlotte. Joanna was upset that things had been so strained between them since their argument in the hallway. There'd been text messages back and forth but they'd been functional rather than friendly. And neither had apologised or tried to make amends.

'You need to call her.' Sally had been adamant. 'You haven't got Steve here to smooth it all out between you.'

Though she was right, it was the reminder of what she'd lost that'd made Joanna less than tactful. 'That's easy for you to say. You don't know what it's like. I'm worried about her every hour of every day.'

There'd been a pause at the other end. 'I don't know what it's like to worry about a child?'

Joanna had known she'd been tactless, but she was still cross. 'Of course I'm not saying that. But you know where

Harry is. He's not out there hanging around with who knows what.'

Sally's raised voice had come as a shock. 'Believe me, I would much rather be worried about Harry's choice of girl-friend than how the hell he's going to navigate the real world. You don't know how lucky you are.'

'Lucky? Lucky? Did you remember that my husband just died?'

'Of course I remember. I was there. But you need to start looking at what you've got, Joanna.'

She wasn't sure who'd hung up first. But she remembered sitting there shaking, staring at the phone and wondering what the hell had caused the two of them to speak to each other like that.

Now she reached for her friend's hand. 'I'm sorry, too. You were right. I should've looked at what I have. My beautiful daughter. Over the years, I got so used to Steve making it better when Charlotte and I had a falling out that I've forgotten how to do it. And I feel like such an awful friend for what I said. I know how hard it's been for you and Graham looking after Harry.'

Sally frowned into her coffee cup. Was Joanna being over-sensitive or was something else going on here? 'Yes, well. That's a conversation for another day.'

They sat and sipped their coffees, either side of the bed. Sally had sat with her like this for days after Steve's death. Not leaving her side for a moment. She'd brought Harry with her to stay at Joanna's house. He'd looked for Steve – one of his favourite people – each day until he'd finally understood that Steve was gone. Joanna had felt as bewildered by his absence as Harry was. Steve had been the linchpin in that house, their family. He was the one who made everything work. She needed him as much as oxygen right now. 'What do you think Steve would say if he was here?'

Sally's face softened into memory. She'd loved Steve almost as much as her own husband. The four of them had been such good friends. 'I think he'd be telling one of his stories. You know those awful ones he'd tell the kids when they were little. With bodily functions and crazy animals who did the most ludicrous things?'

The memory of his animated face – the children screaming with delight at the naughty animal characters he'd invent – brought a smile to Joanna's face that almost hurt her cheeks. 'I used to tell him off about those. I'd imagine Charlotte going into school and reciting them and then me getting a call from social services.'

Sally's laugh was soft. 'Do you remember Vampire Rabbit and his murderous sprees?'

Joanna groaned. 'Don't remind me.'

'The kids loved them though, didn't they? Harry used to roar with laughter.' She sighed and frowned at her coffee. 'Steve was so good with Harry.'

All kids had loved Steve. There was something childlike about him that they just gravitated towards. He was safe. Kind. They knew they could trust him. 'I wish he was here now.' Her voice wobbled but her eyes seemed to have run out of tears.

Sally reached across the bed for her hand. 'Me, too, Jo.'

A wave of loneliness washed over Joanna. 'It's not right. Losing Steve was the worst thing that ever happened to me. How can it be fair that this has happened to our daughter only a year later?'

Sally rubbed her thumb over Joanna's hand, her voice was gentle. 'Yeah, life isn't fair. But she's a fighter. Like her dad. She'll come through this, Jo. She will. Give her time.'

Joanna wanted to believe that, she really did. But Sally hadn't seen the expression on the doctor's face. Hadn't heard the tone of his voice. She had to be strong though. Like Steve would've been if he was here. 'I was googling cases last night. People who've been in comas and come around.'

Sally squeezed her hand before letting it go and sitting back in her chair. 'There you go then. And if they can do it, you can bet that Charlotte will.'

She was right. There was nothing to be gained from thinking the worst. They had to be positive. 'Can I take you up on your offer of going to the house and getting me some fresh clothes? I think I'd feel better if I could get out of these gardening trousers.'

Sally stood immediately. She was like Steve: a doer. Never happier than when they had a job to do. 'Of course. Just tell me what you need and give me your door key.'

Not knowing how long she was going to be staying here, Joanna wanted to be prepared with enough things to last her. While Joanna described and explained where to find them, Sally wrote a list on her phone of the clothes that she wanted her to bring, then looked at her with a frown. 'Don't you want something more comfortable than that? Jogging bottoms, maybe? Leggings?'

Joanna shook her head. 'I don't own jogging bottoms and, as for leggings, I want to look smart. I want to look like me when she wakes up.'

What would she give right now to have Charlotte roll her eyes at her mother's insistence that appearances matter? That people judge you, and treat you differently, because of what you wear and how you look and where you come from. Until she'd shared with her why it was so important, Charlotte hadn't understood how deeply it mattered to Joanna. Maybe that was a good thing. Protecting her from experiencing that pain had been her driving force since Charlotte was born. Although she couldn't help but wonder if she'd got that wrong, too.

Sally held up her hands to give in. 'Okay. Whatever you want.'

Once she was gone, the silence crept back in the door. Joanna cleared her throat with a cough and made her voice as strong and as upbeat as she could manage. 'We've just been talking about your dad, love. And those crazy stories he used to tell you. Do you remember?'

The only response was the sound of the ventilator, but she forced herself to continue. 'Well, we'll have to remember them, won't we, so you can tell your little one when he or she arrives. You'll have to do them because I can't remember all the voices. I think I'll stick to the *Each Peach Pear Plum* book. I know how to read that one.'

The coffee in her hands was cold now, but it still soothed the tightness of her throat. Though she'd promised to try and stay positive, here – on her own – it was so hard. Maybe when Sally brought her clothes, when she'd had a shower, she might feel a bit stronger. When a nurse came to do the checks, she took the opportunity to go and splash some cold water on her face at least.

In the bathroom, there was a young mum helping her daughter to wash her hands. The little girl watched as her mother waved her own hands under the automatic soap dispenser, then followed her lead. It seemed like yesterday and forever ago that Charlotte was that small. When she was little, she wanted to be just like Joanna, even liking them to dress the same. But then teenage hormones had got their claws into her and, almost overnight, everything that Joanna did was wrong.

The hand dryer roared into action and the little girl jumped back. Her mother took her hand and held it in hers under the dryer, showing her that there was nothing to be afraid of. All Joanna had wanted was to make Charlotte's life easier and better. Maybe she didn't get it right all the time, but she'd only ever wanted the best for her.

She waited for the little girl and her mother to leave before splashing some cold water on her tired face. Her eyes seemed to have aged another decade in the last twenty-four hours. Not wanting to leave Charlotte alone, she shook her hands under the dryer only a couple of times before hurrying back to her room.

When she got there, the door was ajar. Expecting to see the nurse checking Charlotte's blood pressure and oxygen saturation, Joanna was surprised to see someone else standing just inside the room, staring at her daughter. A young man. Not only were they not in any kind of uniform, but they were wearing a hooded jacket and trainers, like they were on the way to the gym. Who the heck was it?

NINE

To her relief, the slight figure with close-cropped black hair in Charlotte's room wasn't – as Joanna had feared – a boy who might've been connected to Freddie. When she turned, Joanna could see from her perfectly made-up face that she was a woman nearer her own age, wearing a brand of fitness clothes she'd only seen on the celebrities in her Instagram feed. 'Hello? Can I help you?'

The woman looked her up and down, her face hard and unfriendly. 'No, I'm fine. I'm just visiting someone.'

The heckles rose on the back of Joanna's neck. 'I can see that. I'm Charlotte's mother. Are you a friend of hers?'

Like a light being switched on, the woman's face opened in recognition. 'Oh, I'm terribly sorry. I didn't realise. No, I mean, yes, I mean...' she tailed off. 'I'll start again. Hello, I'm Annabelle Knight-Crossley. Freddie's mother.'

Joanna's whole body went rigid with shock. Freddie's *mother*? What was she doing here? In what world would she imagine her presence was welcome? Open-mouthed, she stared at her. She was an attractive woman and, now she'd introduced herself, Joanna could see the likeness with her son. She also recognised the assured clipped tone that reinforced the effect of the polished hair and make-up. The confidence with which she held herself as she took a step towards Joanna.

Annabelle either didn't register the look of horror on Joanna's face or didn't care about it. People like her rarely did. 'I came as soon as I heard what happened. Is Charlotte going to be alright?'

Despite believing with every ounce of her being that Charlotte *was* going to recover, Joanna wanted this woman to know the severity of what her son had done. Arms crossed in front of her chest, she poured as much blame into her words as she could. 'We don't know what's going to happen. She's in a coma. They've told me to prepare for the worst.'

Annabelle's hand flew to her face; her perfectly manicured fingernails fluttered in front of her mouth. 'Oh no. I can't believe it. Poor Charlotte. Freddie will be devastated.'

Joanna moved nearer to the bed, ready to defend her daughter if this woman came a step closer. 'I'm not sure that Freddie gets to feel anything, given he was the one who put her here.'

Even saying his name felt like poison in her mouth, but his mother was quick to shake her head. 'No. You have it wrong. Freddie is a gentle soul who wouldn't have hurt a hair on her head. He adores Charlotte. We all do.'

Joanna gritted her teeth at this description of the arrogant entitled boy who'd put her daughter in hospital. But as this woman spoke, she couldn't shake off the idea that there was something about her that Joanna recognised. Was it, perhaps, just that she looked like her son? Regardless, Joanna knew about people like her and their attitude towards anyone not in their social sphere. Ordinarily, she'd have crossed the street rather than face this woman. But circumstances made her brave. 'That's not what the police think.'

Annabelle's face stiffened, but her patronising smile stayed firmly in place. 'Freddie is merely helping them with their enquiries. He'll want to make sure that they find whoever is responsible for this. I will be telling them myself that he wouldn't have hurt her. He worshipped the ground that girl walked on.'

Joanna had been primed for an argument, but if she'd expected this woman to be angry at her accusations, that wasn't what she got. Annabelle seemed more focused on making her understand that Freddie was innocent. And she wasn't about to let her do that. 'Well, the evidence speaks for itself. He was there and my daughter is lying here.'

Annabelle stepped closer to the bed; Joanna wanted to lay herself across Charlotte's body like a blanket to stop this woman from even looking at her innocent daughter, as if she'd contaminate her by her mere presence. Annabelle shook her head woefully. 'She's such a beautiful girl. You must be terribly proud of her.'

The change of subject wrong-footed Joanna for a moment. 'I am.'

'I was so pleased when Freddie brought her home. What a well-brought-up young girl. That's what I thought.'

Joanna didn't believe that for a second. And what did Annabelle expect her to say? Was she trying to manipulate her into believing her perspective? 'Well, it's a shame he didn't look after her better.'

Annabelle's voice had the cut-glass edge of someone who was used to being listened to. 'Look. I understand that you are worried about your daughter, of course I do. I'm worried about her myself. But I'm also worried about my son. He's being questioned by the police when he should be here with Charlotte. He must be worried sick about her, too.'

Was she seriously here to lobby on her son's behalf? Joanna

wasn't able to listen to this. 'I don't want to talk about your son right now. I think it's best if you go.'

Annabelle looked panicked then. 'No. Sorry. Ignore me, please. I'd just like to sit with her for a while. I've rushed here and... I just don't know what to do with myself.'

She did look genuinely upset. Did Charlotte have a relationship with this woman? She'd have been very surprised if she did; Charlotte hadn't ever bad-mouthed Freddie's mother, but she'd told Joanna on many occasions that Freddie was 'nothing like his family'.

Once, Joanna had pushed her to expand on that comment and she'd chewed at her thumbnail, a habit from childhood. 'They want him to work in the City. Like his dad did. But he wants more out of life. He wants to travel. Make art and music.'

Joanna hadn't been able to keep the mockery from her laugh. 'It's easy to want to do those things when someone else is footing the bill.'

'And that's why I don't talk to you about him.' Charlotte had flounced off. Lately, their conversations had all seemed to end that way.

Whether or not Charlotte had liked his mother, Annabelle did look genuinely distraught at seeing Charlotte in this state and Joanna didn't want to cause a scene by insisting that she leave. In any case, she didn't know if security would remove someone if they weren't causing a disturbance. 'The nurse will be here soon to do her observations. You can stay here for a little while.'

Annabelle looked positively grateful. 'Thank you. I know you must be terrified for her. I can't even imagine how I'd feel if it was my child lying there.'

Joanna had to push her hand to her mouth to prevent herself from saying she wished it was Annabelle's son laying there instead of her innocent daughter. Instead, she nodded towards the second chair, which had been pushed against the wall. 'You can bring that over if you want to. The nurse said it might help to talk to her.'

Annabelle pulled the chair across the room, the legs scraping the floor. She kept a slight distance between her and the bed. 'Hello, Charlotte, darling. It's me. Annabelle. Come to check on you. Freddie can't be here at the moment—' she moved an imaginary stray hair from her forehead with her middle finger '—but I know he's thinking about you. And about the baby.'

Across the bed, Joanna felt as if she'd been slapped. The baby? Annabelle knew about the baby? They'd told Freddie's mother that they were expecting and not her? Joanna's chest burned with the pain of the betrayal; grief squeezed her throat. Had she been so awful that Joanna would rather confide her news in this woman than in her? Did she really deserve that?

For the next few moments, the sound of the ventilator filled the silence in the room. When Annabelle spoke, her voice was suspiciously light. 'Did they say whether the baby would be okay?'

Was that the real reason that she was here? Nothing to do with concern for Charlotte. Why was she surprised? 'Right now, the baby is fine.'

Not for a moment was she going to admit that she knew nothing about the child her daughter was carrying. Annabelle seemed to assume that she'd known all about it. 'The baby will be a first grandchild for both of us, I assume?'

She hadn't even thought about the baby in those terms. Mainly because it still felt completely surreal that there was a child at all. 'Yes.'

Then it happened. Was it the way Annabelle raised an eyebrow? Or the look in her eyes? Or the downturn of her mouth? Whatever it was, that was the moment when Joanna

realised exactly who Annabelle Knight-Crossley was and a chill
ran down her spine. Just like that, she travelled back over three
decades and her body tensed for attack. How could she be here
now, in her life, in her daughter's life?

Annabelle's cut-glass voice, delivered down her nose, sliced
through Joanna like a razor. 'Freddie is my only one, too. I was
so glad to have a son.'

All this time and she hadn't realised who Freddie's mother
was. How cruel was fate that it would bring her back into her
life. Especially now, in the midst of all this? And Charlotte had
told her about the baby? And not told her own mother? Blood
boiling, Joanna tried to swallow down the hot tears of rage. 'I
was happy to have a daughter. She was everything I ever
wanted.'

They had tried for more children, but it'd never happened
and Joanna hadn't been too disappointed. They were very
happy as a family of three and it'd meant that they had enough
money to give Charlotte the kind of life she'd wanted for her.
Foreign holidays and riding lessons and music tuition. All the
things that she'd had to give up as a child.

Annabelle was looking at her now with eyes that were
aggravatingly sympathetic. 'Charlotte told me about her dad.
Your husband. I'm sorry for your loss.'

In all the time that Joanna had kept Freddie at arm's length,
hoping that the relationship would run its course sooner rather
than later, she'd had no idea that Charlotte was spending time
with his family. With his mother. Annabelle Knight-Crossley.
Annabelle Miles, as she'd known her all those years ago. To
really rub salt in the wound, Annabelle was looking at her with
the annoying head tilt she'd grown to hate since Steve died.
Joanna wasn't about to let this woman see how upset she was.
She stuck out her chin. 'Yes, it was a shock.'

'They were close, weren't they? Charlotte and her father?
Bit of a daddy's girl?'

Was she trying to suggest that Joanna wasn't as close to her daughter? Yes, Charlotte and Steve had been close. Whether it was passing him tools in his workshop, or the improvised stories that made her squeal at bedtime, she'd loved to be with him. This last year, they'd both missed him so much that it'd been difficult for them to learn how to live without him there. Their glue, their buffer. 'Yes. She misses him a great deal.'

This time, it was impossible to stop her eyes from misting over with tears. Annabelle reached for the box of tissues beside Charlotte's bed and passed it to her. 'I lost Freddie's father when he was only ten. I know how hard it is.' Annabelle smiled at her. 'We've got quite a lot in common, haven't we?'

If only she knew. But what would be the point of bringing that up now? She just wanted to get this conversation over with and get this woman out of here. 'Maybe.'

Annabelle narrowed her eyes. 'Is it just because of the likeness with Charlotte, or do I know you from somewhere?'

That was the last thing she needed. 'No. I don't think so.'

'Are you sure, because... it really feels as if we've met before.'

Joanna was saved by the nurse arriving to check on Charlotte. 'Sorry, I need to speak to the nurse.'

This time Annabelle took the hint; the chair scraped backwards as she stood. 'Of course. Look, let me give you my number. In case you need anything. And to let me know how poor Charlotte is doing.'

That voice grated on Joanna's tender nerves. The last thing she wanted was Annabelle having her number, but what could she say? She already had her phone out of her bag and was waiting, red fingernail poised over the keypad, for Joanna to give it to her. Once she'd repeated it back for confirmation, she leaned over the bed and kissed Charlotte on the forehead. 'Bye, sweetie. See you soon.'

Joanna stayed seated and waved goodbye. As soon as

Annabelle was out of the door, she pulled a wipe from the packet on the table and leaned across Charlotte to clean the smudge of red lipstick from her forehead.

An hour later, when Sally returned with a small suitcase of clothes and toiletries, the first thing she said after thanking her was, 'You're never going to guess who Freddie's mother is.'

TEN

FREDDIE

Weeks after it happened, Freddie had told Charlotte what her mother had overheard – Dominic's voice booming from the FaceTime call on her doorstep – and she'd almost fallen from her chair laughing.

Their first date had only confirmed to him how fantastic she was. He could've spent the whole night listening to her talk, the way her hands would punctuate her sentences and her eyes glimmer with her plans. 'We're going to make the band work. I've started to write some songs. I want us to play our own stuff.'

'That's amazing.'

He'd meant it, too. To have both the talent and the ambition to make it work was quite something.

She'd tilted her head, flicked her long blonde hair over her shoulder. 'What about you? What do you want to do?'

He'd shrugged. 'I have to go into the family business. Financial stuff.' He didn't want to talk about it in detail, it bored him enough; he didn't want to bore her, too.

She'd laughed. 'That doesn't sound like it's setting your world on fire.'

'It's not. But what can you do?'

She'd frowned at him as if he was speaking a foreign language that she didn't understand. 'Just... not do it?'

His laugh had been hollow. 'Not an option. Since my father died, my mother has been attending every boring board meeting in his place to keep my seat warm, as she'd put it. She was convinced my cousins might try and squeeze me out.' He raised an eyebrow. 'No such luck.'

Charlotte had shuffled back in her seat, placed her drink down on the table and looked him dead in the eye. God, she was beautiful. 'That's ridiculous. If you don't want to do it, you should tell her. You can't choose your whole career based on what your mother wants you to do.'

Said like that, he'd seen why she was surprised. It was more complex than he'd wanted to get into on their first date, though. 'What about your parents? What do they want you to do?'

She'd picked up her glass and sipped at her beer. 'They just want me to be happy.'

There was something about her expression that had told him there was more. 'Really?'

She'd laughed the warm throaty laugh that had made him want to pull her close. 'Well, my dad just wants me to be happy. My mum wants me to be happy as long as I do it the way she wants.'

That'd made him grin. 'Which is...?'

'Which is, get my degree, get a great job, travel the world, solve world peace.'

He'd just taken a large gulp of his beer and he'd choked on it as she'd got to the end of her list. 'Not much then.'

'No. Should have it done by the end of the week.' She'd sighed. 'I'm exaggerating, but she does have pretty high expectations. She went to private school, my mum. Like you. But she had to leave and I think the whole thing has left her with a bit of a chip on her shoulder about your type.'

Under the table, she'd nudged his legs with her knee to

show she was teasing him. Electricity had run through his whole body. He'd cleared his throat before he could speak. 'Mothers, eh?'

She'd nodded and taken another sip of her beer. 'Absolutely.'

Freddie had had enough girlfriends that he was an old hand at knowing the right time to go in for the first kiss. But being around Charlotte made him feel like a novice. In the end, it'd been her who'd reached for him as they'd left the bar and, when their lips touched, he'd known that he never wanted it to end.

That summer had been the best of his life. She'd been working as a waitress in a small cafe and he would wait for her to finish her shift and then pick her up with a plan for what they'd do that night. Sometimes it would involve their friends, others it would just be the two of them and he would bring a small picnic or a bottle of wine and take her to the nature reserve. They would lay a blanket on the grass and stretch out side by side, eyes closed, holding hands, talking about their hopes and dreams for the future. He'd never wanted the long warm days to end.

When she'd gone back to university in late September, he'd missed her like a limb, but they'd both been determined to make it work. They'd alternate the travel: one weekend he'd visit her; the following weekend she'd take the train home. Dominic wasn't impressed, but Freddie had known – with every inch of him – that she was worth it. She was the one.

Which is why he was so angry with himself for messing it up. For risking everything he had with her on one stupid night. For what he did that Christmas.

ELEVEN

When Joanna told her who Freddie's mother was, Sally made a huge exaggerated O with her mouth just as she might've done when they were fourteen. 'You're kidding! Annabelle Miles? From the private school? Are you sure?'

Joanna nodded. 'Completely sure. I just can't believe what a horrible coincidence it is.'

From the moment she started at Brent Hall school, Joanna hadn't fit in.

It wouldn't have been easy to start any school in the fourth year. But being transferred from a state school, once her father was making enough to be able to afford the fees, had been cripplingly difficult. Though her parents now had a very comfortable life due to the success of her father's law practice, she was a minnow in the big pond of wealth at the private boarding school in Suffolk.

Joanna hadn't boarded. Instead, her mother would drive her over an hour to school every day. A sacrifice she said that she was willing to make 'so that you meet the right kind of people'.

Whether they were 'right' or not, the students she met there seemed in no doubt that she was wrong. Whether it was her estuary English accent, the car her mother drove or the fact that she was quickly outed as a 'state schooler', she was made to feel that she didn't belong.

Beautiful Annabelle Miles, on the other hand, most definitely did belong. Coated with the confidence of wealth, she and her entourage would sweep around the school as if they were the ones in charge.

Now Sally was shaking her head in amazement. 'I can't believe it's her. All this time and you never knew. Was it horrible talking to her?'

'Yes. It was pretty unpleasant.' The moment she'd recognised her, Joanna had felt sucked back into the feelings of shame and isolation that had dogged most of her time at the school. From the beginning, Annabelle Miles had made her life hell. Whispering behind her hand about her in class, louder in the corridors. No one wanted to be friends with Joanna knowing that they would also be putting themselves in the Annabelle firing line.

She'd never known loneliness like it. At the local comprehensive she'd come from, she'd got on with everyone. And she'd had Sally there. Maybe the only thing that got her through the move to the private school was having Sally to unload on each night. Her parents hadn't wanted to listen. They'd been so adamant that Brent Hall was the right place for her.

Sally screwed up her face. 'I can remember you telling me what she was like. How awful she was when you started dating Jacob.'

The bullying had stepped up a notch then. Jacob was one of the boys in their year and, when he'd started to pay her attention, Annabelle had done everything she could to keep them apart. When they'd started going out, Jacob had defended her, been her protector. For a while, things had got better for her at school. Until everything had got much much worse.

Sally had brought two coffees with her and, after kissing

Charlotte very gently, she settled herself next to the bed and took the lid off to blow on the scalding liquid. 'Did she recognise you?'

For a horrible moment, it had seemed that she might and that was the last thing Joanna needed. 'I think I got away with it. It was horrible, though. Speaking to her just reminded me what she was like. What they were all like. It reminded me why I didn't want Charlotte mixing with Freddie. People like that, they think they're different from us. They can't be trusted.'

Sally frowned into her coffee. 'To be fair, you don't really know what she's like now. You were both kids back then. People change. What did she seem like?'

Joanna hated having to admit that she'd been very kind. 'She was fine. And she did tell me to call her if I needed anything. But she was so adamant that Freddie couldn't have hurt Joanna.'

Sally shrugged. 'Well, he is her son. I suppose we're all protective of our children.'

It was understandable that Sally would say that. Her Harry had had his fair share of unpleasantness from other people over the years. People who had clearly judged his behaviour as if he was a naughty boy rather than a child with autism trying to make sense of his world. 'I know, but how can you defend someone who has done this? She tried to tell me that she thought the world of Charlotte, but you can't say that and then let him get away with what he's done.'

Sally kept her voice gentle. 'We don't know the facts yet, Jo.'

She sounded like Steve. Whenever she'd gone off on a rant about something or someone, he'd tried to make her think about the other side of the argument. But when your child was lying hurt, there was no other side. She could hear her voice rising, feel the panic taking over. 'I know it's him, Sally. From the moment I knew that they were together, I knew this was going to end badly. Why didn't I stop it? This is all my fault.'

Sally reached out for her hand. 'This is not your fault. Charlotte's twenty-two. She's an adult. You can't tell her what to do. You just have to hope she makes good choices and then be there to mop up the consequences when she doesn't.'

Again, she sounded like Steve. How many times had she accused the two of them of being siblings from different mothers? Her best friend and her husband seemed to view the world through rose-coloured spectacles. They didn't know what it was like to be on the outside looking in like she did. They'd never had the rug of life pulled out from beneath their feet and had to fight to stay balanced.

'Annabelle tried to say that the police are just talking to Freddie, but I know that it's more than that. He's the only other person who was there. I'm not just being horrible here, Sally. I'm not being prejudiced. He hurt my baby.'

As she collapsed into tears again, Sally's face softened. 'I know you're not being horrible. But let's focus on getting our girl better and let the police do their job with the other part.'

Joanna nodded, but deep down she was certain that Freddie had done this. The only thing she didn't know was why. Particularly if Charlotte was carrying his child. When Charlotte regained consciousness, she was going to make sure that she and the baby had nothing to do with that family ever again.

She couldn't help but wonder what she'd said about him to Sally. 'Did Charlotte talk about Freddie a lot when she was with you?'

Head tilted, Sally considered the question. 'I suppose she did. I mean, we had our monthly lunch date. And she called a few times, too. Just chatting about what they'd been up to and the things she was doing to the flat. She wanted my advice on places to go for the furnishings. She wanted something different. Not like everyone else.'

As she was a designer, it made sense for Charlotte to talk to

Sally about those things, but Joanna couldn't help but feel jealous. 'And she talked about him? About Freddie?'

One of the things she loved about her best friend was how frank she was. It was also one of the things she found most difficult. The eyebrow she raised spoke volumes. 'I guess she just wanted me to know that he was a good guy.'

Sally was being soft on her because of the situation, but the implication was clear. Charlotte hadn't wanted Sally's opinion of Freddie to be coloured by anything that Joanna might've said about him. 'Did you meet him?'

'Only once. He came to collect her from a lunch a couple of months ago. He was a bit early and we hadn't finished our coffee, so he joined us for a little while.'

That sounded very controlling of him. Charlotte would've been quite capable of making her own way home. And arriving early? 'What was he like?'

Sally smiled. 'Clearly infatuated with Charlotte. So careful when he helped her on with her coat and holding on to her hand. Of course, now we know that she was pregnant at the time, I suppose it makes sense.'

The reminder that Charlotte had been pregnant for weeks – months – without telling her heaped more blame on her head. She'd told Freddie's mother she was going to be a grandmother, but not her. Joanna had promised Steve that she would look after Charlotte, but she'd pushed her away to the extent that she hadn't even shared the most life-changing thing that had ever happened to her.

Joanna's phone was on charge on the bedside table and it moved across the top as it buzzed. She steeled herself for another call from the bank, but it wasn't a number that she recognised.

'Mrs Woodley?'

'Yes. Speaking.'

'It's DC Abbie Lineham. I was wondering if I could arrange

to come and see you tomorrow to talk further about your daughter?'

She swallowed the bile that rose in her throat. 'Yes. I'll be at the hospital with Charlotte. Can you come to talk to me here?'

'Of course. Is about ten a.m. okay?'

'Yes. Do you have any news for me? Has Freddie been charged?'

'No one has been charged at present. I'll explain everything when I see you tomorrow. I know that we've already spoken briefly, but if there's anything else you remember that might be relevant, please do let me know.'

Once the call was ended, she took Charlotte's hand before speaking to Sally. 'The police are coming to speak to me again tomorrow. I think they've got news. And they want to know if there's anything else we need to tell them about her and Freddie.'

Though Sally had brought her enough clothes for the next few days, the matron in charge of Charlotte's ward wouldn't countenance her staying in her room another night. Insisting that it had been a very special dispensation to let her stay there the first night, she sent her home around nine o'clock. 'If there is any change at all, we will call you immediately.'

Joanna didn't want to let go of Charlotte's hand. She thought of the young nurse leaving her son for the first time. It didn't matter how old they were, it was never easy to leave. 'Will someone be watching her? All the time?'

'Yes. I'll be here with her.' Another nurse she hadn't seen before stepped forwards and raised her hand.

'And you've got my number?'

Sally took her elbow. 'Come on, Jo. Let's go home and get some sleep and then we can come back first thing in the morning.'

After kissing Charlotte gently on the cheek, she allowed herself to be led away, leaving part of herself behind. It was a good job that Sally was there to drive her home because she'd come in a police car the night before. How had that only been yesterday?

On the way out of the ward, Sally's phone rang in the pocket of her jeans. She slipped it out, frowned at the display, then cancelled the call. 'Sorry. I forgot to put it on silent. It was just Graham.'

'You can take the call if you want.'

Sally never ignored her phone if she was away from Harry. So Joanna was surprised when she shook her head. 'No, it's fine. I don't need to talk to him.'

There was something in her tone that made an alarm bell ring. 'Is everything okay? I know you said you were going through some stuff, but it's nothing to do with Graham, is it?'

Though she'd asked the question, Joanna didn't think for a second it would be. Sally and Graham were solid. Their marriage second only to her own in how committed they were.

But Sally wasn't shaking her head emphatically, or telling her to 'behave yourself, we're fine'. Instead, she was chewing on her lip and looking shifty. 'It's nothing. Just a silly argument.'

It didn't look like a silly argument from her face. 'Then you need to talk to him. Don't leave it, Sally.'

It was only a few days ago that Sally had urged Joanna to speak to Charlotte and make things right, so the weight of that statement wasn't lost on her.

She sighed. 'I will. I just need some space. It'll be fine. And right now, there's more important things to think about. Like getting our girl to wake up and what that detective is going to tell you tomorrow.'

TWELVE

The following morning, a nurse had just been to do her checks and they were waiting to see the doctor when DC Lineham arrived.

Joanna had had a terrible night's sleep. Waking every hour from around 2 a.m. with guilt and fear whispering in her ear like gossiping gargoyles. All the arguments she'd had with Charlotte about Freddie replaying in her mind like reels of torture. How should she have handled it differently? What should she have said? Each time she rolled over in bed, she pulled another layer of blame over her with the duvet.

At 6 a.m. she'd given in and had a shower. After that, she'd been catatonic on the sofa doomscrolling until Sally got up and forced her to eat some toast and scrambled eggs. From 8.45 a.m., they were standing outside the doors to Charlotte's ward, ready to enter as soon as visitors were allowed in at nine.

At ten on the dot, DC Lineham knocked on the doorframe before stepping inside Charlotte's room. 'Hi, Mrs Woodley. I hope it was okay to come straight through?'

She was pleased that they were being so proactive. 'Of course. And call me Joanna. Please.'

DC Lineham smiled. She had the most perfect teeth Joanna had ever seen. 'And I'm Abbie. Do you want to talk in here or shall we go and get a coffee?'

Joanna glanced at Charlotte. She didn't like to leave her, but she wasn't sure how much she could hear and this conversation might not be the most positive thing. Sally came to her rescue. 'She'll be fine with me, Jo. And you can bring me back a latte.'

The coffee shop was directly inside the main entrance; they must've just missed the morning rush because it was very quiet. They ordered a coffee and took the sofas in the far corner. Abbie's tone was kind. 'How is your daughter?'

That was the million-dollar question. She gave the same response she kept getting from the nurses. 'She's stable.'

'That's good. My main reason for wanting to see you in person again was to give you an update on the case.' She paused. 'We've formally arrested Freddie Knight-Crossley in conjunction with the attack.'

Relief flooded through Joanna that at least this meant he couldn't turn up at the hospital. Last night, her 4 a.m. thoughts had included him storming the ward, demanding to see his girl-friend. At least that was one thing she wouldn't have to think about. 'So you know he definitely did it?'

In the wake of her relief, anger surged through her. Among the maelstrom of thoughts and worries and regrets plaguing her last night, she'd had a creeping fear that maybe she'd been too harsh on Freddie in the last few months, even that she'd jumped to conclusions too quickly. But now the police had arrested him, her anger returned with the force of a tiger that's been caged.

However, Abbie's response was less certain than she'd hoped. 'The situation is that we don't currently have a huge amount of evidence other than circumstantial, but if we don't charge him, we would have to let him go. We went in front of the magistrate this morning and it was a fight to prevent him being bailed. As I'm sure you can imagine, he presented a very clean cut image in court. But the family has a second home on the continent so we were able to argue that he might be a flight risk. Thankfully the magistrate agreed and he's been remanded in custody.'

In Abbie's tone of voice and raised eyebrow, Joanna was sure that the detective knew of old the type of entitled rich boy they were dealing with. It gave her hope. 'I'm glad you've got him locked up.'

Abbie inclined her head but didn't comment. 'The next step is to gather enough evidence to build a case. We've been trying to track down anyone who might've seen the two of them on Sunday, to build up a picture of what prefaced the altercation between them. We know from the apartment above that there'd been some shouting heard. Do you know if this was ordinary behaviour?'

Joanna's face burned. Did she know whether it was usual for her daughter to be in the kind of relationship where they screamed at one another, loud enough for their neighbours to hear? This was not the way Charlotte had portrayed their relationship. She'd always taken great pains to tell Joanna how calm and kind Freddie was. What could have made them yell at one another like that? Was it something to do with the pregnancy? 'I don't know. I haven't spent a lot of time with them as a couple.'

Abbie paused. 'But they've been together since she was twenty? And they live together? Did you not approve of the relationship?'

Not approve was the understatement of the century. She'd tried the first time they were together. Bitten her tongue as often as she could while unloading her concerns to her patient husband. But after he'd betrayed her, it'd been agony watching Charlotte – her beautiful confident girl – struggle to come to terms with their break-up. Compounded by the knowledge that – when they finally told her about Steve – there was so much more pain to come for her darling girl, that summer had been the biggest struggle of her life.

'To be honest, no. I didn't feel that he was an appropriate partner for my daughter. And yes, they did meet when they were twenty. But he broke up with her for several months. A few months before her father died.'

Abbie's eyes widened, but she continued to make notes in her small black book. This was what Charlotte hadn't been able to understand. When she and Freddie got back together, she'd expected Joanna to accept him, forgive him, believe that he wouldn't hurt her daughter again. How could she do that? How could she trust him with the most precious thing in her entire world when he'd proven that he could throw it away on a whim when it didn't suit him?

Abbie flicked back in her notes. 'When we last spoke, you mentioned the bruises on your daughter's arms. Have any other instances or suspicions come to mind?'

She looked expectant. If only Joanna could reel off a list of things that they could use to bolster their case. None of the suspicions she had were anything more than that; a gut feeling that Freddie Knight-Crossley was bad news. 'I'm sorry. I can't think of anything.'

'That's okay. As I say, we've been trying to build a picture of what happened that day. We've tried to speak to neighbours but, unfortunately, we haven't had much luck so far. They're very high-end apartments for such a young couple. I'm assuming they had some help with the deposit? Neither of them have a high income from what I've seen?'

Joanna could feel her cheeks burn. 'The apartment belongs to Freddie's family. Charlotte moved in with him several months ago. You said the neighbour upstairs had told you about the argument they heard?'

'Yes. They did. We'll speak to them again. But, in the meantime, are there any friends of Charlotte's who might've spent the day with her or at least heard from her on Saturday? Or Friday night?'

That was a much easier question to answer. 'She has two really close friends, Rachael and Lucy. They're in a band together. She's known them since school. I can ask them if they've seen her in the last few days?'

She should've called them anyway to tell them about Charlotte being in hospital. Pretty soon she'd have to start thinking about all the other people she needed to call. She'd hoped that Charlotte would've been awake by now. But maybe her friends coming might be the stimulation she needed. Everything she was reading online suggested talking to the patient. Sally had been wonderful, but maybe her friends would be even better.

Abbie smiled. 'That would be great. The other thing I wanted to ask you about was whether your daughter had a mobile phone? There was no mobile on her person or at the flat. We checked whether there was a phone in her name registered to her address, but there was nothing. I'm just checking because it's quite unusual for someone of her age not to have a phone.'

That was really strange. 'Yes. She definitely has a phone. She used to get statements about it delivered to our house but then I assume it all went online. Maybe she didn't change the address?'

Abbie nodded and made a note in her pad. 'Great. We'll look into that, then. If you can give us the number, we might be able to get a lead from phone records even if we can't locate the phone.'

It was curious that they hadn't been able to find Charlotte's phone. It was usually welded to her hand. 'Could Freddie have taken it? Might there have been something on it he wouldn't want you to see?'

Abbie's face betrayed nothing. 'We can't speculate, but it would obviously be very useful if it came to light.'

After she'd said goodbye to Abbie, Joanna ordered a latte for

Sally and, while she waited, scrolled through her own phone to find the numbers she needed. Charlotte had been friends with Rachael and Lucy since she was at school, so she knew their mothers well enough to have their telephone numbers for the teenage sleepovers where the girls would be awake giggling until the small hours. On the way back to Charlotte's room, she called both and told them – very briefly – what had happened, asking if they could break the news to their daughters and have them contact her. Both mothers were very kind and, obviously, shocked to hear about Charlotte's accident.

Beside Charlotte's bed, Sally was in the middle of a conversation on her phone and took the coffee from her gratefully. Pointing at her phone and mouthing 'work', she backed out of the room.

She'd only been gone for about two minutes when there was a gentle knock on the door and Freddie's mother, Annabelle, appeared, carrying a brown paper bag. 'Hi. It's only me. Just popping in to see how Charlotte is.'

She was the last person Joanna wanted to see. Her designer fitness clothes had been eschewed in favour of a Breton top and cropped trousers. Navy pumps squeaked on the floor and a trail of strong perfume caught in Joanna's throat. Around Charlotte's side of the bed, she pushed the bag towards Joanna.

It was heavier than she'd expected. Joanna peered inside. It was full of small pots and packets: olives, houmous with carrot sticks, thick-cut crisps, pastel-coloured cans of Kombucha. 'What's all this for?'

'For you, of course.' She strode around to the chair on the other side of Charlotte's bed. 'Provisions to keep you going.'

Joanna could barely manage a slice of toast at the moment, but the thought was unexpectedly kind. 'Thank you.'

Annabelle's scarlet fingernails waived her gratitude. 'No problem at all. Any updates on Charlotte's condition?'

Joanna hid her awkwardness – in trying to avoid being

recognised and the fact she'd just been speaking to the police about Freddie – by taking her time in slipping the bag of food onto the tray table by the side of Charlotte's bed. 'No change at the moment. But that means she's stable.'

She was clinging to this word like a drowning man might cling to a shipwreck. No worse was a good thing. Charlotte just needed time for her brain to recover.

There was a pause before Annabelle spoke again. 'I've had a conversation with Freddie.'

Joanna kept her eyes on Charlotte, not wanting to betray to Annabelle the hatred she was sure must be in them. 'Have you?'

'You know they've actually arrested him for this? I'm distraught about the way he's being treated as if he were a common criminal. He should be here. He's going crazy worrying about Charlotte and the baby.'

Joanna swallowed, kept her eyes on her daughter. What was unbelievable was that her daughter was lying here. 'I knew that, yes.'

'But he didn't do it, Joanna. I know my son and he doesn't have a bad bone in his body. There's no way he's guilty of this.'

Joanna wasn't sure that this woman would know the difference between a good bone and a bad one. She didn't want to argue with her, though. 'Well, that'll be for the police to investigate.'

'The police?' She looked as if the word was poison in her mouth. 'I have lost all faith in them. The way they spoke to Freddie was absolutely awful. My poor boy is an easy target for them.'

The more she spoke, the more anger bubbled in Joanna's stomach. How dare she come here – to Charlotte's bedside – and talk about 'poor Freddie'? Her anger made her brave and she turned to face Annabelle's hard stare. 'Well, I trust them to do their job.'

Annabelle narrowed her eyes. 'Well, I'm sure our family lawyer will do what's needed to ensure justice is done.'

Joanna gripped the sides of her plastic chair, but kept her lips tightly closed and merely nodded. Hopefully, the less she said, the sooner this woman would leave them alone.

After a few moments, Annabelle spoke again – this time her voice calculatedly gentle. 'That's something I wanted to talk to you about actually. I wondered if you could speak to the police. About Freddie and Charlotte. Tell them how much they were in love. How she wouldn't have wanted them to suspect him.'

Joanna couldn't help her mouth falling open, like something from one of the comics Charlotte used to like as a little girl. 'Me? Tell them to go easy on him?'

She couldn't believe the arrogance of her request. The entitlement. This was the Annabelle she'd known at school, expecting the world to revolve around her. She spoke and others ran around to do her bidding. That's what Joanna had liked about Jacob. He hadn't been like the other rich privileged kids at school. In the first weeks they were together, she hadn't even realised how wealthy his parents were. While Annabelle and the other girls had looked down their noses at Joanna's background, he hadn't cared. At least that's what she'd thought. She'd believed in him. The way Charlotte had believed in Freddie. She'd been wrong, too.

Annabelle's tone was so saccharine sweet it made Joanna's teeth hurt. 'I just want you to tell them that he loved Charlotte too much to possibly hurt her.'

Acid gathered in the back of Joanna's mouth. 'I don't know that. I hardly saw them together.'

Already poker straight, Annabelle sat even taller in her seat. 'Well, I saw them together all the time and my son doted on her. Once they found out she was pregnant, he treated her like a crystal glass.'

Jealousy twisted Joanna's stomach at the reminder that, not

only had Annabelle spent time with Charlotte, she'd known about the pregnancy. Had maybe spoken to Charlotte about being a mother. All the things that would've happened for her if it hadn't been for her own stubborn refusal to tolerate Charlotte's choice of partner. 'I'll have to take your word for that. But I cannot tell the police that when I don't know it.'

Annabelle got louder. 'Well, I know it. And I keep telling you. He didn't do it.'

'You can't possibly be sure of that.'

'I know my son. There's no way he'd do this on purpose. If he did do it, it would've been an accident.'

There it was. She knew as well as Joanna did that Freddie had pushed her daughter. Probably in anger. Whether or not he meant her to hit her head was neither here nor there. She had. And now he had to pay the consequences. 'I don't want to have this conversation with you. I think you should go.'

Annabelle's face fell. 'I'm sorry. I didn't mean to raise my voice. I'm just frightened for my son. This baby is part of my family as much as yours, Joanna. And you need to consider something. If it isn't going to have a mother, at least we should make sure it has a father.'

Joanna sat frozen in shock for minutes after Annabelle left, having listened to her strident footsteps as they receded down the corridor.

How dare she ask Joanna to speak to Freddie? And how could she be so cruel as to suggest that Charlotte wasn't going to make it? Furious tears sprang to Joanna's eyes and she wiped them away before leaning in to Charlotte. 'Don't listen to that awful woman, sweetheart. You're going to get better soon and we're going to look after that baby of yours and make sure that that family don't get anywhere near her.'

Sally reappeared, out of breath as if she'd hurried back. 'So sorry about that. I'd completely forgotten that I had a meeting scheduled this morning.'

She couldn't bear the thought of Sally leaving her yet. 'Do you need to get back for it?'

'No, it's okay. I made my apologies. But there's another one this afternoon that might be trickier to rearrange. It's only an hour away. I could go, do the meeting and be back in three hours. Do you mind?'

'Of course not. Do what you need to do. And I love having you here, but you don't have to come back again straight away. Go and spend the night at home if you need to?'

Something unreadable flashed across Sally's face. 'No, it's fine. Graham and Harry can spend some time together. I want to be here. I'll be back as soon as I can.'

She picked up Charlotte's hand and kissed it, gave Joanna a hug and left. Shortly afterwards, Joanna got a text message from Lucy to say that she and Rachael would come to the hospital that evening to see Charlotte.

The police needed evidence to make sure that Freddie didn't get away with what he'd done. Hopefully, the girls might be able to provide that. After all, they'd lived through those months when he let her down before and probably knew a whole lot more about what'd happened than she did.

THIRTEEN

FREDDIE

Freddie was out with Dominic when Charlotte found them.

He hadn't even realised that she was home from university. As far as he knew, she had two more days before the planned 'last night on campus' in the student union bar with her friends. It'd been loud in the White Lion on the High Street and he hadn't heard his phone ring or beep with a text until he got it out of his pocket to check the time and discovered a string of messages from Charlotte that sounded increasingly urgent. And very angry.

Immediately, he sent her a message to ask where she was, tell her the name of the pub and suggest he come to her. She didn't reply for another fifteen minutes when she sent a terse: 'I'm outside.'

Even outside, the music was loud. On the facing pavement, she had her back to him and he was across the road in three strides, desperate to see her face. He'd been counting down the days to her coming home. 'Hey, I'm here. How come you're home early?'

When she turned, her cheeks were scarlet, eyes puffy with tears. 'I needed you. I wanted to see you. I had to speak to you.'

There was a desperation in her voice that made his heart thud in trepidation. 'Why? What's happened? Are you okay?'

He reached for her, but she shook her head and shrugged him off. 'When you didn't answer my messages, I went to your house to find you. I needed to tell you...'

Her voice cracked and broke as she gasped back sobs. He tried again to put his arms around her but she stepped back from him, held out her hands to keep him away. What was going on? 'Charlotte, whatever it is, I—'

Her arms dropped to her sides and her hands formed into fists. He'd never seen her like this. 'And when I knocked on your door your mum... your mum...'

His heart sank. He could imagine how she'd been. Her recent comments to him about the 'kind of girl' she thought he should be with. 'Don't listen to my mother, she—'

She jutted her chin in his direction, fire in her eyes. 'She told me that you'd started seeing another girl. That you'd met someone else.'

Contorted with rage, her face was almost unrecognisable. His heart plummeted to his stomach. 'That's not true. It's not true.'

'Then why would she say it?' Her voice tore through the air; it was agony to hear the pain in it.

His mind was racing for the best way to explain it. The way to make her realise that it didn't matter. He chose the wrong one. 'It was nothing. Just a kiss and I regretted it immediately.'

He'd been such an idiot. Afterwards, he'd accused Dominic of setting him up. A drink for just the two of them turned out to be a night out with two girls Dom worked with. They'd all got drunk. Before he knew what was going on, Dom and one of the girls had disappeared. He wasn't sure quite how he'd ended up kissing her friend, but it'd happened. It was one kiss, one stupid mistake, and then he'd woken up to himself. A bigger mistake had been telling his mother. Asking her advice. Getting angry when her 'advice' had been that 'it's probably for the best' because 'you're too young to know the kind of girl that will make you happy'.

The pain on Charlotte's face as he told her would stay with him forever.

She turned and ran, he followed her, wind rushing in his ears. 'Wait, Charlotte, please wait.'

She turned so sharply, that he almost ran into her, her face a mess of tears. 'Do not follow me. I'm going home.'

He couldn't breathe. This couldn't be happening. 'Please, Charlotte, please listen to me. I need to make you understand.'

She screamed at him then, loud enough to make a couple on the other side of the road stop and watch. 'Leave me alone!'

What could he do? Like a fool, he stood and watched her go.

It wasn't until much later, after he'd sent her a million texts to try and explain, that he realised that she hadn't actually told him why she'd been so desperate to find him in the first place.

FOURTEEN

Waiting by a hospital bed, time loses all meaning. If the patient isn't eating, the hours aren't even punctuated by mealtimes. At least when Steve was really unwell, they'd managed to ease the minutes along with a crossword or Sudoku or, when he was too tired even to open his eyes, she'd read the letters of a Wordle aloud.

Without Sally there for company, the hours had dragged and she checked the time on her phone several times, willing the girls to arrive. She knew them both very well. When they were young, they used to be over at their house all the time. Now, of course, as Charlotte no longer lived at home, she hadn't seen them in months. If only this meeting were in better circumstances.

Because Charlotte was in a private room, the nurses had confirmed that they'd relax the usual two visitors rule. When there was a gentle knock on the door, Joanna was quick to let them in.

Rachael – blonde, beautiful and the most chaotic of their tribe of three – carried a helium balloon emblazoned with Get

Well Soon. She held it out apologetically. 'I felt like I needed to bring something.'

Joanna took it and tied it to the end of the bed, it's bright hopeful bobbing incongruous in this room. 'Charlotte would love it.'

Lucy – whose gorgeous red hair always seemed at odds with her quiet studious nature – carried a basket of fruit and cereal bars. 'These are for you. We thought you could use some sustenance while you were in here.'

Their kindness brought tears to Joanna's eyes and she had to turn away. How much Charlotte loved these two; the three of them had brought so much joy and laughter to her house. 'You're so thoughtful. Please, come and sit down and talk to her.'

She realised how quickly she'd got used to seeing Charlotte like this when she saw the shock on their faces. Rachael's hand fluttered to her mouth and tears came immediately. 'Oh.'

Lucy seemed more determined to be brave. 'What shall we do? Can she hear us if we talk to her?'

'The doctor says it's possible.'

Rachael's eyes were as round as dinner plates, she was frozen in place. 'What shall we say?'

Joanna could understand her fear. The three of them shouldn't be here, they should be propping up a bar, or dancing at a night club or just hanging out in Charlotte's bedroom like the old days, cackling like a coven. 'It doesn't matter, really. Just the sound of your voices will help. You can just chatter away about anything.'

Lucy took her friend by the hand. 'Come on, Rach. You can talk to her about that bloke at the dry cleaners that you keep trying to chat up. You can do that for hours.'

Rachael's smile was grateful; she let Lucy lead her to the bedside where the nurse had kindly brought an extra two seats for them. Her bottom lip wobbled as she looked at her friend. 'Hey Charlotte. It's me, Rachael.'

Lucy rolled her eyes at Joanna. Gosh, these girls were a breath of fresh air. 'You're not going to believe what she did today, Charlotte. That cute guy in the dry cleaners, the one with the big brown eyes? She left her phone number in the pocket of her coat and then asked him if they check the pockets before they, you know, do the cleaning.'

For the next forty minutes, Joanna watched these remarkable girls talk to her daughter. Sometimes they faltered; at one point, Rachael started to cry and Lucy pulled her close for a tight hug while keeping up her commentary to Charlotte in a slightly broken voice. If ever she needed evidence of how amazing her daughter was, it was right here in this room. Only a special person would attract, and keep, two friends like these.

When they ran out of things to say, Lucy suggested music. 'I'm pretty sure I saw it on a film once. And Charlotte loves music.'

Of course, why hadn't she thought of that? 'That's a great idea.'

Lucy found something on her phone and they played it close to Charlotte's ear. They even tried singing along, but both of their voices gave way almost immediately. It was too hard.

Watching them reminded Joanna of something that DC Abbie had asked. 'I don't suppose either of you know if Charlotte has lost her phone? The police couldn't find it at her flat.'

They both shook their heads. Lucy looked surprised. 'That's really weird. She's always got her phone with her.'

Joanna had thought the same thing. 'Had either of you heard from her on Sunday? Do you know where she'd been that day?'

Again, they both shook their heads. Rachael sighed. 'To be honest, we haven't seen that much of her the last few weeks.

She always seems to be busy with Freddie. I wish I'd pushed to see her.'

Her bottom lip wobbled and her eyes filled with tears. Joanna didn't want to upset them. 'It's okay, love. None of us knew this was going to happen.'

When they got up to go, both of them gave Joanna the tightest of hugs. Then Rachael needed to find the ladies before they left.

Lucy glanced at her watch. 'I'll wait with Joanna while you go.'

In the quiet, they both looked at Charlotte. Lucy's voice was softer than it had been when she was talking to Charlotte. 'I can't believe this has happened.'

'I know. It's surreal. Sometimes it doesn't seem possible that that's Charlotte lying there.'

Chewing on her lip, Lucy nodded. 'I've never seen her so still for so long.'

Joanna had to smile at that. It was true that Charlotte was always on the go, dashing here and there, organising everyone. Even watching her lying there, she could imagine that – any moment – she was going to jump up, pull out the wires and ask them why they were all staring at her. 'I wish I'd done more. I wish I'd managed to stop her from seeing him.'

Lucy was shaking her head. 'I just can't believe that Freddie would've hurt her. He worships the ground she walks on. I mean, *really*. I know people say that, but he really does.'

What seems a good thing in your early twenties can sound like a red flag from the perspective of three decades away. 'You mean he was obsessive? Jealous?'

Lucy shook her head. 'No. Not like that. He was gentle. It's just, I don't know, we used to laugh about the look he got on his face whenever she was around. Like he'd won the lottery or something.'

Joanna remembered Steve saying something similar when

Freddie and Charlotte were first an item. The brief times they'd seen the two of them together, he'd certainly given the appearance that he was besotted with her. But that hadn't prevented him from breaking her heart. 'But he let her down so badly. I still don't understand why she'd give him a second chance.'

Lucy stared down at her brown boots. 'I know you didn't want her to be with him. Charlotte told us. But it was just one kiss with another girl. He made a mistake. He was so sorry. Charlotte forgave him so we did, too.'

Sometimes sorry wasn't good enough. Lucy and Rachael were away travelling for most of that dark and terrible year. They hadn't seen how long it took Charlotte to get over him the first time. 'The thing is, Lucy, I know how boys like that behave. I went to school with boys like that. Rich kids who are used to getting what they want. Entitled and arrogant. Their lives are very different from the rest of us.'

Lucy looked up. 'Charlotte didn't see it that way. She said they were the same. I mean, as people. Although some of his friends were like you just described. Particularly that Dominic.'

This was the first time Joanna had heard the name Dominic. 'Who's he?'

Lucy's face left her in no doubt what her feelings were about the man. 'He's Freddie's best mate. Likes to throw money around. It was his fault they split up the first time, trying to get Freddie to hook up with other girls. And he was really weird around Charlotte.'

No, Joanna wanted to say, Freddie was the one who hooked up with another girl. It was his fault. But she was more interested in the last thing Lucy said. 'Weird how?'

'I don't know. Sometimes he would be all smarmy and creepy, like he was chatting her up. Other times he'd be snarky and mean. Sometimes he would just stare at her. I don't know how she could bear it.'

Fear rose in Joanna's chest. She reached down to Charlotte's arm and stroked it. 'What did Freddie say about it?'

'I don't know that he really noticed. Charlotte never said anything to him. She said he was just jealous. It didn't bother her.'

The most difficult part of having a daughter is living in fear of her being vulnerable around men. From the time Charlotte first started going to bars and nightclubs, her last words to her had always been about keeping her hand over her drink, staying with her friends, calling her dad rather than taking a taxi home alone. But once she'd left home, all she could do was hope that they'd done enough that she knew how to keep herself safe when she was out. How ironic that it hadn't been when she was out that they should've worried about.

Something else occurred to her. 'Did you know that Charlotte was pregnant?'

Lucy's hands flew to her face; her gasp made it clear that she hadn't known a thing about it. 'What? Pregnant? Are you sure?'

'Very sure. And very surprised. So, she didn't talk to you about it?'

On the one hand, she was glad that Lucy shook her head. It didn't feel so bad to have been kept out of the loop if she hadn't even told her closest friends. Then again, she'd never known Charlotte to keep a secret from Lucy and Rachael in her life. Had she not been happy about the pregnancy? Had that been the subject of the argument that the neighbour had overheard?

Lucy was still shaking her head. 'I can't believe it. Why wouldn't she have told me? And Rachael. We're her best friends.'

Joanna didn't want to make Lucy feel as bad as she did about it. 'I think they must've wanted to keep it to themselves. Maybe they were waiting to do a big Instagram reveal or something?' She forced herself to sound as if their secrecy wasn't tearing her apart, too.

Lucy seemed to be mollified and then Rachael reappeared from the toilet, the redness of her eyes making it obvious that she'd been crying. Her own heart aching, she pulled the two of them into another hug before they left, blowing kisses to Charlotte from the door and promising to come again soon.

Once they'd gone, the room felt even more empty of life. Her chair scraped across the floor as she pulled it closer to the bed, to Charlotte. 'That was nice, wasn't it, love? I'm so lucky you always had such nice friends.'

And she had been lucky. When other people talked about the problems their daughters had with their friendship groups – fallings out, silent treatment, snippy text messages – she and Steve had thanked the gods of friendship that Charlotte had Rachael and Lucy. Even her early boyfriends had been nice boys – polite, kind, treating her well.

Was that the problem? Everyone in Charlotte's life had been too similar, too safe? Is that why she'd been attracted by someone like Freddie Knight-Crossley? And who was this creepy Dominic that Lucy had spoken about?

She fired off a quick text update to Sally. It was surprising how adamant she'd been about coming back tonight. She knew how difficult it was for Harry if there was a break in his routine. Was this small argument with Graham a lot bigger than she was making out? Though Sally wouldn't want to worry her at the moment, she didn't like to think that her friend was upset about something and not telling her.

She was so lucky to have Sally. Good friends got you through the worst that life threw at you. Seeing Charlotte's friends and their love for her was a reminder that she'd had so much in her life, so much to live for.

A wave of exhaustion washed over her and, still sitting beside the bed, she closed her eyes for a few moments. She knew the doctor had said that Charlotte's prognosis wasn't good, but he didn't know her daughter. He didn't know the strength of character, the stubbornness, the passion for life that she had. Seeing her friends here with her this evening had reminded her of that. If anyone was going to come round from this, her daughter was.

She must've dozed off in the chair, because she was jolted awake by a loud alarm, piercing the air around her. Shrill beeps joined it. Then more. Until it was a cacophony of sounds. People started to appear from everywhere. What was going on?

Fear shook every ounce of sleep from her. Almost knocked out of the way by a nurse who was checking the ventilator, terrified by the look on the faces of the people around her, she tried to catch on to what they were saying. Amidst all the medical jargon, nothing made sense. 'What's happening? Please tell me. What's going on?'

One of the younger nurses took her by the elbow and tried to lead her away. 'You need to come outside, Mrs Woodley. Let the medical team do their job.'

Carts were being wheeled in, complicated equipment produced from within them. Everyone's face was serious and focused. She wasn't going anywhere. 'No, I can't leave her. I need to be here.'

A doctor was opening Charlotte's eyelids, shining a torch into them. Again the nurse tried to persuade her to leave. 'They need room to work. We can wait outside and then—'

'Get the mother out of here!'

She wasn't sure which doctor had shouted that at her, but she allowed the nurse to lead her outside and take her to the small room at the end of the corridor from which, like a recurring nightmare, she never seemed to escape.

FIFTEEN

The room Joanna was shepherded to this time was at the other end of the corridor and smaller than the one she'd last waited in. Intimate and quiet, the muted restful colours clearly chosen for their calming effects did nothing for the trembling that had overtaken her whole body. In place of the torn and curling posters instructing viewers how to wash their hands, a solitary painting hung on the pale-green wall.

Inside the gold frame, a wild rugged landscape covered half the canvas, sloping towards the left where, at the very top, a small wooden house balanced at the edge of a clifftop. It's rough-hewn weather-worn planks so precarious that one breath of the sea air would be enough to make it fall over the lip of rock into the crashing waves below. In the foreground, a small clutch of wild flowers pushed up through the coarse grass, fragile yet determined.

Since Steve's funeral, people had been so kind, but still the loneliness of his absence had hollowed her, battered her, left her a shell. Through the last year, Charlotte had been the only thing that had kept her upright, moving on, living. Knowing that she had to be there to comfort her daughter had got her out of bed in the morning. How would she live if Charlotte didn't?

Waiting for news was unbearable. What was going on in there? According to her watch it'd only been four minutes since the young nurse had backed out of the room with an apologetic promise to be back soon, but it felt like forty. It could be a good thing, couldn't it? Charlotte might be waking up? She tried to hold on to that hope with her fingernails and not think of the tone of the doctor's voice – *get the mother out of here!* – which terrified the very breath from her lungs. Pacing up and down, up and down, in that tiny room intensified the thudding of her heart, the beating of her blood through her veins. Every atom of her was on high alert. What was going on? When would someone come? Was Charlotte going to be okay? *I'll do anything. Please let her be okay.*

When the door opened, she almost jumped on the young nurse who'd brought her here. 'What are they doing? What happened in there?'

Her voice was kind, but painfully calm. 'The monitors registered a change in Charlotte's condition. I'm sure we'll get an update soon.'

Change? That could be a good thing, couldn't it? Maybe she was starting to breathe on her own? Maybe the visit from her friends had worked? 'Could you go and find out? See if there's any news?'

'I'm sure the—'

The door opened to cut her off and one of the doctors from Charlotte's room came in. 'Please sit, Mrs Woodley.'

She couldn't feel her legs but somehow Joanna managed to do as he'd asked. Her breath was ragged and she battled to get it under control; gripping the arms of the chair so hard that her knuckles turned as white as the doctor's face. 'What is it? What's happening?'

'Charlotte's vital signs dropped and that's what caused the

alarms that you heard. We believe that she's had a further bleed on the brain and she's being prepped for surgery as we speak.'

A further bleed? Surgery? How bad was that? Dizzy and weak, she couldn't quite organise her thoughts. He'd paused to let her take his words in, but she wanted him to keep going until she'd heard all of it. 'Does surgery mean you can repair it? You can stop the bleeding?'

He had that face on. The kind face she recognised from the doctors who'd looked after Steve. She couldn't bear it. She pushed her fist into her mouth to stop herself from screaming at him to tell her everything.

When he spoke, it was agonisingly slow. 'Until the surgeon has been able to locate the bleed and found the extent of it, we won't know what we're dealing with. Unfortunately, because of your daughter's existing brain injury, she's already in a weakened state so I'm afraid it's just a case of waiting to see what happens. I'm sorry, I know that this isn't easy to hear.'

He did look sorry, but that didn't help one bit. She could barely get the words out, but – as if she had her head under the guillotine and her own hand on the rope to bring it down – she needed to know. She needed to know everything. 'Could this bleed... could it kill her?'

He took a deep breath. 'We can't speculate about anything until the surgeon is able to locate the bleed. We'll keep you informed as much as we can.'

He already had his hand on the door handle when another question occurred to her. There was more than one life at stake here. 'What about the baby? What will happen to the baby? You know that she's pregnant?'

Still with his hand on the door, he nodded. Too slowly. Too slowly. The clock ticked another three times before he answered. 'The body is designed to prioritise the life of the mother before the baby. It may be that the shock of this bleed could cause the body to terminate the pregnancy. But as we got

to Charlotte almost immediately, we will obviously do all that
we can to keep the foetus alive.'

She didn't want this textbook response. She wanted to know
what he thought. *Will they live? Will they both live?* But she
knew he couldn't tell her. 'How long will she be in surgery?'

'It might be a while. If you wanted to go home, we could call
you?'

As if she would be anywhere in the world except here. 'No.
I'll stay. I'll be here if you have any news.'

He nodded and left. The nurse must need to go back to
work, too. There was no point them sitting here just looking at
each other. 'Can I stay here while she's in surgery?'

She smiled. 'You can. But we have a Visitors' Lounge nearer
to the surgical wards which might be nicer. It has a coffee
machine and a little garden, too, if you want some fresh air. Is
there anyone who can come and wait with you?'

Sally would be here soon. 'My friend is on her way.'

'Good. Shall I show you where it is?'

Lounge was a bit of a euphemism for the three rows of chairs
and a vending machine. But it was empty, at least, and an
improvement over the claustrophobic room she'd come from.
Outside the heavy-duty glass doors, there was a large square of
grass with two benches and weighty plant pots. According to
the sign on the window, it was looked after by the 'Friends of
the Hospital'. She pushed open the door and walked outside.

Encased in the slate-grey walls of the building, the dark-
blue night spilled around her. Carefully tended plants softened
the industrial architecture. Blinds pulled down at the windows
allowed a harsh metallic light from the corridors only the merest
escape. Behind, the muted glow from the glass door dissolved
across the courtyard, not quite reaching the far corner, where a
fountain peered over a shallow upturned cask. Dark orange

flecked its surface. Heavy and suffocating, a neatly ruled square of sky pushed downwards. Beneath her feet, the sharp gravel path cast tiny shadows of charcoal and darkness.

How long had it been since she'd breathed in the outside air? Was it really only forty-eight hours since she'd got the visit from the two police officers? The warmth of the sun had left behind traces of its strength and – when Joanna sat on the bench, closed her eyes and let her shoulders drop from her ears – for the briefest of moments, she let her mind travel back to summer holidays with Steve and Charlotte. As a child, she'd loved the beach and Steve would have endless resources of patience building the most elaborate sandcastles. He'd run into the cold sea with her on his shoulders. Buy her the biggest ice creams with all the sauces and wafers and sprinkles that she wanted. He made life fun.

Beneath her closed lids, tears warmed her eyes. In this quiet empty garden, there was no one to hear her whisper to him, 'Why did you have to go?'

Right up until the end, he'd tried to look after them both. It'd been his idea that she had to book a party for her fiftieth birthday last month. How stupidly hopeful she'd been to go along with it, to book a hall and a band. He'd promised her he would still be here. 'I'll whirl you round the dancefloor one last time.' But he hadn't and she'd cancelled it and, if it hadn't been for Charlotte's stubborn insistence, she'd have pretended her birthday wasn't happening at all. Nothing was worth celebrating once he was gone. Nothing.

The tears pushed under her lids onto her eyelashes, but she didn't move to wipe them away. With her eyes closed, she could see him. Tall, broad shouldered, sandy haired. Dressed in jeans and a shirt with a V-neck jumper. Blue. He always liked blue. Charlotte used to tell him that it matched his eyes and he would smile. That smile, which could say so many things. *I love you. I'm ready. You sound crazy but I'm going to go along with it anyway*. How she missed it. Her quiet, strong, dependable husband. 'Oh, Steve. I need you here. I really need you.'

Why hadn't she pushed him to go to the doctors sooner? If it'd been caught early, maybe he wouldn't have got so sick, maybe he'd still be here with her.

And if Charlotte hadn't wanted to be at home with him, she would've gone travelling with her friends, seen the world, realised that there was more to life than Freddie Knight-Crossley.

And later, once Charlotte had announced that they were serious and she was going to move into his flat, Steve would've handled it so much better than she did. He wouldn't have had the rows that they'd had. He would've oiled the sticking points, eased the tension, made them realise what was important. With him there, it would never have got to the point where they hadn't spoken for the last two weeks.

How had she let that happen? She'd dealt with this so badly. How many times over the years had Steve tried to tell her that she couldn't keep such a tight rein on Charlotte? That she had to let her find her own way?

A breeze whispered past the back of her neck and she shivered. When she opened her eyes, it seemed darker than it was before. From the bag slung across her chest, she pulled out her mobile to text Sally to tell her where she was. She didn't want to call her while she was driving, didn't want to cause her to drive fast to get here.

Once the text was sent, she stared at her screen, the picture of the three of them on holiday. What would she give to be back there now? Why had she not realised how lucky she was? How easy life had been then. So much time spent worrying about the most ridiculous things. When Steve had told her that they didn't matter, why hadn't she listened to him? Why did it have to take such awful events to wake her up to what was important in life?

She only realised there was someone else there when the door squeaked as it opened onto the garden. When she turned towards it, Dr Doherty was in the opening, framed by electric light. The shadow cast on his face by the canopy above the door made it impossible to read his expression. He called out to her. 'Mrs Woodley?'

'Yes, I'm here.'

As she walked towards the door, she sent up a silent prayer. *Please let her be okay.*

SIXTEEN

FREDDIE

If Charlotte's father hadn't got ill, she might never have given Freddie a second chance.

For the first month after they'd broken up, he'd tried to get Charlotte to speak to him but she refused to answer any of his messages. He even tried writing a letter and posting it through her front door. She wanted nothing to do with him. Eventually, he had to stop before it became harassment.

At the beginning of November, Dominic's dad was complaining that the van was still parked behind the barn on his land. Even though getting rid of it seemed like the final nail in the coffin for his and Charlotte's relationship, Freddie agreed to get it cleaned up and sold.

It was amazing how many sweet wrappers and crisp packets could be stuffed into edges of the back of a van. Clearing them out, he couldn't help but think of all the gigs he'd taken Charlotte to. The times they'd driven home singing along to the latest band she was into. It didn't matter how many times Dominic – and his mother – had told him he'd get over it, he just couldn't forget her.

It was when he was pulling out the car mats at the front of

the van to vacuum the carpet that he found her necklace. A silver chain with a heart that her parents had bought her for her eighteenth birthday. He remembered her taking it off one night because he'd bought her a necklace and she wanted to wear it immediately. She'd tucked it into her bag, but it must've fallen out and they'd searched everywhere for it. It felt like fate was giving him a second chance by offering it up now.

The next day, heart thumping out of his chest, he was on her doorstep, with the necklace in a brand-new box. He rang the bell, then knocked, but there was no reply. Still, he hesitated. Her dad's car was on the drive. Were they actually not in or just ignoring him?

He was just about to leave, when a neighbour from next door shuffled out onto his own front porch. 'They're at the hospital, son.' He shook his head. 'Poor old Steve. It doesn't sound good.'

For about ten minutes, Freddie sat in his car further down the street, just staring into space. Charlotte's father was ill? Maybe dying? He knew what it was like to lose a father and he also knew how close Charlotte was with hers. He made up his mind. He'd drop the necklace through the letterbox. But before he did, he sent her a text:

Hi Charlotte. I found your heart necklace in the van, so I dropped it through your door. I heard about your dad being ill. I'm so sorry. If there's anything I can do, I'm here x

That night, at the gym with Dominic, he made the mistake of telling him what'd happened. Dominic pushed the bar upwards with a grunt. 'This could work in your favour.'

He watched him lower it back to its rest. 'What do you mean?'

Another grunt as he pushed it upwards. 'She gets upset, you

swoop in and comfort her. Before she knows what's hit her you can...'

He was supposed to be spotting for his friend, but he could quite cheerfully have let the bar fall directly on him. 'Don't you dare talk about her like that.'

Dominic sat up on the weights bench. 'Alright, mate. Calm down. I was just joking.'

He was still in love with Charlotte, but that's not what she needed right now. He knew that she had other friends, but he'd lost a parent. If he could be a friend to her right now, that was all he'd want to be.

The next day, she sent him a message: *Thank you for the necklace x*

He replied immediately: *No problem. Hope you're okay. If you ever want to go for a coffee and just talk, give me a shout x*

Two days later, she replied: *Coffee tomorrow?*

She didn't want him to collect her from her house, so they met in a Starbucks. He got there thirty minutes early, his heart lurching every time the door opened. When she walked towards his table – thin, pale and so very sad – it took everything he had not to wrap his arms around her. 'Hi. Shall I get you a latte?'

Twirling her paper cup in her hands, she told him all about her father's illness. 'It's really bad. It's cancer. In his brain. We don't think he's got very long with us now.'

His heart actually hurt to listen to her. 'Charlotte, I'm so sorry.'

She frowned into her coffee. 'That night. When I found you and you told me that you kissed the girl? That was the day after they told me he was ill.'

She couldn't have taken the wind out of him more if she'd punched him in the stomach. 'That's why you wanted to find me?'

She nodded, staring into his eyes as if to make sure that he understood just how awful that'd been for her. 'Yes. And then your mother told me you had someone else and then you told me about the kiss and I just... lost it.'

He thought about her screaming at him in the street. No wonder she wouldn't listen to what he had to say. 'Charlotte, I am so so sorry.'

She waved away his apology. 'I was so angry. With you. With your mother. But with my parents, too. They'd known for months about my dad's diagnosis. Both of them. And they kept it from me.'

He was out of his depth here. 'Maybe they wanted to protect you?'

From the look on her face, that hadn't been the right thing to say. 'That's what they said! Protect me? I'm an adult. All that time, all that time they knew and they let me carry on as normal, going to university, playing gigs. And all that time my dad had been really, really sick.'

He wanted to pull her to him, comfort her, make the pain go away. 'Come here.'

As he reached across to her chair, she looked at him with such pain in her eyes that it ripped his heart out. 'He's going to die, Freddie. My lovely dad is going to die.'

She collapsed into his arms and he held her close, never wanting to let her go.

After she'd been to the bathroom and splashed some cold water on her face, they talked for another two hours. She told him how she'd insisted that Rachael and Lucy still go through with their planned travels to South America, which meant that she spent all day at home with her parents. 'I just don't want to miss a minute with him.'

'Of course.'

These days, though, her father slept an awful lot and it was getting difficult to keep her mind occupied. 'Me and mum keep arguing about stupid stuff. Then realising it's just stupid stuff and then we start crying.'

'Well, if you ever want another coffee or just to go for a walk. I'm here.'

She smiled at him then. A watery smile that shattered his heart. 'Thank you.'

After that, they met three or four times a week in the afternoons when her dad was asleep, and they texted back and forth late into the night. It was friendship, but it was intimate; he didn't let himself get carried away. It was his kindness she needed, nothing else.

Then, the night after her father passed away, she sent him a message just after midnight. *Are you awake?*

He picked her up and took her back to the apartment. It'd belonged to his uncle who'd emigrated the year before and left him the keys. Though he and his friends stayed there a lot, he still lived at home. That night, he held her until she cried herself to sleep. Then, as promised, woke her at 5 a.m. and dropped her home before her mother woke up.

It became a routine in the days before the funeral. She'd spend them with her mother and then, once her mother was asleep, she'd call Freddie. On the third night, she'd whispered to him in the darkness, 'I don't know how I would've got through the last few weeks without you.'

When she reached for him, it'd felt like the most natural thing in the world, but he'd wanted to be sure. 'You're going through a lot, Charlotte. I don't want you to do anything that you'd regret.'

She'd shaken her head, smiled and pulled him closer.

Lying awake afterwards, listening to her breathing, he thought about his own father's funeral. Business associates with their hands on his ten-year-old shoulder, telling him that he had to be the man of the family now. His mother, circulating, making sure that everyone was catered for, then finding her alone in the kitchen that night, weeping into a large glass of red wine.

Though he'd missed his dad, his mother had done every-thing in her power to make his life as good as it was. Every week at university, she'd sent packages of food and treats. Anything he wanted or needed, she'd get it for him. He knew it was her dream to see him working at his father's family business with his cousins. It wasn't as if he knew what else he wanted to do, so it wasn't really a huge sacrifice. She'd done so much. If he could do anything to make this easier for Charlotte, he would do it.

He woke her at 5 a.m. the next morning, ready to drop her home as usual, not wanting to presume that their night together meant anything more to her than comfort, but hoping with every part of him that it might.

'Hey, you. Time to drop you back home.'

She'd smiled at him. 'So... last night?'

He held his breath for a moment, weighed up how to respond. Honesty seemed the only option. 'I love you, Char-lotte. I always have. But I don't expect you to forgive me or to feel the same. And you have much more important things going on right now. I'm here for you whatever. For as long as you need.'

She pulled her knees up to her chest. 'I have forgiven you. I'm not saying that what you did was okay, but I might've listened to your explanation if circumstances were different.'

He waited. There was no way he was going to push her to say any more than she wanted to.

She rested her chin on her knees and looked up at him through her eyelashes. 'And I love you, too. This is the most terrible timing in the world, but I do want to give us another chance.'

Tears pricked the back of his eyes. 'Are you sure?'

He could see tears in her eyes, too. 'Yes. But I'm also sure that if you *ever*—'

He was beside her on the bed in less than a second. 'I will

never *ever* do anything that stupid again. I promise you, Charlotte. I will spend the rest of my life making it up to you.'

She smiled then. The first he'd seen in days. 'Well, that sounds like a good plan.'

He kissed her lips – salty with the mix of their tears – and then held her close. Muffled by his shoulder, her words were warm against his body. 'Now we just need to deal with our mothers.'

SEVENTEEN

Later, when she looked back at her conversation with the doctor, Joanna was angry at herself. Stupidly, she'd hoped it was a good sign that he hadn't taken her away into another small room. In reality, there wasn't a soul in the lounge so he'd spoken to her there.

When Steve had been ill, they'd looked to the doctors to be their saviours. Believing in their ability to know what to do, what to try, to predict the future and know how to prevent it. Even when things go badly, doctors are expected to stay stoic, professional, unflappable.

But the surgeon in front of Joanna wasn't infallible. Or a superhero. He looked human and exhausted and utterly dejected. 'I'm so sorry.'

They were the last words on Earth she wanted to hear. 'Please,' she whispered. 'Please don't be sorry.'

Sorry was what people said when there was nothing more to be done. No more drugs to try. No more trials to undertake. No more methods to employ. She didn't want to hear sorry. Sorry meant they were giving up. That it was over.

They sat halfway along the first row of chairs. She kept her hands in her lap, twisting her wedding band as she listened to, but couldn't hear, what he had to say.

The doctor was gentle, but his words were devastating. 'The brain bleed was too severe. We tried to locate it but it was very deep and Charlotte's brain was already damaged. It was too much.'

She cursed herself for hoping that he'd have better news. 'So she's still in a coma?'

The doctor took a deep breath before he spoke. 'I'm afraid we lost her.'

Lost. That was another word she hated. Sorry. Lost. Sorry for your loss. It was a platitude. A euphemism. A sticking plaster on a gaping wound. 'I don't understand.'

'The bleed on the brain was too severe. Coming so closely after the initial injury... I'm afraid Charlotte has suffered a permanent and irreversible loss of brain function.'

In the reflection on the glass doors that led to the garden, she could see herself and the doctor. He was leaning forwards, hands on his knees. She was upright, immobile. This could have been a scene from a play. It couldn't be real. In the silent room, all she could hear was the ringing in her own ears. She tried again to understand. 'I... don't... What does this mean?'

The doctor looked confused. He cleared his throat. 'Charlotte is not going to recover. Her brain function will not come back.'

The ringing in her ears got louder. Charlotte was gone? 'But she's pregnant. She can't be gone. What about the baby?'

'We're keeping Charlotte on life support to give the baby as long as possible in the womb. We don't know how long that will be, but every day will make a difference. It's still possible that the child might survive.'

She was listening to what he said, but she didn't, couldn't, believe it. She needed to go to Charlotte. 'Can I see her? Can I see my daughter?'

'Of course. She will be back from surgery shortly. I'll ask one of the nurses to come and get you.'

The door at the back of the lounge flew open and Sally hurried towards them. The look on Joanna's face must've been enough because she slowed and her legs almost buckled beneath her. 'No. Oh, no.'

The doctor looked relieved to be able to hand her over. 'I'll leave you with your friend. We can talk again tomorrow.'

Sally reached her as the doctor moved away. She held out her arms and pulled Joanna close. 'I've got you. Oh, Joanna. I've got you, my darling.'

She wasn't sure how long they stayed like that, clutching on to each other as if they were drowning. At some point, she'd managed to explain to Sally what had happened.

'I just can't believe it.' Sally's words echoed her own thoughts. 'How can she be gone?'

'And how can she be gone but still be on life support?' She couldn't get her head around that. Might there not be a chance – however slim – that she might come back from this?

Sally blew her nose, then stuffed the tissue into her pocket. 'And he said that the baby is going to be okay? They're sure about that?'

Joanna could barely remember what the doctor had said. 'I don't know. He just said that they were going to keep Charlotte on life support. But the baby is twenty-eight weeks. Babies survive at twenty-eight weeks, don't they?'

She wasn't sure of anything any longer, but Sally nodded as she rubbed her arm. 'I'm sure they do.'

It was as if Joanna's brain was split into two: one half was still trying to accept that her daughter was gone, the other had to worry about her unborn grandchild. And between the two halves, like a serrated edge, was an excruciating, unbearable pain. She wanted to collapse on the floor and never get up, but she couldn't. She had to take care of Charlotte's child. 'I will get custody, won't I? Of the baby?'

Why she expected Sally to know the answer to that question, she didn't know. But she was nodding in support if not in agreement. 'Well, if her father is in prison, I can't imagine that they would give him custody, will they? It must be you.'

Would Freddie have any rights to this baby once he was convicted? Would he be able to apply for custody? He'd taken her child away from her. She wasn't going to let him take her grandchild too. 'I don't want him to get anywhere near the baby. I will not let that happen.'

'Absolutely.' Sally sat up straight in her chair, back into action. 'We need to get you a solicitor.'

She was right. And Joanna knew that practical things to do were the footholds that got you through these early days of grief. But she hadn't been in a solicitor's office since visiting her father's partnership when she was fifteen and even the thought of it made her nervous. When they'd bought the house, Steve had dealt with that side of things because she hadn't been able to. 'Yes. I'll have to ask around and see if anyone can recommend one.'

Again, Sally came to her rescue. 'Leave it to me, I'll find someone for you.'

The door squeaked open at the back of the room and a nurse approached. 'Mrs Woodley? Your daughter is back from theatre. You wanted to see her?'

Charlotte was in a different ward to before, but still in a room on her own. To Joanna's eye, she looked exactly the same as she had earlier. There were still machines beeping and her hand felt warm to the touch. 'She looks like she's still breathing.'

The nurse was very kind. 'It's the machine. I know how it looks, but I'm afraid everything the doctor told you was correct.'

The nurse continued to hover. Was she expecting Joanna to leave shortly? 'Can I still visit? Can I still come and sit with her?'

'Of course. Just the same as you could before.'

'And... how long... I mean, how long will you keep her like this?'

'We don't know. It depends on the baby. While the baby continues to thrive, we'll keep things the way they are. But if anything changes, we might need to deliver the baby straight away.'

'She's only twenty-eight weeks. Will the baby be okay?'

'The survival rate at twenty-eight weeks is really good. But every day the baby can stay in the womb will help its development.'

Joanna looked at Charlotte. 'Did you hear that, sweetheart? Your baby is still doing well. You clever girl.'

A buzzer sounded outside and the nurse stuck her head out of the door and looked up the ward, before returning to Joanna. 'I really need to see to some other patients.'

'That's okay. We're fine here.'

She looked uncomfortable. 'Actually, we're a long way outside visiting hours. You can come back in the morning from nine?'

For a moment, she considered refusing to go, but Sally held out her hand. 'Come on. Let's go home and get some sleep and then we'll come and see her tomorrow.'

But once she got home, she was too wired to go to bed. Sally found a bottle of red wine in the cupboard and poured them both a glass. 'It might help us sleep.'

It wasn't just the going to sleep that was the problem. 'I don't want to wake up tomorrow and know that she's not here.'

Sally's head dropped and she gazed into her glass. 'I wish I knew what to say but there isn't anything. Except the baby. You have to stay strong for the baby.'

She knew Sally was right. 'That poor child. Born without a mother and with a father who...'

She couldn't bring herself to finish the sentence. She didn't need to. Sally understood. 'But he or she'll have you and they'll have me.'

Another fear bubbled to the surface. 'What if she wouldn't want me to look after the baby?'

'That's your exhaustion talking. Of course she would want you to look after her baby if she couldn't.'

Joanna wasn't so sure. 'She hadn't even told me she was pregnant.'

Sally paused for a moment, sipping at her wine before she replied. 'That was just the two of you being stubborn. Once the baby came, she would've needed you more than ever.'

Joanna screwed her eyes tight, trying not to let her mind play out a fantasy future of her helping Charlotte with a newborn baby. 'How did I get it so wrong?'

'Oh love, you didn't get it wrong. You've been a wonderful mum. She loved you and you loved her.'

That wasn't how it felt right now. 'It was okay when Steve was alive. He knew how to... how to manage it all. Without him here, I've just made a mess of things.'

Sally put her wine glass on the coffee table and took Joanna's hand. 'That's just not true. None of us get it right all the time. It's impossible to be a mother, you're either doing too much or not enough. No one tells you what the rules are and yet you are judged when you break them. There're just so many decisions to make and no idea what the right thing is, and the stakes are always so damn high that it's terrifying. You love them so much that you want to wrap them up and protect them from this terrible cruel world and then... and then...'

As she spoke, her voice became more and more strangled

until she burst into tears. Joanna reached out to grab hold of her hand and searched her face for the reason for her reaction. 'What is it? Is this to do with the argument you had with Graham?'

Sally wiped away her tears and picked up her wine. 'It's not important right now. Ignore me.'

Joanna squeezed Sally's hand. 'No, it is important. I'm not going to sleep anytime soon. Tell me, Sally. Please.'

Sally took a deep breath. 'Graham has found a place for Harry to live. A sheltered housing kind of thing.'

'That sounds good?'

Sally frowned. 'No. It doesn't. Graham thinks that Harry is ready to leave home, but I think he just wants us to get our life back.'

Joanna knew that she had to tread carefully. 'Is that the worst thing?'

'Yes. He's not ready for that. We wouldn't know whether he'd got home safely every night. What he was eating. Who he was with.'

'That feeling is a normal feeling for a parent. We all worry.'

Sally's voice rose. 'It's not the same and you know it.'

She did know it, but that didn't mean she agreed that Harry wasn't ready for the next step. 'What is Graham saying?'

'He says that Harry is a young man now. That he should be able to have his independence. But he's only twenty-three. Loads of kids still live at home at that age.'

She was right. Hadn't she begged Charlotte to stay with her and not move in with Freddie? Although that was a different situation altogether. 'Did you tell Graham that? I mean, would you consider it in a few years' time? Work towards it, maybe?'

Sally didn't answer her question directly. 'Graham thinks that if we wait too long, he'll get too used to being at home with us. His college have been working with him to build his independence. They think this will be a good step for him. Graham thinks we should trust them. Says they're the experts.' When she looked up, she had tears in her eyes. 'But I'm the expert. He's *my* son. I know what's best for him.'

Before all this happened, Joanna might've agreed with her. Now she wasn't so sure that it was true. 'What kind of things has he been doing at college?'

'Life skills. Shopping. Cooking. Ordering things over the telephone. It's not as if I've been mollycoddling him. I've always encouraged him to do things for himself.'

She had always made sure he helped out at home and taken him to whatever groups were going to help him socialise. But Joanna also knew that Sally wouldn't leave Harry alone in the house for more than a few hours. That she'd cut short plenty of evenings because Harry wasn't answering his phone. That she and Graham hadn't been on holiday abroad since he was born because he didn't like the noise of a busy airport or train station. Graham wasn't a villain for wanting a little more freedom to enjoy life with his wife. 'The thing is, most people with a twenty-three year old at home don't have to worry about what time they get home or cooking their meals for them. You're a brilliant mum, Sally. And Graham is a brilliant dad. Isn't it worth just having a look at the place he's found? Where is it?'

Sally wrinkled her nose. 'Ten minutes from where we live.'

Joanna reached for her hand. 'Could you just take a look at it? See what Harry thinks. You don't have to commit to anything. And give Graham a break. He's a good man.'

Sally breathed out slowly; her shoulders relaxed from where they'd been almost at her ears. She looked Joanna in the eyes and nodded. 'Okay. I'll look at it. But I'm not making any promises and I'll only go if you give yourself a break, too. Charlotte loved you, Jo. All families have arguments. And you were doing what you thought was best for her. You can't beat yourself up about this.'

She could beat herself up about the fact she pushed her away, straight into his arms. 'I wish I could've saved her.'

'We need to focus on that baby now. First thing in the morning, I'm going to contact a solicitor and find out what we need to do when the baby comes.'

Joanna nodded, but inside she was still thinking about Charlotte. Still hoping there was a chance that she could save them both.

EIGHTEEN

The corner of the hospital canteen was quiet. Joanna had bought a fresh notepad and pen from the hospital shop to make sure she wrote everything down. Her head was such a fog these days that she didn't want to run the risk of forgetting anything.

True to form, Sally had a recommendation for a family solicitor by ten o'clock the next morning. Now she was sitting with Charlotte so that Joanna could focus on speaking to the solicitor. She wanted to make sure that she knew her rights. Maybe even start to get the process in motion.

In the circumstances, the solicitor had agreed to conduct their first meeting over FaceTime. Joanna hadn't known what to expect, but speaking to a woman who looked to be around her age helped to put her at her ease.

'Hi, I'm Louise, one of the partners here. I've been given the details of your case. Firstly, I wanted to offer my condolences for your situation.'

Joanna swallowed. The only way she was going to get through this was to not think about Charlotte and just focus on the legal side of things. 'Thank you.'

'I know that you have some questions for me, so this will be a preliminary discussion to make you aware of the issues to consider and then we can talk about how you might like to go forward.'

Joanna already knew how she wanted to go forward. 'If my daughter doesn't regain consciousness, I'd like to apply for custody of her child.'

Louise made a temple with her hands and rested her chin on the top. 'Well, firstly, it's not called custody any longer. It would be a Child Arrangements Order and there are two types. Lives with and spends time with.'

Joanna was scribbling everything down as Louise spoke, so she had to reread the two phrases to grasp the difference between them. 'So, if the baby's father is in prison, then the baby definitely won't be able to live with him. So can I have a—' she looked at her notes '—a child arrangement order so that the baby lives with me?'

Louise's smile was kind but professional. 'Mrs Woodley. Joanna. We're getting ahead of ourselves here. Am I right in saying that your grandchild hasn't yet been born?'

'Yes, they're...' she pushed the image of Charlotte from her mind and tried to concentrate, 'they're waiting as long as they can to give them the best chance.'

Now it was Louise's turn to make a note of what she was saying. 'I see. And the baby's father is on remand, awaiting trial?'

Joanna squeezed her pen so tight that she almost snapped it. 'That's right.'

She could only imagine some of the things this solicitor had heard in her career, because she didn't look fazed by this information at all. 'Right. Well, there's a lot of unknowns at the moment, but I can understand that you want to be ready for any eventuality. Why don't I put you through to my assistant so that she can make an appointment for you to come into the office?'

She couldn't wait that long to know what her chances were.

'Please. I just need to know if there's something I can do now. Something that will prevent him from coming for my grandchild. I know he is legally her parent, but I can't risk him or his family taking her from me.'

Louise held her pencil at either end and leaned forwards towards the screen. 'Is your daughter married to the baby's father?'

She couldn't bear the thought. 'No, they just lived together.'

'Then, actually, he doesn't have parental responsibility for your grandchild.'

That sounded more hopeful. 'What do you mean?'

Louise sat back in her seat. Joanna could tell that she'd explained this more than a few times. 'A mother automatically has parental responsibility for a child. But there are only three ways that a man can get it. Being married to the mother, which you've already said he isn't, being registered on the birth certificate or by court order.'

Joanna's heart lifted for the first time in days. This was so much better than she could've hoped for. 'So he doesn't have any right to the baby?'

Louise shook her head. 'No. He doesn't. In a case like this, if your daughter doesn't recover, social services will apply for an interim care order for the child.'

Social services? The warm flicker of hope she'd had was extinguished by a bucket of cold fear. 'But it doesn't need to go into care. I'm here. I'll look after it.'

Louise's voice was kind. 'It's just how it works. When the baby is born, the hospital will notify social services and the emergency team will take the baby into emergency foster care. They will apply for an emergency protection order and will then speak to family members and any associated persons who wish to apply for guardianship.'

Joanna's throat was so dry that she had to swallow before she could speak. 'Associated persons? What does that mean?'

Louise held out her hands as if she was encompassing the whole world. 'Anyone who is connected with the child who wants to look after it. For example, the father, grandparents, aunts or uncles, older siblings.'

This didn't make sense. 'But if Freddie, the father, is found guilty, surely they won't let his mother have the baby?'

Louise's head tilt said otherwise. 'If the paternal grand-mother wants to apply for guardianship, she will have an opportunity to do so.'

This was terrible, terrible news. 'And Freddie? The baby's father. What if he is found not guilty? Will he be able to have parental responsibility? Will they just give the baby to him?'

'No. Not necessarily. Everything is decided in the best interests of the child.'

Anxiety fluttered in Joanna's chest. The best interests of Charlotte's child would be to stay with her, where he or she would be safe. 'How will they decide what that is?'

'We can talk about this in more detail when you come in. But assessments are completed on each person. The social worker and the team will run police checks, look at their financial position, everything that relates to the person's capacity to look after the child.'

Financial checks? Those calls from the bank about the mortgage. Would that count against her? 'And all the while, the baby would be in a foster home? With complete strangers? How long does that take?'

Even one night would be too long, but she wasn't prepared for the response that came after a pause. 'The reports must be completed within twenty-eight weeks.'

Joanna folded her arm tight against her stomach to stop the anxiety prickling there. Twenty-eight weeks? Seven months? The baby would be half a year old before she could bring her home? 'But that's awful!'

'I can understand how it looks that way, really I can. But it's all done in the best interests of the child. They need to be very sure that they are placing the baby in the best possible circumstances.'

Joanna needed time to get her head around all of this. Not for one moment had she considered that Charlotte's child would be taken into care. When she was here, waiting, wanting to love that baby.

Leaving her coffee to get cold, she made her way back to the ward. When she opened the door to Charlotte's room, Sally looked up from her crossword and over the top of her reading glasses. 'How did you get on?'

Being back in the room with Charlotte, the weight of the solicitor's words weighed even heavier and she couldn't even articulate them. All she could do was shake her head at Sally as her eyes filled with bitter, fearful tears.

Sally laid down her newspaper and patted the chair beside her. 'Come and sit down. What's the matter? What did she say?'

Using her notes, Joanna explained what the solicitor had said. With each new piece of information, Sally's eyes got wider, her mouth rounder. Once Joanna had finished, her anger was palpable. 'That's madness! Why wouldn't they just let you raise the baby? You're Charlotte's mother.'

Second time through, Joanna could at least understand a little of what the solicitor had tried to tell her. 'They don't know me from Adam, though, do they? I could be a terrible person. They can't just hand over a newborn baby.'

'Well, I know that, but... social care? A foster family?'

The words were obviously as distasteful to Sally as they were to Joanna. It didn't matter how nice the people were, they weren't family. They wouldn't love the baby like she would.

She could only heap hope onto the fact that it wouldn't get to that. 'We just need to get Charlotte better. She's going to recover, I know she is. She's going to be here to raise the child herself.'

Sally sagged in her seat. Her voice was gentle. 'She's gone, Joanna. The doctor explained that.'

The doctor didn't know her daughter. She leaned forwards and placed a hand on Charlotte's arm. 'All the while she's breathing, there is still a chance.'

Sally closed her eyes for a second as if gathering strength. 'It's the machine that's breathing, love. Not Charlotte. You have to accept that.'

So much pain threatened to overwhelm Joanna, she had to hold it back. 'No! I don't want to accept it. I can't accept it.'

Sally gave a little nod. It wasn't acquiescence, but it was a reprieve from talking about it now.

When Sally went to hunt them down a sandwich at lunchtime, Joanna took the opportunity to call the bank. Considering how desperate they'd seemed to talk to her in the last couple of weeks, it took a lot of waiting and pressing of buttons before she got to speak to a real human being. If social services were going to investigate her suitability as a carer for Charlotte's baby, she would need to make sure everything was perfect. And that meant she couldn't have this problem with the house and mortgage hanging over her head.

It took so long to actually speak to someone, that Sally was back in the room to hear the tail of her conversation. When she ended the call, she was looking at her with concern. 'Is everything okay, Jo? What's going on?'

There was little point in hiding it. 'That was the bank. They've been trying to call me about the mortgage on the house.'

Sally frowned. 'But wasn't that paid off when Steve passed away? Surely the life insurance would've paid it off?'

Not for the first time, she kicked herself. 'We had to remortgage a few years back. When Steve had those problems with the business. He managed to get us locked into a good rate, but we stopped the life insurance to save some money.'

The rate at which Sally's hand flew to her mouth in shock merely confirmed how stupid they'd been. 'Oh, Jo. I had no idea. How have you been paying the mortgage?'

Financial worries had added a further layer to the most difficult year of her life. She hadn't told anybody – even Charlotte – how close to the wire things were getting. 'I've been paying the mortgage from our savings. Which has been okay up until now. But we're – I'm – getting low on funds and the fixed rate on the mortgage ends soon. I'm not going to be able to afford it. I've been looking for a job, but I'm not qualified for anything.'

That wasn't entirely true. She'd been in such a bad place those first few months after Steve died. It had just been easier to use their savings, stick her head in the sand.

Sally passed her a mozzarella and basil panini. 'What are you going to do now?'

That was another question to add to her list. 'I've explained the situation and they've said that I can apply for a mortgage holiday. But I have to go and see them in that time so that we can come up with a solution.'

'Are you going to have to sell the house?'

She could see from Sally's face that she knew what that would mean. Joanna had never intended to live in this area for the rest of her life. After university, she'd only come home to stay a few months, get some money together. But then she'd met Steve when they were working at the Orsett Hall as wait staff. He'd just graduated, too. Was doing the same as her: a part-time job while he'd looked for work. Then her mum had needed her. Then his dad had got sick. Then Charlotte had started school. And, somehow, they'd never actually moved away.

Buying that house had been the only thing that'd made it

okay. She loved it from the minute they viewed it for the first time. The Georgian windows, the red front door, the picture-perfect front garden. It'd been outside their price range, but Steve – as always – had found a way to make it happen. Of course, she was still working then, too.

Now it wasn't only the house itself that she might have to give up, but the memories that lived within it. It was the place where Charlotte had brought friends home for sleepovers, where Joanna had baked birthday cakes. It was the last place she'd laughed with Steve. The place they'd been a family.

Her eyes filled as she looked at Sally. 'I don't know.'

'Oh, love. We'll sort it out somehow. Maybe you can come and work for me?'

That made them both laugh at the mere thought of her joining the small team in Sally's design company. Joanna didn't have a creative bone in her body and Sally was a perfectionist of the highest order when it came to her work. 'Well, I think that might be the end of a beautiful friendship.'

Sally shrugged. 'Oh well, it was good while it lasted. Eat your sandwich.'

Thought she didn't feel remotely hungry, she knew better than to argue. But she was just about to take a bite when her phone rang again. This time it wasn't the bank.

'Hi, Joanna? It's Abbie. DC Lineham. I was wondering if I could come and meet with you tomorrow? We have some potential new information and I was wondering if you might be able to discuss it with me.'

NINETEEN

Over breakfast the following morning, Joanna insisted that Sally go home to her family. 'You need to talk to Graham.'

Sally seemed to be particularly meticulous about making sure the jam was spread evenly on her toast. 'Yes, I know. But I'm not leaving you yet.'

Much as she would've loved to keep Sally here, she insisted. 'I'll be fine. I'm just keeping Charlotte company until the baby comes.'

That's how she was phrasing it to herself, the only way she could deal with it. It didn't matter what the doctors told her; she hadn't given up hope that Charlotte was still in there, holding on.

Sally paused her clinical knife work and looked up at her. 'You could have a day off today. Rest?'

The nurse had suggested the same thing when she showed them out the previous evening. With an unspoken expression of 'it won't make any difference now'. But she couldn't bear to think about Charlotte alone in that room. 'I want to go in and, anyway, I've arranged to meet Abbie there at ten. She said she's got updates.'

Awake at three o'clock this morning – and four, and five – she'd tried to consider what those updates might be. If Freddie had confessed, surely Abbie would've just told her? What else could it be?

'Well, I'll come in and keep you company, then.' Sally held up a hand to prevent Joanna from arguing. 'No, don't object. I want Graham to spend some time with Harry on his own.'

On the outside, this might sound like a nice thing. But Joanna smelled an ulterior motive. 'Why?'

Sally cut her toast into four perfect triangles, just like she used to when Charlotte and Harry were toddlers and they'd have to try and slot the toast into their mouths as they ran past them in the garden. 'Because Graham thinks that Harry can cope with living on his own. Graham is at work from early in the morning until late at night. Not his fault, I know. But it does mean that he doesn't understand how much I do for Harry.'

Joanna suspected that he did know and that this was one of the motivating factors behind looking at supported accommodation for their son. But she wasn't going to push. 'I see. And you think that spending time with Harry on his own will make him realise?'

Pointing one of the quarters of toast at Joanna, she used it to punctuate each syllable of her reply. 'Exactly.'

Her determination was admirable, but knowing how capable Graham was as a father, Joanna couldn't help but wonder if Sally was shooting herself in the foot with this plan. She might find that Graham proved something else that she wasn't ready for. 'In that case, I'd love to have your company at the hospital.'

She could only imagine that the hospital had been keeping the police informed about Charlotte's condition, because Abbie already knew when she arrived. 'I'm so sorry, Joanna.'

This time, they were walking around the hospital building. It was cool and overcast, but there was no rain and Sally had suggested – forced her into the idea – that she needed to get some fresh air. Abbie had been happy to oblige. 'Thank you. What was it you wanted to talk to me about? Has Freddie admitted to it?'

She shook her head. 'No. Freddie still denies that he attacked Charlotte. His version of events is that he came home and found her on the floor. He says she must've fallen because there was no one else at the house. But her injuries are not consistent with an accident. The forensic pathologist is certain that she must've been pushed backwards with some force.'

She tactfully waited a couple of moments before continuing. Even though Joanna knew this was what had happened, it was still not easy to hear.

When she spoke again, Abbie's voice was calm and measured. 'There was also no sign of forced entry at the flat. Which means that Charlotte is likely to have known whoever it was and let them in. We've been to speak to the residents of neighbouring flats and the next-door neighbour gave us some new information. He said that there was another man who came to the flat before Freddie did.'

Joanna gasped and stopped dead in her tracks, her head spinning with the news. Someone else there? Someone Charlotte knew? 'Who was it?'

From behind them, an orderly with a large basket on wheels full of laundry rattled up the path, the whole contraption jolting as it banged over the uneven paving stones under their feet. When he was out of hearing distance, Abbie continued. 'At the moment, we haven't identified this man. The neighbour can't be sure whether he left before or after Freddie arrived home. He can't provide us with a description because he didn't pay much attention at the time. But he thinks he was a similar build to

Freddie because, when he first saw him, that's who he thought it was.'

A dark cloud spread over the roof of the hospital like ink in a glass of water, its outer reaches curled into the air. Abbie held out her arm to suggest they continue their walk and Joanna followed her lead. 'What did Freddie say about it?'

'Freddie is denying that there was anyone else there, but we are checking CCTV footage in the area for anyone of a similar height and build to him. Unfortunately, there are no cameras on that road so we don't have much hope of spotting anyone.'

Joanna remembered a heated discussion at home one evening when Charlotte had been reading about surveillance cameras in a magazine and was practically apoplectic about the invasion of privacy. It was funny how, the older Joanna got, the more she'd become willing to trade privacy for safety. Especially where her daughter was concerned. 'What else can we do?'

'I wanted to ask you whether there are any young men you know who might've visited Charlotte that afternoon? A male friend, perhaps? Or a relative that she was close to?'

The tattoo of their footsteps on the path beat the depths of Joanna's silence. She couldn't think of anyone. Apart from when she was at university, all of Charlotte's close friends were girls. She'd had various part-time jobs in the last year since graduation but had never mentioned keeping in touch with anyone from those. Although, there were plenty of bigger things that she'd also neglected to tell Joanna about. 'I can't think of anyone. But I can speak to her friends again to see if they can.'

Abbie nodded. 'That would be great.'

Something else occurred to her. 'Actually. There is someone. Apparently, Freddie has a friend. Dominic. Charlotte's friends told me that he's been hanging around with them a lot. That he seemed quite interested in Charlotte.'

Abbie pulled a notebook from her pocket and scribbled his

name inside. 'We'll speak to him and see what his whereabouts were that day. If anyone else comes to mind, you can call me.' She looked up at Joanna. 'Now that the hospital has updated us on Charlotte's condition, things have changed a little. This is a murder enquiry now.'

This is a murder enquiry now. They'd decided Charlotte wasn't going to make it? The words bit into Joanna like fangs that spread their poison throughout her body. According to the police, her daughter had been murdered. Her precious life was over. She squeezed her hands together to stop them from trembling, then realised her whole body was shaking, her breath coming in short bursts. She couldn't be murdered if she wasn't dead. Why had everyone given up on her? *She hasn't gone. She's still here.*

They'd completed their loop of the hospital and were back at the entrance. A mother was kneeling in front of a small child with a bandage on his arm, an old lady was being helped down the steps by a smiling man in a grey uniform, a couple – his arm around her shoulders – looked stricken by bad news. Life – and death – was happening all around them. She understood what Abbie was saying, she just didn't believe it. 'I need to get back to Charlotte.'

Abbie nodded. 'Of course. I'll be in touch if we have any news.'

Joanna turned and watched Abbie walk back to the car, trying to process what she'd said about this other man. Why wouldn't Freddie tell the police if there was someone else there? Was he worried that they would reveal what'd happened?

Joanna hurried back to the ward, to Charlotte, her mind spinning with the news. She was on the main corridor when her phone rang. Fishing it out of her bag, she half expected it to be Abbie with more news, but it was the bank. Thinking back to what the solicitor had said about her financial affairs affecting her custody bid, she had to answer it.

She was just ending the call when she turned to see a familiar figure, heels clicking towards her along the corridor. Annabelle. 'What's happened? I went to Charlotte's bed and she wasn't there?'

Aside from her son, Annabelle was the last person Joanna wanted to see. 'She's been moved to a different ward. After the surgery.'

She still couldn't say aloud what the doctor had said, what Abbie had known. But this time it served to confuse matters as Annabelle's eyes widened. 'But the solicitor said she wasn't going to recover. Has that changed? Is she going to come round?'

If only that was the case. 'No. She had another brain bleed. They're saying that... that she won't come back from this.'

Irritation flushed Annabelle's face red. 'Why did no one call me? We only found out because Freddie's solicitor called for an update. He needs to be told what is happening with the baby.'

A tsunami of anger rolled through Joanna. She squeezed her fists either side of her. It was all she could do not to fly at Annabelle. How dare she worry about herself and Freddie at a time like this? *What about my baby?* she wanted to scream. *What about what is happening with my baby?*

The look on her face must've told Annabelle how insensitive she was being. 'I'm sorry. I'm so sorry about Charlotte. I'm just worried about the baby. It's only tiny. I'm worried it won't survive.'

It was only by pressing her fingernails hard into her palms that Joanna could refrain from shaking her, from shouting at her to go away. 'The baby is fine.'

Annabelle looked as if she'd spent the morning at a salon. Her hair was freshly blow-dried and her make-up perfect. Yet her face softened as she reached out to pat Joanna's arm. 'So

Charlotte's body is still looking after her baby when she can't. That's a mother, alright. Protecting her child with her dying breath.'

Coming from Annabelle, this unexpected kindness hit Joanna hard and softened her anger. It made her feel guilty, too. Was she in the wrong for holding Annabelle accountable for what Freddie had done? Was Sally right in suggesting that she was allowing Annabelle's behaviour at school to inform what she thought of her now? She certainly looked as if she was genuinely upset about Charlotte.

She remembered what DC Abbie had said about this mystery man who'd been to Charlotte's flat. Though she was jealous at the thought that Charlotte and Annabelle had shared confidences, maybe Annabelle might have an idea who it was. 'Do you know if Dominic was there that day?'

Annabelle frowned. 'Dominic? Freddie's schoolfriend?'

'Yes. They're close, aren't they?'

Annabelle's proud smile was still irritating. 'Freddie is close with all his friends. Everyone loves him.'

Joanna wasn't sure that she should share any of the details that the police had told her about the mystery of the other man. 'Did he like Charlotte?'

A frown clouded Annabelle's brow. 'I have no idea. What are you getting at?'

It was difficult to explain what she wanted to ask without repeating the information from DC Abbie. 'Just that sometimes boys don't like it if one of their friends gets a girlfriend.'

She knew this for a fact. When she'd dated Jacob at fifteen, his friends had been decidedly unfriendly. A memory she was clearly not about to share with Annabelle. 'Well, I doubt that was a problem for Freddie's friends. They'd be used to it. He always had girls interested in him. When he was tiny, my mother used to say that he could charm the birds from the trees. He was such a beautiful baby. I wonder if their child will have the same dark curls that he had. I didn't want to cut them, but my husband insisted. Said he looked like a girl. What was Charlotte like as a baby? Was she fair?'

Charlotte had been the most beautiful baby. Her hair hadn't been blonde so much as gold. And her eyes... they were the roundest, bluest eyes she'd ever seen. 'She was beautiful. Everyone would remark on her when I took her out in the pram.'

'I can imagine. She's a very pretty girl. I'm sure the baby will make us proud.'

Though Annabelle's voice was firm, her eyes were misted and Joanna realised that she was on the brink of tears. Her words hung on the air between them. They both wanted the best for this baby. Maybe she could appeal to Annabelle, mother to mother. Of course she wanted to protect her son, but surely she could see that someone with the potential for violence shouldn't be raising a child?

Once Annabelle had gone, Joanna leaned against the wall and closed her eyes. She was utterly exhausted. Who was this Dominic? If he was a friend of Freddie's, what did he have to do with Charlotte? And was he the man who'd been in their apartment that day?

Just as she was about to get going again, her phone rang in her pocket. It was Sally.

'You need to come, Joanna. Something's happening, they've made me leave the room. You need to come right now.'

TWENTY

FREDDIE

Dominic was not happy when Freddie told him that Charlotte was moving into the apartment with him full time.

It was around three months since she'd lost her father. Though she'd mentioned to her mother that they were back in touch, they'd agreed to keep their relationship quiet for a while, and he hadn't expected to go to the funeral. As soon as he'd got her text from the wake, though – *I need you* – he'd been on his way. She'd met him at the door as soon as he arrived.

'Thanks so much for coming.'

'Of course. I've been thinking about you all day.'

He'd put his arms around her and pulled her close, let her cry heaving sobs into his neck. Over her shoulder, he saw her mother's eyes, watching them. He tried to convey his silent condolences over the heads of the people in black, eating sandwiches from the paper plates in their hands, but her eyes were dark and unforgiving before she turned away. What did he have to do to make her realise he only wanted to look after Charlotte?

Today, he'd invited Dominic over to the flat to tell him what they'd decided. Hangover-killing black coffee in hand, Dominic was looking at him as if he'd lost his mind. 'You've got to be kidding me. You're twenty-one, mate. You shouldn't be playing house.'

Things had moved quickly since her father's funeral. Over the last couple of months, since finding out about the two of them being back together, her relationship with her mother had been increasingly difficult.

Last week, she met him at the apartment for lunch and got quite upset talking about the change in her mother since the funeral. 'She doesn't want to do anything. It's like someone turned out the lights for her and she can't see a way out. Was your mum like that?'

Freddie had been only ten at the time. 'I don't really remember. And I was boarding from eleven, so I wasn't around.'

He was still a little tentative about mentioning his mother after her role in their break-up, but she had asked.

Charlotte pulled the serviette into pieces in her lap. 'My mum can be hard work.'

He'd got that impression from the frosty reception he received every time he collected Charlotte from her house. 'You don't get on?'

'It's not that. We do. I love her. And sometimes we get along really well. But other times she's quite... demanding? I don't think that's the right word. She just has strong opinions about how things should be done. She wants me to have everything and do everything. My dad, he was always the laid-back one. He kept us from driving each other crazy.'

Her face crumpled into tears and he wrapped an arm around her. 'It's hard for you both.'

She wiped the tears away. 'I feel like she's pushing me away. She keeps asking if I'm going to go travelling now Dad's gone. She thinks he would've wanted me to go and do it.'

Anxiety prickled in Freddie's stomach. He tried to keep his voice calm. 'Do you think you will?'

He'd been relieved to see her shake her head. 'No. Lucy and Rachael will be home soon and they won't have the money to go again for a while. Unless you want to go?'

If only he could. 'I have to start my job. Mum wants to take me out suit shopping next week.'

He made a face and she laughed. Then sighed. 'I need to do something though. Me and my mum are dragging ourselves around that house like a pair of ghosts. I need to start thinking about the future, too.'

'What about moving in here?' He hadn't planned to ask but now realised that he wanted it more than anything. When he wasn't with Charlotte, he missed her like a limb.

She pulled away from him and raised an eyebrow. 'Are you asking me to move in with you?'

The more he thought about it, the more it seemed like a brilliant idea. 'It's closer to the station for me to get to work. And it means I'll be able to see you every night, even if I'm home late.'

For a few moments, he thought he'd pushed her too far, too soon. But then her face broke into a tearful smile. 'Yes. Let's do it. Life's for living, right? I need to do something and it'll be fun living together. But I have to get a proper job and pay my way.'

That was the last thing he was bothered about. 'We can argue about that later.'

Now, sitting on the same sofa at the apartment, Dominic was still shaking his head in disbelief. 'I suppose you're going to want me to give you my key back if you're moving her in?'

He'd given Dom a key to the apartment back when his uncle first emigrated. Had even let him bring a girl back here more than once. 'Yeah, I don't want you just wandering in on us. But there's no rush. I've got a spare one for Charlotte.'

'How does your mother feel about her precious boy moving out?'

He hadn't actually told her yet, but she seemed to have changed her mind about Charlotte now that she could see how happy he was and it really would be easier for him to get to the station from the apartment. He was sure she'd be okay with it. It was Charlotte's mother that he was more worried about. Would it make her like him even less if he took her daughter away to live with him?

TWENTY-ONE

Joanna ran through the corridors, her breath tearing through her body. Either side of her, a sea of faces turned to watch her go. Her legs wobbled beneath her but she needed to get there, she needed to get to her baby.

When she got closer to Charlotte's ward, she saw Sally pacing the corridor. Sally opened her mouth to speak but Joanna didn't have time. She pushed open the doors into the ward and kept going. Nausea threatened. She wanted to bend and empty the contents of her stomach onto the floor. But she kept going, kept going. Rushing, running, stumbling. Legs faltering, hands shaking, breath coming in short jagged bursts. *Charlotte?* Did she call that aloud? *Charlotte, I'm coming. Mummy's coming. Wait for me. Wait. I'm coming. I'm coming.*

Rounding a corner, a medication trolley caught her hip a glancing blow and the pain shot through her. Still, she didn't stop. It was nothing to the pain lying in wait for her in that hospital room.

But when she got there, the room was empty.

She caught a nurse on his way to another bed. 'Where is she? Where have they taken Charlotte?'

Recognition dawned on his face as he realised who she was. 'They had to take her down to surgery. Do you want me to find someone to talk to you?'

No, she wanted to go to her daughter, but what choice did she have? 'Yes. Quickly. Please be quick. Yes.'

As soon as he'd left the room, she bent double, hands on her thighs. Her vision blurred as the blood rushed to her head. Why had she left the room? Was this the last time she could see her daughter?

A nurse she knew came back with the first nurse. 'Joanna? I didn't expect you to get here this fast.'

Joanna's heart was beating so loudly in her ears and her breath was coming so quickly that it was difficult to talk. 'I was nearby. Where is she? Can I see her?'

The nurse nodded to the first nurse as if to excuse him leaving. 'Shall we sit down?'

No. She didn't want to sit down. 'Can I go to her?'

The nurse's face was full of sympathy. 'Not right now. Please, sit down before I have to find a bed for you.'

Reluctantly, she sank onto the chair she was offered, her legs like jelly on a paper plate. 'Where is she?'

The nurse sat opposite her and leaned forwards. 'The baby's heart rate dropped. It was an emergency. They're performing the C-section now.'

She felt sick. Not nauseous. She put a hand over her mouth for fear that she might actually throw up on the floor right here.

The nurse continued. 'The plan was always to keep the baby in the womb as long as it was continuing to thrive. The doctor thinks that we've got to the point where the baby has a better chance outside of the womb.'

A better chance? Chance? 'Does he think the baby will be okay?'

The nurse reached out and took the hand that was

clutching at the fabric of her dress. 'The baby is nearly twenty-nine weeks. Charlotte has given them a great start.'

A sobbed escaped from under the hand over Joanna's mouth. 'How long will it take?'

'I can't give you an exact time. But it should be soon.'

'And will we know straight away if the baby is okay?'

'As soon as we know anything, we'll tell you.'

And then the question that she didn't want to ask. 'And what about Charlotte? What will happen to her?'

The nurse looked at her carefully, as if judging how much she could take. 'You know that Charlotte has gone. That her brain injury meant she can no longer support her own life.'

She knew that's what the doctors had said. But they didn't know her daughter. Didn't know the tiny hope in Joanna's heart that Charlotte would prove them wrong. 'But what will they do once the baby is delivered? Will they take away her life support?'

The nurse swallowed. Joanna didn't envy her the conversations like this that she must have to have on a regular basis. 'No. They will bring her back to the ward and then you'll be able to say goodbye.'

Joanna couldn't look at her any longer. She needed to be alone. 'Where can I wait?'

'Wherever is best for you. We'll call you as soon as they're out of surgery. You can use our relatives' room or—'

Joanna shook her head. She didn't want to go in a room like that ever again. 'No. My friend is outside. We'll find somewhere. But you promise you'll call me? As soon as they're out?'

The nurse nodded. 'I promise.'

Sally was waiting for her outside the ward. 'I'm sorry. I didn't know whether to follow you in or stay out here. What's happening?'

Having to say it out loud made it all the more real. 'They've taken her down to theatre. The baby. They need to...'

Her voice dissolved into sobs. She couldn't say it. Thankfully, she didn't need to. Sally took her into her arms and held her as she cried.

Holding her tight, Sally spoke into her hair. 'The baby is nearly twenty-nine weeks. Most babies are okay if they're born at twenty-nine weeks. I've been reading about it.'

But it wasn't the baby that Joanna was thinking about. There was her other, secret hope, that Charlotte would shock them all and wake up. It didn't matter what anyone told her, she'd wouldn't give up hoping until there was no hope left. If she didn't hope, she would fall back down into the abyss. And – this time – she might not be able to climb out again.

Sally gave her another squeeze then held her at arms' length and looked deep into her eyes. 'Come on, let's go and wash our faces and then let me buy you a coffee while we wait.'

'You were going to go home and see Graham. You need to sort everything out.'

'I'll call Graham in a while. He'll be fine.'

All the way to the coffee shop, they walked in silence. Neither of them knew what to say. Passing a trio of young nurses, two of them laughing at whatever the third was saying, Joanna wanted to tell them to make the most of every minute of life.

At this time of day, the coffee shop was full of visitors and patients and hospital staff on their break or at the end of a shift. She couldn't bear to sit among them staring into space. She pointed out the one free table to Sally. 'You go and sit down. I'll get the drinks. It'll give me something to do.'

The air was full of voices and rattling crockery, the hiss of the coffee machine and the call of the barista delivering the drinks to those waiting. For once, she wasn't bothered about the long queue, which snaked almost to the entrance. In fact, she would happily let people in front of her, and stay in that line forever. Because, all the time she was here, Charlotte was still in the world, the baby was okay and she didn't have to face a life without her in it.

She was two people behind the person being served when her phone rang in her hand. It was a hospital number. With a trembling finger, she pressed the screen to take the call.

TWENTY-TWO

The paediatric Intensive Therapy Unit was in a completely different part of the hospital. Joanna pressed the buzzer to the right of the door and waited for a response.

Until now, she hadn't even dared to believe that the baby would survive. The nurse had been as good as her word and had called to let her know that the delivery had gone smoothly. She'd also offered to call ahead to the ITU to let them know that Joanna would be on her way there. Her kindness – and the utter relief that the baby was okay – had made Joanna weep silent tears in the middle of the coffee shop queue. People had watched her from behind their paper cups.

Sally had been beside her in moments and led her away from the counter and back out into the corridor. 'What is it? What's happened?'

Her throat had been so thick with emotion that she'd barely been able to speak. 'The baby is here. She's doing really well.'

Sally had put her hand to her mouth, then her heart. 'Her? A little girl?'

A little girl. She could hardly believe it. 'The nurse said that I can go and see her straight away.'

'Oh, that's wonderful. Jo. Go now. I'll wait for you.'

She hesitated and looked at Sally, wanting her to read her mind. 'I asked when I can see Charlotte. But she didn't know.'

Sally nodded. 'I'll go and find out. You go and check on that baby.'

She was just about to press the buzzer again when the door opened and a nurse smiled at her. 'Mrs Woodley?'

'Yes. Joanna. Nurse Asenyi said I should come.'

The nurse stood back to let her pass. 'We've been expecting you. Would you like to come and meet your grandaughter?'

Joanna had never been in a special care baby unit before, let alone an ITU. Nurses – some wearing plastic aprons – moved quietly around the room past two rows of plastic cribs. Beside five of the six cribs, mothers – and sometimes fathers – were intent on the precious contents. Joanna's heart ached; Charlotte should be here, just like them. But right now, she needed to focus on the baby. Fear curled at her heart at the thought of whether she was going to be okay, whether she had enough strength to make it through these first important hours.

The nurse who'd met Joanna at the door stopped beside the crib in the far corner and spoke quietly to the nurse sitting beside it. She smiled at Joanna. 'Hello, I'm Jenny. Baby is doing really well. She's a little fighter.'

Though she was trying not to draw attention to herself, a sob escaped from Joanna. Relief, pride, sadness; all mingled together. 'Her mother was a fighter, too.'

Kindness and sympathy lit up Jenny's face. 'I'm so sorry you lost your daughter. She did so well to hang on for this little one. She gave her the best chance possible.'

Grief threatened to overtake Joanna, but she refused to let it be here in the moment. This was about new life. 'Can I come closer?'

'Of course.' Jenny made way for her. 'Here she is.'

And then she was there. Wearing just a nappy, which

looked enormous next to her bird-like frame. Tiny arms and legs akimbo as if she was sunbathing without a care in the world. Although much of her face was obscured with what she assumed was an oxygen mask, Joanna could see enough to know that she was exactly as she should be. 'She's so perfect.'

The nurse smiled. 'Would you like to touch her? If you sterilise your hands here—' Jenny showed her the tub '—you can reach into the crib if you'd like to come and sit here.'

She followed the nurse's direction to the seat next to the crib. There was a flap on the side and she showed her how to pull this down and reach her hand inside. She stroked the baby's tiny fist, each finger a miniature work of art. 'How can she be so tiny and yet still have all the bits and pieces inside her that she needs?'

Jenny smiled. 'A lot of people say that. The human body is amazing, isn't it?'

Amazing, yet so fragile. The baby's skin was the softest tissue. She stroked her arm. 'Hello, little one. I'm your granny.'

Jenny took a step back. 'I'll leave you both alone for a while. But I'll be just over here if you need me.'

Joanna barely heard her: she was absolutely transfixed. Though she'd had a few days to get used to the idea that Charlotte was pregnant, it was still a completely surreal experience to be here with her child. 'You have a very brave mummy, you know. She used everything she had to make sure that you'll be well. And you will be. Because you're like your mummy. Beautiful and strong and determined. And I'll be here, little one. I'll be here for all of it.'

Aside from a huge white nappy, the baby was naked and Joanna could see her tiny bones beneath the skin. Covered in circular stickers, which were attached to wires, attached to monitors, it was difficult not to think of Charlotte in the hospital bed and her heart ached so much. Not only for her loss, but for this baby's loss. That she would never know her mother and what a wonderful human being she was. 'She would've loved you so much, your mummy. She would have done everything right. I just know she would.'

The baby stirred in the cot and opened a hand. Gently, Joanna slid her finger into the baby's palm and, when she closed her fingers around it, a wave of love washed over her, almost strong enough to bowl her over. She could remember these same precious moments when Charlotte was a baby. The joy on Steve's face when he'd held Charlotte's hand just as she was doing now. 'And your grandpa would've loved you, too. He was such a soft touch. When your mummy was little, she used to wrap him around her little finger. He would do anything to keep her smiling. I've got so many stories to tell you.'

As she spoke, tears coursed down her cheeks. She had a lifetime of stories to tell. Though it was over two decades ago, it didn't feel that long since Charlotte was almost as tiny as this. It'd felt so difficult, the responsibility of keeping her safe. When she first brought her home, she'd had her crib beside the bed and would lay awake watching her little chest rise and fall before exhaustion claimed her. Then as a toddler, she followed her around the room determined to catch her if she fell. If only she could've kept her safe this time.

Around the bed, monitors beeped and the familiar hiss of an oxygen tube punctuated her one-way conversation. But this was different and she had to keep reminding herself of that. This baby was going to survive and thrive and she would make sure that she had the best life she could possibly have.

Above the crib, on a white board, were details about the baby's care. At the top, her name was written as Baby Woodley.

She was going to need a name. And soon. Joanna didn't want to keep thinking about her – or talking about her – as 'the baby'. But what should it be? Her mind drew a blank. Charlotte had never talked about having children so she had no idea what she would've wanted to call her. She tried to remember if she'd had any favourite names when she'd played games as a child. But she'd always been more into tools and cars than dolls and dresses. Maybe Sally would know something. Or her friends.

She wriggled the finger in the baby's grasp. 'We'll come up with something your mummy would like.'

Much as she wanted to stay here and stare at the baby all day, half of her mind and heart were still with Charlotte on that operating table. When Jenny came over to check the monitors, she asked her who she should speak to, to find out whether Charlotte would be out of surgery, and where she was right now.

'I'll find out for you as soon as I've finished these obs.'

How many times in her life would she be pulled in different directions? Between caring for her mother and leaving home, between grieving for her husband and trying to look out for her daughter. And now, between her daughter and her grandchild. If Joanna could've torn herself in two, she would've done. It was a wrench to leave the baby, but she wanted to go to her daughter. Joanna watched Jenny work, trying to read her face as she wrote on her clipboard. 'Is she doing well? Is she going to be okay?'

'All the numbers are right where we want them, so that's a great sign.' She nodded at Joanna's hand in the crib. 'What you're doing right now is really helpful. Contact is good. Will you be visiting frequently?'

'Yes. Every day if I can?'

'You can come as often as you'd like. The only times we ask parents to wait outside is during handover and if we have to have a private conversation with other parents about one of the babies, but mostly we'd like you to be with your babies as much as you can.'

Joanna didn't know if the nurse had slipped up by calling

her a parent or whether she wanted her to know that that's how they saw her. 'Will I be able to hold her at some point?'

Jenny ticked the last box on her sheet then nodded. 'We just want to keep her warm in there a bit longer before bringing her out, but it's good to get some skin on skin going as soon as we can. Maybe in a few hours, or tomorrow, we can have her out for a little cuddle with granny. I'm all done here, so I'll call through to surgical for an update on your daughter.'

Once she'd walked away, Joanna leaned towards the cot and whispered to the baby, 'Did you hear that? You're doing really well. We're going to get through this and then take you home.'

She did her best not to think about the solicitor's words. That it would be up to a social worker to decide where this baby's home would be. With every fibre of her being, she was going to make sure this child was going to be safe. With her.

Jenny came back with news that it would be about another half an hour before she could go to Charlotte and, shortly afterwards, a message came through on her phone from Sally saying the same thing. Time seemed to stand still in the ward. Chairs were faced towards the wall, to give people privacy she'd imagine, but glancing to the left and the right, she saw two mothers cradling their child, singing to them. The mass of wires attached to the babies served as a reminder of how much was going on to keep them alive. Again she asked the nurse for reassurance. 'Is the baby going to be okay?'

Jenny lowered her clipboard so that Joanna could see what she was writing.

'She's getting a big tick from me on everything. A doctor will be in later and they'll give you an update. She just needs time to grow.'

Time to grow. Joanna couldn't help but think that she needed that, too.

. . .

Outside the ward, Sally – her precious loyal supportive friend – was still waiting for her.

'I can't believe you're still here.'

She held out her arms for Joanna to walk into. 'How's the baby?'

Joanna accepted a big squeeze then pulled away. 'She's doing so well. She's so tiny, Sally. So so tiny. But she's perfect.'

Sally smiled. 'Of course she is. Look at who her mother is.'

Tears filled Joanna's eyes. 'I wish she could've seen her. Held her.'

'I know. Me, too.' She paused, her voice growing hoarse. 'Are you going to her now?'

Apart from the baby's side, she wouldn't be anywhere else. But dread lay heavy as stone in the pit of her stomach. This was the final time she would see her daughter. 'I can't do it, Sally. How can I say goodbye to her?'

It was inconceivable. Unnatural. No mother should ever outlive her child.

Sally was fighting to keep the crippling grief from her face. 'You have to, Jo. I'm so sorry. I know this is so hard.'

Hard didn't even come close. Grounding her when she begged to go out was hard. Holding her when she cried about the end of her first relationship was hard. This was impossible. 'I can't. I can't, Sally.'

Sally was crying now. 'I know. I know. But you don't have a choice. I can come with you?'

For a moment, she might have taken her up on it, but she knew that wasn't how it should be. 'No. It's okay. Thank you, but I have to do it on my own.'

Though everyone says you forget, she could remember every moment of Charlotte's birth. Though Steve had been there – along with the midwife – it'd been as if she was all alone. In the final stages, she'd retreated so far inside herself it was as if no one existed except her and her baby. When Charlotte was born, she recognised her immediately.

And now, at the end of her life, it would be just the two of them again. Just her and her baby girl. Just like those final stages of labour, she would have to find the strength from somewhere.

Sally held out her arms and gave her the tightest squeeze she could. 'I'll be right here. I won't move an inch.'

TWENTY-THREE

The hardest goodbye is the one you never thought you'd have to say.

Joanna's soft knock was answered immediately by a nurse she hadn't seen before. In the room, the lights were low and there was an air of calm which was in direct contrast to the turmoil in Joanna's chest. Covered by only a hospital sheet, Charlotte looked all the world as if she only needed to be shaken by the shoulder to wake and ask her for 'just five more minutes, Mum'.

The nurse had left the chair close to the bed, ready for her. 'Once you're settled, I'll take the ventilator off. Then I'll leave you alone together.'

Joanna took a seat and Charlotte's hand. It was warm and soft and she never wanted to let it go. 'How long will I have with her?'

The nurse's eyes reached out in sympathy. 'Usually, once someone is taken off the ventilator, they stop breathing in a few minutes. But you can stay with her as long as you like.'

A few minutes? How could she say everything she wanted to say in that time? 'Thank you.'

Nothing was hurried or cold. The nurse was gentle and kind as she made her way around the bed. Once she got to the ventilator, she looked at Joanna. 'Are you ready?'

No. She wanted to say. *No. I will never be ready for you to take out that tube and watch my daughter take her last breaths.* Unable to trust her voice, she nodded.

Gently the nurse slipped the mask from Charlotte's face, then turned the machine off. Those mechanical breaths had been the background music to Joanna's life for the last few days. Without them, the air was totally silent. The only sound was the squeak of the nurse's shoes as she left the room and clicked the door shut behind her.

Music. She'd forgotten to have it ready. She wanted her to hear her favourite music. Fumbling with her phone, she found the playlist Charlotte had made for her months ago and set it to play.

Sitting beside her wasn't enough. It wasn't as close as she needed to be. The time for asking permission was past. She climbed on the bed next to Charlotte and held her daughter in her arms for the last time.

Without the ventilator, she could see the whole of Charlotte's beautiful face. With her forefinger, she traced a circle around it, the way she used to when she was trying to get her to sleep as a baby. Starting at her hairline, sweeping past her eyes, the round of her cheek, down to her chin and then up the other side. Then she leaned in close and whispered across the pillow, 'You did good, sweetheart. Your baby girl is perfect, just like her mama. She is almost as beautiful as you were. She has your heart-shaped face and the same long fingers. I wonder if she'll be a pianist too.'

Her voice broke and she held her breath for a few moments, trying to regain control. She didn't want her cries to be the last thing that Charlotte heard in this world.

'It doesn't matter if she doesn't want to play the piano. Or play anything at all. Because she can be anything she wants to be. I know you would tell me that I just need to let her do her own thing. So that's exactly what I'm going to do. You don't need to worry about her. I'm going to look after her for you now.'

She wasn't sure if she was imagining it, but Charlotte's breaths seemed to be getting shallower. Maybe she only had a couple of minutes more.

'I'm going to miss you so much, my darling girl. But it's okay to go now. Your dad will be there waiting for you. He'll be so glad to see you. Don't the two of you be talking about me like you used to.'

What would she give to see Charlotte roll her eyes at Steve behind her back. To see him laugh at her and then quickly rearrange his face into a faux-serious expression when she turned to face him. How had she not seen each of these moments as the precious gold of life that they were?

Hard as she tried, she couldn't control the tears spilling from her eyes. She laid a hand on the far side of Charlotte's face and pressed her lips into the cheek closest to her. She was still warm. How could she be leaving the world?

'You can go to sleep now, my precious girl. Just rest. I've got you.'

If it weren't for the baby, she'd want to close her eyes now, too. Close them and never wake up again. But she had to stay. She had to make sure that little girl knew just how incredible her mother was. She'd spend the rest of her life telling her.

She wasn't sure how long she lay there next to Charlotte. After some time, the nurse came and spoke to her quietly, to check that she was okay. It seemed like an appropriate time to go. Still, she stood at the door, terrified to leave. This would be the last time she ever stood in a room with her daughter and she didn't want it to end. For one last time, she tiptoed over to her darling girl and kissed her goodnight.

When she left the ward, Sally was sitting in the waiting area, her own face red where she'd wiped away tears. Her watery smile was a welcome sight. 'Okay, love?'

'No.' Joanna's heart squeezed in pain. 'I don't think I'll ever be okay again.'

Sally held her as she cried, rocking her gently. Down the corridor, two young boys were running and she could hear their mother calling them, telling them to slow down. How could the world still be going about its business? She wanted everything and everyone to stop. Her daughter had died. Nothing should ever be the same again.

Eventually, her body calmed and she sat up. 'I'm so glad you're here.'

'There's nowhere else I'd rather be.'

'Did you want to go and say goodbye? I'm sure it'd be okay?'

Sally shook her head. 'No. Thank you, but I'd rather remember her the way she was the last time we met. Making me almost wet myself by impersonating the arrogant waiter at our afternoon tea.'

Despite her pain, she had to smile at that. 'She was a really good mimic, wasn't she?'

'She was. She was a really good girl.'

This pain was so raw that every word was agony. But thinking and talking and reminiscing about Charlotte was going to be something she always wanted to do, however painful it was. 'We have to remember all these stories, you know. Because her daughter will want to know all of them.'

'Oh, I've got plenty. We'll get a book and we'll write them all down. We can ask those nice friends of hers, too.'

Joanna liked that idea. Although that made her think about something else. 'I'm going to have to organise a funeral. How can I be doing that again so soon?'

Sally shook her head. 'You don't need to worry about that. Just tell me what you want and I'll do it.'

She was very grateful, but knowing what she wanted was the hardest part of it. She couldn't bear to even think about it.

Sally must've read her mind. 'But you don't need to think about that today. Today is the first goodbye, the next one can wait.'

She knew exactly what Sally meant. There was never one goodbye when you lost someone you love. When you know you are going to lose them, the goodbye begins. Then the moment they slip away. Then the funeral. And after that, every time you do something without them for the first time – a meal out, Christmas Day, a holiday – you say goodbye again.

'Thank you, Sally. For everything. For being here. I don't know if I'd still be standing upright without you.'

'That's what friends are for. You'd do the same for me.'

She was absolutely right. 'I would. And now I need you to do something else for me. I need you to go home and see Graham. I'm going to be with the baby for the rest of the day until they kick me out of here. And then I'll be back in the morning. You need to go and be with your family.'

Sally was shaking her head from the first sentence. 'No. I'm not leaving you to go home alone.'

'You are. Because it's what I want. Please, Sally. Go and see Graham and sort out this thing between you. And then come back. With both of them. I'd love to see Harry. I need one of his hugs.'

Sally's eyes filled. 'I could do with one of those, too. But I don't want to leave you.'

'I know that. And I love you for it. But please. Go home tonight.'

Sally took a deep breath. 'Okay. I will. But if you need me...'

'I know. I'll be straight on the phone. Now go home.'

Sally picked up the jacket on the chair beside her. Then she wrinkled her nose. 'Before I go, there's something I need to tell you. While you were in with Charlotte, Freddie's mother arrived. She was coming to visit Charlotte. She said she had a letter to read out to her.'

Sally looked at her, waiting for her to join the dots. 'A letter from him? From Freddie?'

Sally nodded. 'I had to tell her what was happening; otherwise I think she would have tried to join you. I'm sorry.'

'It's fine. Of course you had to tell her.'

Sally took a deep breath. 'The other problem is that she obviously wanted to know what the situation was with the baby. So, I kind of had to tell her that, too. I'm really sorry, Joanna. I tried to be vague but it was difficult.'

'It's fine. You've saved me having to tell her. At least she's gone now. I'll deal with her tomorrow.'

Sally pulled a face. 'I also told her that it'd be better if she came back later, but she said she wanted to see the baby. I think that's where she's gone.'

She'd gone to see the baby? Would they let her in? Joanna knew that she was being unfair, but she wasn't ready to share the baby with her yet. She gathered the broken pieces of her heart and started to jog towards the special care baby unit. 'I need to stop her, Sally. I don't want her there.'

As she hurried through the corridors, she couldn't help but think that Annabelle had known about this baby longer than she had. Again, she felt the sting of Charlotte keeping the news from her. If she'd known about the baby, might it have changed everything that happened?

TWENTY-FOUR

FREDDIE

When he first got home, Freddie thought she was about to leave him.

It was a Friday night and everyone from the office was going out for drinks. He'd stayed for one, then battled through the mockery about him leaving early to 'get home to the little woman'.

He didn't come home early every night. Often, she'd have plans to meet up with Rachael and Lucy on a Friday or she'd have dinner with her mother. But she'd sent him a message that afternoon to check that he'd be home and there was something about the tone of it that'd made him concerned. When he walked in to find her sitting on the sofa waiting for him, he was even more worried.

'Hey. What's up?'

'Can you sit down?'

Heart in his mouth, he dropped his bag beside the sofa and joined her. 'You're making me nervous. Is everything okay?'

'I've tried to think about how to tell you this, but I think it's easier if I just come out and say it.'

All his worst fears flashed through his mind. They'd rushed

things. She'd been vulnerable because of her father. She'd just gone off him. 'Charlotte, I—'

'I'm pregnant.'

Pregnant? That was *not* what he thought she was going to say. He froze. Scanned her eyes, her lips, trying to read her face. Was she joking? *Say something. Just say something.* 'Are you sure?'

She held out her hands. 'Pretty sure. I've done three tests.'

He brought his own hands up to his cheeks and rubbed them. He still had no idea how to react. He was twenty-three. He'd just started work. This wasn't part of the plan. Not yet, at least. 'Wow.'

She chewed on her bottom lip; her eyes still unreadable. 'Yeah. Wow.'

Now he realised for sure this was real, he took one of her hands in his. Letting his feelings – confusion, disbelief, uncertainty – settle, there was another, warmer sensation in the pit of his gut. Still, he couldn't read her face. 'How do you feel about it? What are you thinking?'

She swallowed, placed the hand that wasn't in his onto her chest. 'I think, I actually feel pretty good about it.'

The warmth started to spread through him, from his stomach, through his body, across his heart. This was crazy and yet... 'Yes? You're happy?'

A smiled played at the corners of her mouth. 'I actually am. But I understand if you don't...'

She tailed off as he took her other hand, unable to stop the tears from gathering in his eyes. 'I think I'm happy too. I mean, it's a bit nuts, but... I think we can do this. I want to do this.'

Her lips widened into such a smile that it reached her eyes, lighting them with a sunshine she'd been missing for a while. 'I think we can do this, too.'

He wrapped his arms around her and held her close. His heart swelled to see her so happy. A baby was a big step, but –

weirdly – it didn't scare him. They could do anything together. Against his chest, her voice wobbled. 'I wish my dad was here. He would make such a lovely grandad.'

He squeezed her tighter. 'Yes, I wish my father could see this, too. Have you told your mum yet?'

She pulled herself back to sitting and shook her head. 'Not yet. It's early days. Let's keep it just for us for now. And she's been so... difficult. About us. I want her to get to know you properly first. If I tell her now, I don't know that I'd get the reaction I want.'

He understood. It didn't matter how much he'd tried to show Joanna that he loved Charlotte, that he'd never let her down again, he could see that, in her eyes, he was a cheater she couldn't, wouldn't, trust. 'I won't tell my mother yet, either. Like you say, let's keep it just for us for a while.'

TWENTY-FIVE

Hospitals are rabbit warrens at the best of times, and it took two different lifts and five lengthy corridors before Joanna reached the baby unit. With relief, she saw Annabelle waiting outside, punching instructions into her mobile phone, a face like a stormy day. Even from a distance, she intimidated Joanna. Old feelings die hard.

When she looked up, her frown smoothed out into something more sympathetic. 'Joanna. I'm so sorry about Charlotte. But why didn't you tell me that the baby had been born?'

That sentence was exactly why she hadn't called her. That, and the fact that the most precious human being in the world had just died. Her grief made her bold. 'I've had rather a lot to be dealing with, Annabelle.'

Annabelle's shoulders softened beneath her pale-pink tailored jacket. 'I'm sorry. Of course. How was it?'

How was it? Joanna had no idea how to answer that question. How were the last minutes of her daughter's life? Not ten minutes ago she'd held her precious child for the last time ever in this world. Even if she could articulate the deep, debilitating grief that consumed every part of her, she wasn't about to share it here, with her. She kept her response brief. 'Very hard.'

Annabelle dipped her head a little; perhaps she realised how inappropriate her question had been. 'I'm sorry. I can't begin to imagine how you feel. This must be incredibly difficult. She truly was a wonderful girl. We'll all miss her so very much.'

Joanna didn't quite know how to respond. She'd been so knotted up with the knowledge that Annabelle had known about Charlotte's pregnancy that she hadn't stopped to think what that meant. That Annabelle and Charlotte must've had a good relationship.

Her own experience had been very different. The one and only time she'd met Jacob's parents – he'd invited her to his house for a garden party they were throwing – she'd been totally out of her depth. It wasn't that they'd made her unwelcome – they were far too well-mannered to do that – it was that she knew she didn't fit. The outfit she'd chosen, the way she spoke, the references they made to plays and books and music that she knew nothing about. Jacob's family hadn't been unkind, but they hadn't gone out of their way to be kind, either.

From the moment she'd recognised Annabelle, she'd assumed it'd been the same for Charlotte. Having experienced Annabelle's attitude at school, she'd imagined exactly how she would've responded to Freddie's relationship with Charlotte.

But what if she'd been wrong? Annabelle didn't know that Charlotte was the daughter of the girl that Annabelle had bullied at school, did she? Maybe they'd got close and, much as the very thought twisted Joanna's stomach, maybe she needed to stop letting her memory of the younger Annabelle cloud her judgement of the woman who clearly cared for her daughter?

'Thank you. That's kind of you to say.'

Annabelle's smile was gentle. 'And how is the baby... is it a boy or a girl?'

Joanna swallowed the lump in her throat. 'Charlotte had a little girl.'

Annabelle's hand fluttered to her chest. Under the bright-yellow strip light in the corridor, the tears in her eyes glinted almost as much as the large diamond on her finger. 'A girl? Oh, how wonderful. I've always wanted a granddaughter. A girl. Is she very tiny? Is she going to be okay? Who does she look like? Can I come in and see her now?'

Her questions rained down on Joanna's head. She focused on the last one. 'You can't come and see her yet. It's a restricted ward.'

Annabelle's perfectly groomed eyebrows pulled together. 'I don't understand. You're allowed in there and I'm the same relationship to the baby as you are.'

Joanna squeezed her fists at her side; anxiety prickled at the possible implications of that statement. 'It's because I've been here with Charlotte. They won't want too many different visitors. There'll be a risk of infection if there's too many people.'

She was freewheeling here, making it up as she went along. She'd say anything to stop Annabelle getting anywhere near her precious granddaughter. Even as she did so, she knew that she was being unfair. The baby was Annabelle's grandchild as much as hers. But she'd just lost her daughter; didn't she get to keep the baby to herself for a little while at least?

Disbelief flashed across Annabelle's face, but, before she could reply, the door in front of them buzzed then clicked open and an exhausted-looking couple in their mid-thirties emerged blinking against the bright electric light. The man slipped his arm around the woman and kissed the side of her head. 'Come on. It's just a quick coffee. You need a break, love.'

He smiled and nodded at Joanna and Annabelle as they left. Joanna returned the smile, then closed her eyes as she listened to their footsteps tap away from them up the corridor, presumably in the direction of the canteen. If only Charlotte had met someone like that. Someone caring and supportive and kind. When she turned to look at Annabelle, her eyes were full of tears.

'I wish Freddie could be here to meet his daughter. It breaks my heart to think of all he's missing out on.'

Her grief seemed so genuine that it chipped away at the shell of distrust Joanna had protected herself with. Whatever she thought of Freddie, she could understand why Annabelle would feel like this.

Annabelle pulled a packet of tissues from her bag and dabbed one of them under her eyes. 'He's in absolute pieces about Charlotte. Whatever the police are thinking, I know he didn't do it, Joanna. You'd know it, too if you'd seen them together. They were inseparable. They were so happy at their apartment, building their home.'

Joanna felt another twist of jealousy. Followed immediately by guilt. She hadn't seen them together because of her own stupid pride. If she had, she might've known what kind of man he was. She'd know better whether he'd done this awful thing. For the first time, she saw herself through Annabelle's eyes. The mother who'd been so difficult about her daughter's boyfriend that she'd pushed her away. More of the hard shell crumbled away. 'This last year, since losing my husband... it's been really tough.'

Annabelle nodded. 'I know how hard it is to lose a husband.'

Of course, she'd understand. She'd been through the same thing, hadn't she? 'I think I lost myself a little bit, too. Charlotte and I... we struggled.'

Annabelle's face was kind. 'She was close to her father, wasn't she?'

'Yes, but I don't just mean that.' The guilt that'd sat just beneath the surface for the last few days needed to come out. 'We argued. Before this happened. About her and Freddie. We were barely on speaking terms. When she died, we hadn't seen each other for almost two weeks. The last thing I said to her was something about me being right and her being wrong. I can't bear it that she died not knowing how sorry I am for that.'

She fought to keep the tears under control. Annabelle pulled another tissue from the packet and passed it to her. 'You need to be kind to yourself, Joanna. Grief makes us act strangely sometimes. I'm sure she knew you wanted the best for her. We all just want the best for our children.'

She managed to raise a smile at Annabelle. 'Thank you.'

For a few beats they stood opposite one another. Two mothers who only wanted the best for their children, now connected by one tiny little girl.

Joanna nodded her head in the direction of the door. 'I'm just going to go and check on the baby. I have some photos of her. Would you like me to send them to you?'

She slipped her phone from her pocket and showed Annabelle the last picture she'd taken, the baby a fragile little sparrow in a huge plastic crib. But perfect too.

Annabelle gasped. 'Oh, she's beautiful. What a precious little girl. And she's a Knight-Crossley alright, look at that brow. Freddie had that when he was born. Looked just like my father-in-law.'

Joanna's throat tightened. 'Actually, I think she looks just like Charlotte. Her long fingers and toes are just like her mummy's.'

Annabelle tilted her head to get a better look. 'Well, let's hope we get a bit of both of them in there. Yes, please send it and I'll forward it to Freddie, he'll be so pleased to see her. Our solicitor is working on getting him out for the day so he can meet his daughter. But this will keep him going in the meantime.'

The hairs on the back of Joanna's neck rose. Come here? Would they really let him out to come to the hospital if he was being held on suspicion of murder? To avoid Annabelle's eyes, she stared at her phone screen as she sent the photograph to her number.

When it beeped to show the photo had arrived, Annabelle waved her phone. 'Got it. Thank you. Please let me know as soon as I can come in to see the baby.'

Through everything that had happened in the last twenty-four hours, the baby had been the one thing that had kept Joanna upright. And now, when she was barely in the world, she was going to have to consider that Freddie's mother would have just as much of a claim on her as Joanna did.

Annabelle's phone started to ring in her hand and she picked it up and spoke loudly. 'Hello, George? Yes, hang on, the reception is terrible in here.' She held the phone to her chest to mute the call and spoke to Joanna. 'Our family solicitor. I'm hoping to find out when Freddie can get out for a visit here. Keep me informed about our grandaughter.'

She left with a wave and Joanna waited until she'd turned the corner before holding on to the wall to get her breath. She couldn't go into the baby like this; she needed to compose herself. But how could she do that with the threat of her daughter's attacker, her murderer, working out a way that he could come and get his hands on their daughter?

Once she had her breath back, she scrolled through on her phone and found the number for DC Lineham. She answered in a couple of rings. 'Hi Joanna. How are you doing?'

She had no time for the niceties. 'Charlotte's gone.'

The police officer's voice was kind. 'I'm so sorry.'

She had to keep pressing on, not think about Charlotte right now. 'And the baby has been born. She's in the Intensive Therapy Unit. The nurse said she's doing well.'

'That's really great, Joanna. I'm so pleased. Have you seen her?'

'Yes, and I'm about to go back in. But I wanted to ask you about Freddie Knight-Crossley. His mother seems to think that he'll get permission to come and visit the baby. That can't be right, can it?'

There was a moment of quiet on the other end. 'Would you like me to come and see you? I can be there in a couple of hours?'

She didn't like the sound of that. 'No, I'll be in with the baby. But can he come?'

Her voice on the other end of the phone was gentle but firm. 'I can understand your fears, but it is likely that he will get permission to come and see his newborn child. Especially as he hasn't been convicted yet.'

Nausea rose up in Joanna's throat. The door to the special care unit clicked open again and a nurse came out. Joanna backed away from the door and lowered her voice. 'But it's his fault that the baby doesn't have a mother.'

'He hasn't been to trial yet and the thing is...'

She tailed off and fear lurched in Joanna's stomach. 'The thing is what?'

'There's a possibility that we don't have enough evidence to proceed to trial. His solicitor is putting quite a lot of pressure on.'

The last remark had a definite change in tone. Joanna could well imagine the amount of money he made from working for the Knight-Crossley family. 'But you have to get the evidence. You have to make sure he gets convicted. He can't go free.'

'Look. Let me come and see you. It'll be a lot easier to talk about this in person.'

Joanna was almost numb with the different emotions she was having to deal with. Right now, all she wanted to do was make sure that her granddaughter was okay. It was unbearable, imagining her laying there all alone. 'Okay. Tomorrow?'

'Tomorrow is good. Any particular time suit you best? Shall I meet you at home or come to the hospital?'

'The hospital. I'll be here all day.'

'Okay. I'll confirm a time in the morning.'

As soon as she'd ended the call, her phone dinged with a text message. Then another. The first was from Sally. The second from Annabelle.

She read Sally's first. *I'm at the car and about to drive home. If you need me for ANYTHING, just call. ANY time. I mean it xxx*

That was friendship. Knowing that you had someone you could call for support. Who would be there for you, no matter what.

Reluctantly, she opened the message from Annabelle, expecting another demand for photographs of the baby. But her stomach flipped over when she read it. *I've finally worked out where I know you from. You were Joanna Stafford, weren't you? You're the one whose father went to prison.*

TWENTY-SIX

When Charlotte was tiny – and a whole night's sleep was little more than a rumour – Joanna used to get through the day on a conveyor belt of coffee. It meant that she spent most of those months simultaneously bone tired yet artificially wired. That was a little how she felt now: her grief was so immense that it threatened to pull her under at any time, yet the need to look out for her tiny grandaughter kept her alert and determined.

After leaving the brightly lit corridor, the baby ITU was quiet and the lights were low and restful. Sitting beside the baby's cot, Joanna's mind kept wandering back to Annabelle's text. *I've finally worked out where I know you from.*

Joanna had grown up in a very comfortable, middle-class home. Her father was a solicitor who'd done really well for himself. Her mother was a professional committee member on anything going in the local area and they lived in a detached house with a large garden. She was an only child who had access to anything she wanted: horse riding lessons, ballet classes, nice clothes and toys and holidays abroad.

Halfway through senior school, her father's business had

been doing so well that they'd taken her out of the local state school and sent her to Brent Hall. The exorbitant private school fees were met, skiing holidays were taken, dinner party guests entertained.

Until the day that her father was arrested for embezzlement and their whole world came crashing down.

It didn't take long for the news to be the hot topic of gossip among the parents of Brent Hall school. Then, almost immediately, for that gossip to be picked up by their children. Like chickenpox, the news spread throughout the school. It wasn't as if Joanna had many friends to lose, but she did lose the one friendly face that had helped her to keep afloat: Jacob.

He didn't tell her explicitly that her father's arrest was the reason for ending their relationship. His parents, so he said, thought it was important that he 'focus on his studies' and that a girlfriend would get in the way of that. He'd been apologetic, but there was no offer of waiting until they were older or even staying friends. The boy she'd believed had loved her just dropped her like a stone.

Once her father's assets were frozen, there was no money for school fees and Joanna was to be unceremoniously dropped from the school roll as soon as the term her father had already paid for had ended. Dumped by her boyfriend, reeling from the events in her family life, she'd been easy prey for Annabelle Miles and her friends. Scuttling from lesson to lesson, shrinking to the corners of the playground at breaktime, every morning she'd beg her mother to believe that her stomach ache was bad enough to stay home. Her mother hadn't budged. 'We've paid for this term, so you need to make the most of it before you have to leave.' She didn't blame her – her mother had her own issues to deal with – but it was impossible to make her understand just how awful it was at school.

This is why she'd been so worried about Charlotte and

Freddie. She'd known it would end in tears. Charlotte had trusted Freddie the way she'd trusted Jacob. Everything Charlotte had said about Freddie – *he loves me, he's different, he's kind, he cares* – had been the same things she'd thought about Jacob. But when the chips were down, people like that think only of themselves.

And now Annabelle had remembered their shared history. Joanna's face had burned reading that text. What had jogged Annabelle's memory? Admittedly, this was now the third time they'd met in a very short space of time; was that all it had taken? Or had her vulnerability – the way she'd opened up about her arguments with Charlotte – made her more recognisable to the bully who'd ensured her school life had been a misery?

She shook her head. What was the point in thinking about any of this? She wasn't that scared little girl any longer. She'd met and married a wonderful man. Steve had been the most loving and dependable of husbands. The most kind and generous of fathers. He'd given her – and Charlotte – a life of security and fun and love. Now, with Steve and Charlotte gone, she had to step up and do the same; provide all of those things for Charlotte's little girl.

In the crib next to theirs, a mother was being helped to hold her tiny baby. Joanna watched as she laid her precious cargo onto the pillow on her lap. The nurse hovered long enough to rearrange the tubes and wires, then stepped back to give them some space.

The pure love emanating from the mother's face pierced Joanna's heart. She remembered the moment she first held Charlotte. How proud she'd felt. *I made this. This beautiful human being. She came from me.* She could remember Steve's face, his joy when they told him that he had a daughter.

Through the hole in the crib, she stroked the baby's hand,

not sure who was providing strength for whom. 'We've got this, little one.'

Tomorrow she would worry about Freddie and Annabelle and custody. Right now, she just wanted to love this precious child.

TWENTY-SEVEN

The morning after the baby was born had been spent learning to do more for her under the supportive watch of Jenny, the kind nurse. Somehow – around the collection of wires and tubes – Joanna had managed to change her nappy and empty the mask of the moisture that could collect inside. 'Very good, Granny.' Jenny had winked at her and Joanna had almost blushed at her praise. 'How about we get your grandaughter out for a little while?'

Grandaughter. Such a big word. 'Yes, please. As long as it won't hurt her?'

'Not at all. We'll keep all of the wires and the breathing mask attached. We won't have her out for long but I'm sure she'd love a cuddle.'

Joanna would love a cuddle, too. More than anything. 'That would be wonderful.'

Jenny lowered her voice. 'If you're comfortable unbuttoning your shirt, I can place her directly on your skin. We call it kangaroo care. There's lots of benefits for baby.'

Joanna knew all about the benefits of skin-to-skin contact after birth; she'd been a devourer of baby books when she was expecting Charlotte. Steve used to joke that she could've got a job as a midwife by the end of her pregnancy. 'I know that it can calm the baby after the birth. Will it still work if I'm not her mum?'

It was a clumsy question, but Jenny didn't blink. 'Most definitely. And it's even more important for an early one like this little cutie. There's lots of evidence that it improves oxygen saturation and reduces stress levels as well as helping with feeding and lots of other good stuff.'

Anything that would help the baby didn't need thinking about. Joanna turned towards the cot and unbuttoned her shirt.

After lifting the lid on the crib, Jenny reached inside and deftly moved the wires and tubes so that she could pick up the baby. As she laid her on Joanna's chest, she could feel her heart pull towards her. 'Hello, little girl.'

The poignancy of being the one to experience this when it should be Charlotte was almost painful. Her body ached for the child in her arms and the one she'd lost. Why was life so unfair? *Oh Charlotte, she's so perfect.*

Jenny rearranged the tubes, slipping her fingers along them to check for kinks or bends. 'Have you thought of a name for her yet?'

'No, not yet.' She and Sally had talked over a few names on the phone last night, but nothing seemed right. Nothing seemed good enough. She was planning on asking Charlotte's friends Rachael and Lucy if they had any ideas and she'd ordered a baby names book online last night. Maybe something with a poignant meaning might be a good fit. She wasn't even sure she'd be allowed to name her. Would the social worker they'd be assigned let her choose or would she ask Freddie?

'Well, whatever you choose, it will have to be beautiful, just like her.'

She knew that the nurses probably said things like this to all of the babies' parents. But it was true in this case. She was absolutely perfect. She laid a hand across the baby's back, just enough to keep her in place, and then lowered her face onto her soft dark hair and breathed her in. The surge of love she felt for her could have toppled her from her chair. When she did see the social worker, she would need to make her understand. She belonged with her. She was part of her. She was home.

DC Lineham had sent her a text first thing that morning to confirm that she'd be in around eleven. The baby was safely back in her cot when she rang to say she was outside the door to the ITU. Joanna joined her outside and they found an empty bench along the corridor.

'Hello, Joanna. I'm so sorry about Charlotte.'

'Thank you.'

'Is the baby doing well?'

Joanna appreciated the concern. 'She's doing great.'

'Like I said yesterday, it's only a matter of time before Freddie will get permission to meet his daughter. We might want to think about how you want to manage that. I'm assuming you won't want to be there?'

Her first reaction was to agree. The mere thought of him hovering over the baby's crib made her stomach churn. But what was the alternative? Leave her alone with him? 'How soon?'

'I don't know. The hospital might want to set up a private room. But that can't happen unless the baby can be moved a hundred per cent safely. We'll be guided by the staff here.'

That was a temporary relief. At least she could put that thought on the back burner for a few days.

But the police officer didn't look relieved. 'There's more, I'm afraid.' She appraised her as if she was trying to work out just how much more Joanna could take.

What more could there possibly be? 'What is it?'

She took a deep breath before speaking. 'Freddie has requested permission to attend Charlotte's funeral. And it looks likely that he'll get it.'

That was utter madness. 'How? How the hell can he get permission to come to the funeral of the person he killed?'

The police officer kept her hands in her lap, her voice calm. 'Like I said before, he hasn't been convicted. And not allowing him to attend the funeral could be seen as an act of mental cruelty.'

'What about me? Don't I get a say in this? What about the mental cruelty of me having to see him? The man who took my daughter from me.'

'I'm sorry, Joanna. I really am. But they have to take into account the fact that he might not be guilty. Or if...' she paused, 'if the case gets dropped before the trial.'

Joanna's heart thudded in her chest. 'Is that possible? Is that what's going to happen? Are you telling me that he's going to get away with this?'

The police officer shook her head. 'No. I'm just trying to explain why they'll probably allow him to come to the funeral. He will be escorted by two officers and he will be handcuffed to one of them at all times.'

Joanna closed her eyes. Wasn't it bad enough that she was having to bury her only child, but now it was going to be a spectacle of police and handcuffs? Would his mother come? Was it possible to ban people from funerals? And, even if she could, how would she stop them if they just turned up anyway?

She hadn't even begun to think about planning Charlotte's funeral. Sally would help her, she knew that. But it was only a year since she'd had to do the same for Steve.

Most of the preparation for Steve's funeral had passed in a blur. Sally had booked the crematorium, invited the guests, organised catering. Later, when Joanna had come back to herself a little, she'd asked Sally how she knew who to invite. That was when she admitted that Steve had given her a list before he died. 'Because he knew that you and Charlotte wouldn't be in the right frame of mind to do it.' That was the mark of the man. Even in death, he was thinking of her and their daughter.

Though she knew Charlotte was back in contact with Freddie, she'd been told that they were just friends and Charlotte had known better than to invite Freddie to the funeral itself. In the crematorium, Joanna and Charlotte had clung to each other for support. Sally beside them with a hand on their backs when they needed it.

But she had invited him to come to the wake. She'd seen the look on Charlotte's face when he arrived. The way he'd folded her into his arms. That wasn't the kind of hug you gave to a friend. She'd said nothing then, of course, but later that evening, grief, anger and a little too much wine had resulted in an argument between her and her daughter.

'Why was Freddie there?'

'I invited him.'

'He barely even met your father.'

'I know that. That's why he didn't come to the funeral. But I wanted him at the wake. I wanted the support.'

She'd known for sure then. 'Are you seeing him again?'

'Mum, let's not talk about this now. I want to think about Dad today.'

Stupidly, she'd let it go. They'd sat together on the sofa in the lounge, Charlotte holding an old sweatshirt of Steve's, watching one of the war films he loved. Even so, she found it hard not to let her mind wander to Freddie like an itch she couldn't scratch. The boy in whose arms she least wanted to see her daughter. Why had he come? How could Charlotte have forgiven him so easily for all the pain he'd caused?

She made herself forget about him that night. Focused on

Charlotte and tried to trust what Steve had always said. *She's a good girl and she'll choose wisely in the end.*

How wrong she'd been. How would she have felt that night if she'd known that he would still be Charlotte's boyfriend a year later? And what might she have done differently if she'd known that now – only a year later – he was going to be at Charlotte's funeral?

She didn't want him anywhere near there. It was a day for those who'd always wanted the best for Charlotte. But it didn't seem as if she had any choice in the matter.

Okay, then. If he had the front to turn up and pretend to be the grieving boyfriend, she was going to meet him head on. Shame him. Make him admit to what he'd done. She wasn't shy little Joanna at school any longer and she wasn't going to let the Knight-Crossley family bully her into letting her daughter's murderer get away with it.

If he wanted to be there, let him see the consequences of what he'd done. That room was going to be filled with all the people who loved Charlotte.

Annabelle kept telling her that Freddie was innocent. That he hadn't pushed Charlotte. Hadn't caused her death. He might've been able to pull the wool over his mother's eyes, but not hers. Let him say that to her face. She was ready.

TWENTY-EIGHT

There can be no lonelier way to travel than in the hearse behind your daughter's coffin.

Sally reached for Joanna's hand and held it tight, but all Joanna could think about was the car in front. Inside that car, behind the vibrant displays of flowers, inside that wooden box, lay the girl who had held her heart and carried it out into the world for the last two decades.

She didn't turn her head when she spoke to Sally. 'This is so hard.'

Sally squeezed her hand even tighter, bringing the other hand to surround it. 'I know. In an hour it will be over. We'll get through it together.'

Not for the first time, she thanked God for Sally. How she would've planned this funeral, invited these people, even sat in this car without her, she didn't know. Even the people at Brands Funeral home – the same people who had managed Steve's funeral a year ago – had been shocked to see her back so soon. They hid it well, of course, but she could feel the extra sympathy in the insistence that they would provide an extra car for Charlotte's best friends at no additional cost.

It wasn't until the car pulled up at the crematorium that Joanna realised how many people would come. Every direction she looked in, there was a sea of tearful, sombre faces. School friends, university friends, neighbours, family. They parted to let her and Sally through. As she held Joanna's elbow and guided her towards the large wooden door, Sally smiled and nodded at people, thanked them for coming. Joanna could not.

Though the chapel was the largest of the three, the thick sand-coloured carpet and oatmeal upholstered chairs softened any sound except the background music that Sally had asked Charlotte's friends to choose. In the front row, Sally kept hold of Joanna's hand as people filed in quietly. Once the rows were filled, people came down the sides. The room was packed. Sally glanced behind her and then leaned close in to Joanna. 'It's so full. Some people are going to have to listen from outside.'

Charlotte was so loved. This proved it and it warmed her a little to know that all of these people were here because they wanted to say goodbye. She managed a watery smile and nodded her thanks. 'Where is he?'

Sally looked around again, a little longer this time, before she spoke. 'They've just slipped in at the back. Him and two police officers. But don't think about him. He's nothing today. Let's just say goodbye to our girl.'

It didn't matter how long she'd had to try and prepare herself, the day Steve passed away had still been an almighty shock. For the two weeks prior, the nurses had talked about him going into a hospice but none of them had wanted that. The first few weeks after Steve had passed away were absolute agony.

Charlotte had been incredible. Joanna had leaned on her more than she should've done. Charlotte had been the one who'd shopped for their food and made most of their meals. After Freddie's appearance at the funeral, she hadn't mentioned him again. In fact, it wasn't until a month later that she'd realised that she'd been seeing him the whole time.

Charlotte had gone to the supermarket and, for the first time since Steve had gone, Joanna had felt a little parting of the fog she'd been living in. She'd decided to make lunch and surprise Charlotte with it when she got home. Macaroni cheese.

In the kitchen, she'd found her car keys on the counter. The supermarket was a good ten minutes' drive away. Surely Charlotte wouldn't have walked? She'd looked out of the front window. Sure enough, there was her car on the drive. Just as she'd been about to turn away, a car had pulled up at the end of the garden. She'd peered closer. Long enough to see Charlotte kiss Freddie goodbye.

She'd pulled back from the window as if she'd been burned and hurried to the kitchen before Charlotte came through the door.

'Mum? I'm home.'

'Through here.'

Charlotte had plonked two bags of shopping in front of the fridge freezer. 'Sorry I was ages. Tesco was packed.'

She hadn't met Joanna's eyes. She hadn't changed from when she was little. Steve had told her that your eyes changed colour when you told fibs and they could always tell from that point on if she'd been bending the truth. Not that it happened often. Joanna had tried to keep her voice light. 'How come you didn't take the car?'

Charlotte had said nothing for a few beats, then had responded slowly as if she was gauging the weight of each word. 'I got a lift there and back.'

'Really? Who with?'

Again, the pause. 'With Freddie.'

'Are you seeing him again?'

Charlotte had leaned against the counter. 'I know what you think of him, Mum. Which is why I haven't said anything. But he's been really sweet. He lost his dad, too. When he was a lot younger. He gets how I feel. And, yes, I'm seeing him again.'

She hadn't trusted herself to talk about it right then. Knew that she'd say something wrong, and the last thing either of them needed was to fall out. So she'd held her tongue, hoped it would run its course. What a fool she'd been.

Knowing that Joanna wouldn't be able to do it, Sally had offered to write and read a eulogy for Charlotte. When she stood to deliver it, Rachael and Lucy shifted their seats so that they were sitting either side of Joanna.

Sally coughed, swallowed, and then she began.

'For those of you who don't know me, I've had the absolute honour of being Charlotte's godmother. I had a front row seat to watch her grow from a cherub of a child to a beautiful strong woman.'

Joanna pressed her hand to her heart and the two girls either side of her moved in closer. Sally looked straight at her as she delivered the next line. 'When she was very young, her dad Steve coined the line from *A Midsummer Night's Dream* to describe her. "Though she be but little she is fierce."'

Joanna smiled back at her. Every time he said it, she would frown at him for excusing whatever it was that Charlotte had done to drive her crazy. How lovely it was that Sally had remembered that too.

Now Sally looked past Joanna and at the congregation. 'And fierce she was. Even when she was very young, she had an irrepressible spirit. I remember once Joanna put her on the naughty step for something she'd done and, far from being upset about this, Charlotte decided it would be the perfect stage from which to entertain us with her full repertoire of nursery rhymes.'

A ripple of soft laughter moved around Joanna, and her heart warmed at the memory of her cheeky little girl.

Sally had her hand pressed to her chest as if it was getting harder to speak. 'But she loved fiercely too. She had the biggest heart. I've lost count of the times I've see her rescue a baby bird from the garden when a cuckoo had pushed it from its nest. Or wait patiently for a ladybird to crawl onto her finger from the windowsill so that she could let it outside.

'And she was the most loyal and fierce defender of those she loved. She has always been a wonderful friend to my son, Harry, and he has always adored her. Everyone who knew her adored her.'

Joanna tried not to think of her last conversation with Charlotte. When she'd defended Freddie. Tried to make her believe that he was someone to be trusted. Her poor loyal girl.

There was a long pause from the lectern as Sally clearly needed time to compose herself. But she held on to her papers and swept her eyes across the room at all the people who had come to pay their respects. 'Charlotte will leave a huge gap in many of our lives. I hope that we will remember and honour her by trying to be like her. To be fierce, to be brave and to love.'

She turned toward the coffin. 'Sleep tight, my darling girl.'

Sally's words were perfect. Capturing the essence of Charlotte. Her spark, her hatred of injustice, her passion for friendship and life. For a few moments, she was back in this room with them. How could a life so vibrant be extinguished so easily?

Lucy moved to make room for Sally next to Joanna. Joanna rested her head on Sally's shoulder and whispered, 'Thank you.'

Then came the moment Joanna had been dreading all morning. As the curtains closed around the coffin, she had to grip tightly to her chair with her free hand. *Don't go.* She wanted to call out. *Don't leave.*

After the service, she stood at the exit with Sally's hand on her back as people filed through and passed on their sorrow at her loss. So many young girls with faces red and tear-stained. For many, this might be the first loss of someone close that they'd experienced. How cruel it was that they had to learn so soon the fragility of life.

She'd taken one of Charlotte's friends in her arms to console her, when she spotted him. Diplomatically, the escorting officers hadn't brought him past her. They must have exited the building from the entrance – but they stood apart from the crowd. Only Annabelle stood with him and she could see that he was crying.

From somewhere deep inside, a hot rage burned her stomach like she'd never experienced before. As she stepped towards him, Sally caught her arm. 'Ignore him. Let's go back to the house.'

He was a lot thinner than she'd remembered, his skin pale and his dark hair cut much shorter. Gone was the easy stance: he looked broken. There'd be no sympathy from her though. When he looked up and caught her eye, the pain in his face was like petrol on the fire inside her. She gritted her teeth. 'I want to tell him what he's done.'

She was three steps away from him when Annabelle turned to face her. 'Joanna. It was a beautiful service.'

She nodded her thanks, but her eyes were fixed on him. 'Your expensive lawyer made sure you got your own way, then?'

Annabelle took a step between them. 'I don't think you need to—'

'It's okay, Mum. I wanted to speak to you, Joanna. I've been asking to get a message to you. Mum had a letter to bring but... I need you to know that I didn't do it.' His face creased in pain and he slumped down even further into his hips. 'I loved Charlotte. She was my absolute world. I miss her so much.'

Joanna clutched her hands together to stop them from trembling. 'I don't know how you can stand there and say that.'

'Please give me a chance to explain. To make you understand that I wouldn't have done this.'

Her whole body recoiled. 'How can I trust you? My own daughter was keeping secrets from me. Was it you who told her not to tell me about the baby?'

It was the only reason she could think of. The only rational explanation.

Freddie looked pleadingly at the guard, tears running down his face. 'Please. Can I have some time to speak with her? In private?'

The guards looked at one another. The elder one nodded. 'Alright. You can talk in the waiting room. But I can't take off your cuff. Which means I'll have to come with you.'

'And me.' Annabelle pushed herself forwards.

'No.' The other guard shook his head. 'You'll have to wait outside with me, I'm afraid.'

Annabelle looked as if she were about to object, but Freddie shook his head. 'It's fine, Mum. Honestly.'

She folded her arms. 'Well, I'll be right outside, my darling.' She turned defiantly to Joanna. 'You need to listen to him. He'll tell you the truth.'

People were looking over now; Joanna could see them wondering what was happening. Much as she wanted to tell him to go to hell, there was a part of her that wanted to hear what he had to say. She knew from the police that their enquiries hadn't turned up any new information. Was there something he might let slip that she could use against him?

'Okay. I'll listen. But that doesn't mean I'm about to believe a word you say.'

TWENTY-NINE

FREDDIE

Freddie was in the middle of making a veggie curry for dinner when Charlotte crashed into the apartment.

'I've had it with her.'

Knowing she'd been to her mother's house, he didn't need to ask who she was talking about. 'What happened?'

'My mum and her usual issues. One minute I was helping her to straighten a photo frame, the next she'd found a way to criticise our relationship.' She picked up one of the carrots he'd just peeled and took a loud bite from the top of it.

He pulled out one of the stools in the kitchen and motioned for her to sit on it. 'Don't eat angry. You'll choke.'

She took another bite of the carrot and crunched it noisily to make him laugh. Then she laughed herself, which started her coughing.

He watched her to make sure she was okay and, only when he was sure she'd recovered, he waved a finger at her. 'See. I'm always right.'

She sighed. 'I wish my mum could see you like I do. She's just so blinkered by this horrible experience she had at school. Oh, and the you cheating on me thing, of course.'

They'd got far enough past that awful night that it'd become a part of their history, something to joke about, a reason that he had to give her the last M&M from the bag every time.

He returned to chopping the carrots. Like Charlotte, he was frustrated that her mother didn't like him, but he'd given up trying a long while ago. 'Maybe when the baby comes she'll have an epiphany.'

'No.' Charlotte banged the carrot on the table. 'I don't want it to be like that. I want her to love you like I do. So that when I tell her about the baby, she'll be overjoyed. Is that too much to ask?'

He replied the way he always did when they had this conversation. 'It's been a tough time for both of you.'

As always, thinking about her dad combined with pregnancy hormones brought tears to Charlotte's eyes. 'But that makes it even worse. The baby is a good thing. Something lovely for our family. Once we got through the twenty-week scan, I was looking forward to making that big announcement. But since then, she's just been so difficult.'

He turned to look at her and raised an eyebrow. 'We could tell my mother?'

He already knew the answer to that, too. Her tone became more conciliatory. 'I'm sorry. I know you want to tell her, but I really want to wait until I can tell my mum, too. Am I being a total cow?'

From behind, she slipped her arms around his waist and he turned to kiss her. 'Well, as you're the one carrying the baby, I guess you get to choose.'

Truth be told, he wasn't in a hurry to tell his mother either. Though she'd been better lately about accepting that he and Charlotte were serious, he still wasn't sure how she'd react to them having a child together. Especially when he was in his early twenties and had just started work.

Charlotte rested her head on his shoulder. 'So we wait a little longer?'

He chopped in time with his words. 'We wait a little longer.'

THIRTY

The walls of the crematorium waiting room were a pale mint, the carpet a hard-wearing dark blue. Designed to seat early arrivals to the crematorium, there were only ten chairs around the walls. Joanna waited for the officer in charge of Freddie to sit him down on one seat, then turn so his back was to them, giving the illusion of privacy. Over his shoulder, he spoke to Joanna. 'I'm sorry, but we can't be too long. We need to get him back.'

'That's fine.' Her voice was pure ice. 'I don't have a lot to say.'

For the last two weeks, she'd hated this man with a vehemence she didn't know she had in her. In her imagination, he'd become a dark presence, almost a cartoon villain. In front of her now, he looked like a frightened little boy. His clothes were hanging from him. The thick-chested tanned prison guard behind him like an enlarged shadow. The good looks that had attracted Charlotte had been ravaged by fear and grief. In other circumstances, she might've had some sympathy. But not today.

He swallowed, ran the hand that wasn't in cuffs over his face. 'How's the baby?'

She hadn't expected him to start there and it wrong-footed her for a moment. 'She's good. Doing well. Getting stronger.' Then she remembered herself. 'I'm not here to update you on the baby. What did you want to speak to me about?'

The crease at the top of his nose deepened as he looked at her, his bottom lip trembled and she could see him struggling to gain control of his voice. 'I wanted to ask about Charlotte. Did she... was she in pain? In the hospital. Did she suffer?'

His eyes searched hers and, just for a moment, she wanted to torture him with lies. But she couldn't bring herself to even think about Charlotte in pain. 'They don't think so. She didn't regain consciousness.'

His face twitched; it looked as if he was fighting tears. 'I still can't believe she's gone. She was so wonderful. I loved her with everything I had. She was just... perfect.'

Joanna's whole body stiffened; her hands closed into fists. This boy didn't deserve to kiss her daughter's feet, let alone love her. What was he trying to gain by talking to her like this? Was he misguided enough to think that she might feel *sorry* for him? 'Why did you do it, Freddie? Why did you hurt her?'

Between their chairs, a small table held leaflets about bereavement and counselling. Freddie clutched its edge like a life raft, his face a grimace of agony. 'It wasn't me, Joanna. I would never hurt her. Charlotte was my life. She was everything.'

His words just made her more angry. How dare he say he loved her? What about the bruises on her arms? You don't hit the people you love. 'You can stop lying. It was you. The police have the evidence. It was only you and Charlotte in that flat. There was no one else.'

His face darkened. 'There must've been someone else.'

There it was, the cloud of jealousy. That was motive, surely? 'Are you telling me that Charlotte was seeing someone else? Is that what happened? Was it Dominic? Your friend? And that's why you were angry at her?'

Surprise or shock glanced across his face. 'Dominic? No. No! Charlotte wasn't doing anything with Dominic. She didn't even like him that much. Why would someone like Charlotte even look at him? Even I knew that she was way out of my league. I couldn't believe how lucky I was that she wanted to be with me.'

His face was so open, so honest, it would be easy to believe him. But protestations of innocence weren't enough. 'So, if not Dominic, who was the someone else? Why were you so jealous of him?'

He shook his head. 'I wasn't jealous. Charlotte never gave me reason to be. I knew for sure she'd never cheat on me. She was the most honest person I've ever met. You must know that.'

She did know that. Her honesty was brutal at times. Even as a child, she wouldn't think twice about telling Joanna if her outfit was wrong or she'd made a mistake. Steve would laugh at her, choosing to find it endearing. More tactful as she'd grown up, she would still be the person to go to if you wanted a really honest opinion. 'If it wasn't jealousy. What was it? Was it the pregnancy? Were you angry about that?'

Turning slightly to glance sideways at the back of the guard behind him, he lowered his voice to a fierce whisper. 'I was overjoyed that she was pregnant. It was the best thing that could've happened to us. I wanted to run around telling everyone. I loved her so much and she was going to make the best mum ever.'

His teeth clamped together and she could see he was struggling to gain control of himself. He wanted to run around and tell everyone? 'If that was true and you were both so happy, why didn't she tell me she was pregnant?'

Her voice wobbled. It hurt so much that Charlotte had kept this from her. Her own mother. Though she knew she had a big part of the blame for making it clear how she felt about Freddie, surely her daughter knew that she would support her, love her child?

Freddie hung his head. 'She wanted to tell you, but she wanted to be sure first. She didn't want to hurt you.'

'Sure about what?'

'She wanted to get to the twenty-week scan. She didn't want to risk telling you and then...'

'Losing the baby?'

He nodded, looked at her from under his eyelashes. If he was play-acting the bereaved partner, he was doing a pretty convincing job. 'She said you'd had enough pain. Losing her dad. She said she didn't want to put you through it if it didn't work out. Once we'd had that scan, she kept putting it off. She wanted things to be—' he paused '—better between you and me. And then you had that argument and she was so cross. She said she wasn't going to tell you about the baby until you accepted me and then...'

As he trailed off from saying the awful truth, Joanna closed her eyes. All she could see was the face of her beautiful girl. Charlotte hadn't told her about the pregnancy to protect her. To shield her from pain. Just as her dad had looked after her, she'd taken on the role. When all the time it was Charlotte who'd needed protecting. Fresh anger rose in her like lava. 'How could you hurt the mother of your child?'

'I didn't!' His raised voice brought the attention of the guard and he held up his hand to show he'd quieten down. He returned to Joanna. 'I didn't. That's what I'm trying to tell you. I know you don't like me. I know you don't trust me. But you have to believe that I'd never hurt your daughter. Or mine.'

Over the last year, she'd made Freddie into a villain. The boy who'd broken her daughter's heart in the worst year of their lives. But now, sitting across from him, that's not the man she saw. Her head ached and she rubbed at her temples. 'Okay. Let's say I believe you. If it wasn't you, then who was it?'

His open face closed like a slammed door. 'I don't know.'

The way he shut down so quickly was like a slap. How dare he beg her to believe him then react like that? 'You're lying.'

He shook his head but didn't meet her eyes. 'I'm not. I don't know how I'm going to prove it to you, but I'm not. When I got to the apartment, she was already on the floor. I called the ambulance. I tried to save her. I tried so hard.'

Tears sprang to his eyes and he wiped them away with the back of his hand. The guard outside rapped with his knuckles on the glass window in the door. His colleague behind Freddie, rose and shook his wrist that was shackled to Freddie. 'I'm afraid we need to go now.'

Freddie stayed where he was but leaned forwards as if in prayer. 'Please, Joanna. You have to believe me. I didn't hurt Charlotte. And I'm going to get through this and raise our baby and make sure she has everything she needs.'

The guard's voice was deep but kind. 'Come on now, lad. Let's go and leave the lady in peace.'

Fear clutched at Joanna's throat. He thought he was going to raise the baby? 'You won't be able to raise her. You'll be in prison.'

Freddie got to his feet. 'My solicitor says that the evidence is flimsy. I've got a good chance of being out soon. I didn't do it, Joanna.'

Surely this wasn't true? She couldn't bear it. 'I don't want you anywhere near that child. You've taken my daughter from me. You're not going to take her baby, too.'

It only took three steps for the guard and Freddie to make it to the door, where the other guard held it open, then reattached himself to Freddie's other wrist. While he did so, Freddie looked back at Joanna over his shoulder. 'She's our baby. Mine and Charlotte's. And her name is Eliza. Charlotte wanted to call her Eliza if she was a girl. Like the film. She made me watch it with her.'

The door closed with a bang and Joanna sank back into the chair. Eliza. Like the film. Of course. *My Fair Lady*. The film she used to watch with her when she was home ill from school. Their comfort film.

In the silence of the room, Freddie's words hung like icicles. *I didn't do it. She's our baby. I loved her. There's someone else.*

Through the glass in the door, she saw Freddie say goodbye to his mother, his shoulders moving in time with his sobs. Annabelle's face was different than she'd ever seen it. Not the entitled mean girl from decades ago. Not even the supremely confident woman she'd seen arguing for her right to see the baby. No. She looked like a mother whose heart was breaking for her son.

All of her certainty about Freddie's guilt began to show cracks of doubt. What was true? He looked so devastated about Charlotte's death. When he said he loved her, he was so fervent, so bereft. Was he telling the truth that he hadn't been the one to hurt her? The police were certainly not able to come up with anything conclusive. Could he be innocent? And if he was, who was this 'someone else' who he said was to blame?

THIRTY-ONE

Joanna hadn't wanted to host a wake. How could she smile and eat and speak to people when the light had gone from her life? But Sally had persuaded her that Charlotte's friends needed it. 'They're so young, Jo. This might be the first funeral they've ever been to. And, anyway, we need to give our girl the send-off she deserves.'

For a day or two, she'd considered just having everyone back to the house. But Sally had suggested a room at the Orsett Hall. 'That way you won't have any of the clearing up. And you can leave when you want to.'

That sounded appealing. She was already itching to get back to the hospital, back to Charlotte's baby. *Eliza.* 'Thank you for doing all this. I don't know how—'

Sally mimed zipping her lips. 'Don't say another word. You don't need to thank me. I want to do this.'

Three nights ago, Sally had sat with her at home. Helped her to choose photographs of Charlotte to display at the wake. Scrolling through her laptop, watching Charlotte grow up before her eyes, had been a beautiful agony. 'She was so cute.'

Sally had leaned forwards to look closely at a photograph of an eight-year-old Charlotte, missing her two front teeth. 'She certainly was. I can see you in her there. Around the eyes. Not the gap in her mouth.'

Everyone had always remarked on how much Charlotte was like Steve. It was nice to see some of her in there. 'It just went so fast. One minute she was a baby and then next she was a woman.'

How differently might she have lived if she'd known that she would only have two decades with her? What might she have let go? And what would she have focused on?

The room Sally had booked was really lovely. Dark-blue carpet and crystal chandeliers. She could almost see Charlotte rolling her eyes at it. 'Trust you to book somewhere posh, Mum.'

The air was subdued, sombre clumps of people clutching glasses of orange juice or wine. In a while, people would warm up, start to smile, even tell jokes. It was the way of things. Relief from the grief of the day. Would she ever know that relief?

She turned to take a glass of white wine from a server with a tray of drinks, catching sight of Lucy and Rachael joining a larger group in the far corner. It was lovely to see so many of Charlotte's friends, hard to watch as they comforted one another. From here, they would continue their lives – as they should – but Charlotte would always be suspended in this part of their story. The girl they knew. The one that died.

Feeling a hand on her back, she turned towards a sympathetic smile surrounded by the face of one of their neighbours who had lived on the same street since Charlotte was small. 'Joanna. I'm so sorry.'

The next hour was a blur of kind words and offers of 'anything you need'. All she could do was nod and whisper thanks. Making sure she didn't stay long enough with anyone that the cracks in her would start to show. This was a ritual she had to get through. Once it was over, she could go back to the hospital, see the baby, then go home tonight to wrap herself in her grief and shut out the world.

The order of service that Sally had put together included an open invitation to the wake for anyone at the funeral, but Joanna had had no idea that Annabelle Knight-Crossley was there until she got to the bathroom and found her reapplying her lipstick in the mirror.

When she turned, Joanna realised she was reapplying her make-up because she'd been crying. She wasn't sure what to say, but Annabelle got there first. 'How are you holding up, Joanna? Not easy, is it?'

Joanna shook her head. 'No. It's not. To be honest, I just want to go home.'

Annabelle nodded. 'I can imagine. Still, she got a good turnout, didn't she? That must be a comfort?'

Although Joanna wasn't keen on the reference to Charlotte as 'she', she nodded. 'Yes. It's nice to see how loved she was.'

Annabelle seemed distracted. 'Sorry I was late. I stayed to speak to Freddie as long as they'd let me. Don't know when I'll next get to see him. He only gets one visitor a week.'

Joanna didn't remark that she hadn't been expecting Annabelle to be there at all. Instead, she ran the tap until it was cool and rinsed her hands, bringing the soothing dampness to the back of her neck. 'Don't worry about that.'

Annabelle stayed where she was with her feet planted on the dark-blue carpet. When Joanna looked in the mirror, her face was beside hers. She waited until their eyes were connected in the reflection before she spoke. 'Did you listen to what Freddie had to say?'

There was something almost threatening in her tone that was surprising. 'Yes.'

Her eyes were the colour of steel. 'And you know he's innocent now? That he didn't hurt Charlotte?'

She wasn't about to get into a row with Annabelle. It served nothing and she didn't have the capacity today. 'I know what he said. But I'm going to leave it with the police.'

Annabelle stepped in close to her. 'No. You can't do that. You need to tell the police that you know it wasn't him.'

A sense of unease crawled on Joanna's skin. 'I'm not telling them anything.'

She took a step back, but Annabelle didn't get the message that she was too close and came forwards again. 'He's the father of Charlotte's baby. Are you really going to sit back and watch him be imprisoned for something he didn't do?'

Was she trying to *bully* her? The irony that they were having this conversation in the women's toilets. The scene of so many unpleasant encounters in their distant past where Annabelle and her friends would talk about her loudly, knowing she was in one of the stalls.

'I don't know what you're trying to achieve, Annabelle. But I don't actually have any control over whether the police investigate this. Today is my daughter's funeral in case you haven't noticed.'

It was as if she hadn't spoken. 'I know what you want, Joanna. You want Freddie to go down for Charlotte's murder so that you get to keep the baby, but it's not going to work out like that, I'm afraid.'

Ice shot down Joanna's spine and her heart thumped hard against her ribs. 'What are you talking about?'

'That baby is Freddie's child. He will be raising her. I've had my solicitor working on our case. If Freddie is convicted, I'm going to apply for custody of Eliza.'

As if she'd punched her in the stomach, Joanna couldn't breathe. She gripped the cold porcelain of the basin with both hands. 'You can't. You can't do that.'

'I can and I will. I'm the child's grandmother and I can give her a very nice life.' She sneered. 'You don't think they'd give custody to you, do you?'

Joanna's chest tightened. She couldn't feel her legs. 'But I've been looking after her. I've been with her.'

With her arms folded across her chest. Annabelle looked even more menacing. 'Only because you lied to me about not being able to visit. Oh, yes. I know about that, too. Nice little scheme you had to keep me out of the equation.'

Pushing herself off from the basin she'd been clinging to, Joanna forced herself to measure up to Annabelle. 'I'm her grandmother, too. I've got just as much chance of getting guardianship as you.'

'Really?' Annabelle raised an eyebrow. 'What about your financial issues?'

Joanna's mouth was so dry that it was difficult to speak. 'What do you mean?'

'I overheard you. On the phone to your bank, begging them not to repossess your house.'

It hadn't been like that, but Joanna could see how easily it might be spun that way by a clever lawyer with a big retainer. 'That's not—'

'And dear Charlotte,' Annabelle interrupted. 'The fact that the two of you weren't even speaking when she died. I mean, she hadn't even told you she was pregnant. What kind of mother are you?'

Joanna gasped: her vicious words were like knives. She opened her mouth to reply, but what could she say? It was all true.

Knowing she had her on the ropes, Annabelle smiled. 'You better think very carefully about what you want to say to the police about Freddie. Because if you make things worse for him —' she paused and stared intently at Joanna '—when I get custody of Eliza – and I will – you might never see her again.'

Annabelle picked up her handbag from beside the basin and slotted it under her arm. 'I'm going to go home now. Have a think about what I've said.'

As soon as the door banged closed, Joanna collapsed against the wall. She felt as if she'd been beaten up. Was she serious? She was going to apply for custody of Charlotte's daughter?

Terror tore its way through her and she bent double with the pain of it. Annabelle had far more money than she did. Would that sway the decision? And what about her arguments with Charlotte? What an absolute idiot she'd been to confide in her. To be taken in by her fake sympathy.

Pushing herself back to standing, she stared into the mirror. How had she let this woman be more present in her daughter's life than she had been? All those weeks when she could have known about the baby like Annabelle had. It had cost her her daughter. Was it going to cost her her grandaughter, too?

Did Annabelle really want custody or was she trying to scare her into helping Freddie? What if she did have it wrong about him? Whatever she thought of him, he was the baby's – Eliza's – father. If he went to prison when he hadn't committed the crime, she would be robbing her grandaughter of the only parent she had left.

And, if it wasn't Freddie, that meant the person who'd hurt her daughter was still out there, getting away with what they'd done.

It was even more urgent now that she find out what had happened that night. She'd go to their apartment. There could be something there that the police had missed. They didn't know her daughter. There might be something they wouldn't have noticed.

The police had also said how difficult it had been to speak to their neighbours. Except the one who'd seen a man enter the flat before Freddie. They might not want to give too many details to a police officer, but maybe she could persuade them to speak to her?

THIRTY-TWO

Joanna planned to go to the apartment the very next day, but first she needed to check on Eliza.

Up at ridiculous o'clock that morning, she'd been the first one in to ITU, relieved not to find that Annabelle had got there before her. Already on first name terms with some of the nurses, she was pleased to see her favourite on duty.

'Jenny, hi.'

'Morning, Joanna. You're in early. How did the funeral go?'

She took a deep breath and held out her hands. 'Difficult. But there were lots of people there which was lovely. How was her night?'

'Very good. You can see on the chart. She had a little breathing difficulty, but it was only a two and she sorted herself out, didn't you, precious?'

They'd explained to Joanna the scale of one to four they used to record oxygen levels and heart rate – one signifying a drop that the baby is able to sort it out for themselves and four signifying that a nurse had had to intervene – and she knew this was to be expected, but still she worried. 'Is she okay now?'

Jenny seemed reassuringly unconcerned. 'Perfectly. She's a

model patient. While it's quiet, I'm just going over there to have a cuddle with one of the little ones whose mum can't come in today. Do you want me to lift baby out for you first?'

Holding Eliza was the exact medicine she needed this morning. 'Yes, please.'

She would never cease to be amazed at the skill and care of these nurses as they looked after these fragile little birds. Eliza felt like nothing and yet everything as she received her into her arms. Jenny slipped her hands away and checked all the wires were in the right place. 'There you go. One grandaughter ready for cuddles.'

Feeling a little more confident now, Joanna ran her finger gently around Eliza's face, avoiding the edges of the oxygen mask. 'Your mummy used to like this, Eliza. It used to send her to sleep.'

Jenny paused on her way to the cot opposite and turned back. 'Eliza? You decided on a name?'

'Her mummy decided on a name. I found out yesterday.'

She didn't know how much the other nurses knew about her situation. They must know that there was a social worker involved, but no one had spoken to her directly. 'Eliza. I like that. I'll make sure everyone knows.'

She watched Jenny pick up the baby opposite, holding them in the crook of her arm, rocking gently side to side and singing a song in her own language. These nurses couldn't possibly be paid enough for what they did for these babies, these families. How grateful she was for them.

Joanna couldn't imagine not wanting to be here every minute that you could. 'Does that happen often? That parents don't come in?'

Jenny tilted her head and smiled. 'It's life, isn't it? If you've got other children and your partner is at work. You can't be in two places at once. And some of our parents live a distance away. It can be very difficult for them.'

Life was difficult. And confusing. And hard. She leaned towards Eliza in her arms and whispered softly. 'Granny's here for you, Eliza. Always.'

She only prayed that she would be allowed to be.

She stayed at the hospital until around lunchtime when all the parents who were there were asked to step out for a while because one of the babies had a visit from the doctor. She could tell from the white faces of the baby's parents that this might not be good news and she sent up a silent prayer for them as she left. Alongside one of thanks for Eliza's progress.

It'd seemed a good time to make the visit to Charlotte's flat.

The apartment was part of a modern complex. On the ground floor was a coffee shop, a shared workspace and a small gym. The corridors were carpeted and had the feel of a mid-budget hotel. Freddie and Charlotte's apartment was one of four on the second floor. Though Charlotte had given her a spare key to look after when she moved in, this was the first time she'd used it.

Vanilla. The scent hit her the moment she stepped into the small entrance hall. A reed diffuser on a small wooden table an emotional tripwire of Charlotte's favourite scent. Already, a surge of grief washed over her.

The hall had been repainted a pale blue since she was here last but was otherwise the same. It was too much to look in the sitting room yet. The scene of the crime. She'd work her way up to it. The small kitchen was clean and tidy. Of course, no one else had been here since the police had taken both Charlotte and Freddie to different locations.

She hesitated at the doorway to their bedroom before pushing open the door. It felt intimate and intrusive to enter the room Charlotte had shared with Freddie. The bed was unmade – no surprise there – and there was a pile of shoes in the corner.

Again, no shock to see that her daughter's messy nature hadn't changed from when she lived at home. Before she could think, instinct made her reach for the duvet and shake it flat. When she did so, a familiar friend from Charlotte's childhood made her gasp. Lopsy.

When Joanna discovered that she was expecting a baby, her mother had insisted that she knit her something. Joanna wasn't keen on woollen baby clothes, so they'd agreed on a toy rabbit pattern. Sadly, her mother's desire greatly exceeded her talent. And the poor orange bunny had a lopsided face to match its different size legs. She picked Lopsy up to take home for Eliza.

Freddie's side of the room looked much neater. On his bedside table, a fishing magazine and half a glass of water. On Charlotte's, a clutch of used cotton wool balls fought for space with her contact lens case, a paperback thriller with pages swollen – she knew – from being read in the bath, a bottle of nail polish and three silver bracelets. Joanna pressed her hand to her chest. How could these remnants of her life be here when she wasn't? She wanted to take the whole thing home and encase it in glass as a shrine to the daughter who would never again walk between the bathroom and the bedroom telling her all about her night out while scrubbing at her black eyeliner and mascara.

There was nothing here that gave any insight into what had happened. It was time to face the sitting room.

Even more than the kitchen and the bedroom, the sitting room was evidence that this was Charlotte's home. Everywhere she looked, the marks of Charlotte's touch. Where before there'd been a designer but stark navy sofa, now it was softened with mustard and teal cushions. Behind that, the dining table – which from memory had been a glass oval with chrome and leather chairs – had been replaced with an oak square and cream velvet backed chairs. Everything was softer. More feminine. More Charlotte.

On the wall, a copy of Joanna's most favourite photograph in the world. She wasn't in it because she'd taken it. At Aldeburgh beach. Charlotte was about eight and shrieking with horror at the icy wave that had lapped at her skinny legs. Steve had turned at the same moment and was watching her, the love and pride in his eyes clear for anyone to see. Though the original picture was in colour, Charlotte had printed it in black and white. The contrast served to sharpen their expressions. Clarify their joy in each other's company.

'Oh, Steve. Why aren't you here. I can't do this on my own.'

She let her face fall into her hands. What was she doing here? There was nothing to be gained from torturing herself like this. Shaking her head, she crossed the room to look out of the window onto the street below, pushing aside the heavy blue curtain.

On the windowsill there was a gift bag, the tissue scrunched. She peered inside. A tiny knitted rabbit, in yellow and white. Around its neck a ribbon and tag. She read it aloud until her voice faltered. 'Here's a bunny for our baby, just like yours. I can't wait to meet him or her. You'll be the best mum in the world. I love you. Freddie.'

Tears made the last words swim in front of her eyes. How could a man who did something like this have hurt the woman he loved? Did she need to give Freddie a chance? She picked up the bag and dropped Lopsy in as well; she'd take both for Eliza.

She was locking the front door behind her when the next door along opened onto the corridor and a neighbour emerged from his flat. He jumped when he saw Joanna standing there. 'Hello. Are you moving in?'

She shook her head. 'No. This is my daughter's flat.'

Dressed in jeans and a sweatshirt, he looked clean and respectable, probably in his late thirties, early forties. He tilted his head to one side. 'You're Charlotte's mum? How is she?'

This was the first time she'd had to say it out loud. The

words were lumpy in her throat. 'Charlotte passed away a few days ago.'

His eyes widened and he paled in front of her. 'Passed away? But what... I mean... I just thought it was a domestic.'

A domestic? Did he know something? 'Didn't the police speak to you? They said they'd spoken to all of the neighbours.'

He rubbed at the stubble on his chin, flicked his eyes to the ground and back again. 'Like I said, I just thought it was a domestic. Not worth mentioning.' An expression of genuine sorrow ran across his eyes. 'I liked Charlotte a lot. She was a nice girl.'

Joanna reached for her throat to keep it still. 'She was. I miss her very much.'

He glanced down at his feet again. 'Look, I don't know if you know this already, but there was another man. I think I've seen them before. When Freddie wasn't home.'

Joanna stifled her anger that he hadn't mentioned any of this to the police. It was more important that she find out whatever she could. 'Are you sure?'

'I mean, I'm not saying there was anything going on but...' He frowned down at his feet, scuffing the sole of one of his shoes back and forth on the carpet.

She waited for him to go on, sensing that an interruption might stop him talking altogether.

She didn't have to wait long. 'The thing is, they were here that night. I was stretching after my run when I saw them park their car – a white sports car – and then I saw them going into the apartment when I made it upstairs to the landing.'

Her heart was thumping in her chest. What had Freddie said? *There was someone else.* 'Did you tell the police this?'

He shook his head. 'No. I thought Charlotte was going to be okay... But I did hear some shouting shortly afterwards. Although I don't know if Freddie had got home by that point.'

She wanted to scream at him. How often did this happen in

houses around the country, around the world? People turning a deaf ear to a 'domestic'. Not wanting to get involved in other people's business even if they could save them from horrendous things. 'Would you tell the police that now?'

He resumed the scuffing of his sole on the carpet. 'I don't know. I don't know anything for certain, I don't see how it would help.'

'But it might. And my daughter...' she had to stop and regain control of her voice before she could continue, 'my daughter deserves justice for what happened to her.'

He stared at her, then nodded. 'Okay. I'll try to remember as much as I can. But I wouldn't be able to recognise him. I only ever saw him from behind.'

Joanna didn't know what good it would do, but at least it was something. A lead. A possibility of evidence.

Walking back to the car, she ran this piece of information through a million possibilities. Had Charlotte been seeing someone else? Is that what Freddie meant by 'there's someone else'? Had this been an act of jealousy on Freddie's part? Or this other man? She stopped in her tracks when a new, important possibility hit her. Was the baby even Freddie's?

There had to be someone who knew who this man was who visited Charlotte. She needed to call Lucy and find out if she or Rachael knew who he was. And she wanted to find this friend of Freddie's too. Dominic. He must know something.

THIRTY-THREE

FREDDIE

The night of their first ever argument, he'd spent the afternoon with Dominic.

Charlotte had planned to spend the afternoon with her mother. He'd asked her again if she was going to tell her about the pregnancy and she'd shrugged her shoulders. 'I'll see when I get there. Maybe.'

He'd only planned to have a couple of beers with Dominic in a local beer garden, but it had been so nice to sit outside in the sun, a cold pint in hand, that it'd been difficult to leave.

'This is what we should be doing.' Dom leaned back in his chair, legs stretched out and feet crossed at the ankle. 'I know you and Charlotte are all loved up, but don't you miss just having long afternoons on the beer with no time or place to be?'

He did miss it a little. 'She's worth it.'

Dominic didn't know about the baby either, though Freddie really wanted to tell him. He was shaking his head. 'Rather you than me. I'm not getting tied down to one woman until I'm at least thirty.'

His words reminded him of Freddie's mother's when he'd told her about moving into the apartment with Charlotte. 'Why are you rushing into things?' she'd asked. 'You're so young. There's plenty of time. Don't get tied down too soon.'

It wasn't that she didn't like Charlotte. It was impossible not to. But she did seem to have this idea that Charlotte was the one who wanted to settle down. That she had engineered the relationship. She'd feel differently once she knew about the baby, he was sure of that.

Five beers down, it took him three attempts to get his key in the lock before he let himself into the apartment. At the end of the entrance hall, Charlotte was clattering around the kitchen making herself something to eat. 'You're home early. How was your mother?'

'Don't ask.' She slammed another cabinet door and turned to face him with a jar of chocolate spread in one hand and a butter knife in the other. 'Do you know what? I think we should go travelling.'

That fifth beer had definitely dulled his senses. 'What now? What about your pregnancy?'

Jar open, she stuck in the knife and brought out a glut of chocolate to spread on the toast she'd already made. 'Not now. Once the baby is born. Then it won't matter what either of our mothers think.'

Was he imagining it, or was she irritated with him? She wasn't making sense. 'But I have to work. We need money to live on.'

'Well, let's save then. We'll work up until the baby is born and save all our money and then we'll work as we go. Fruit picking. Teaching English. Whatever we can pick up.'

Was it pregnancy hormones making her so crazy? 'It's a nice idea, but it's never going to work. I have a job. I need to work hard and build a life for us, for the baby.'

'Those are your mother's words. She's the one who wants you to stay there. You hate it.'

She wasn't wrong about that. He did hate working there.

For a start, his brain wasn't programmed to do that kind of work. And, also, he hated every boring minute of it. 'But that's changed now that there's a baby coming. There's a reason to go to work.'

She looked on the edge of tears. It must be the hormones. 'I feel like, if we move away, it'll all be easier.'

The doorbell prevented him from getting to the bottom of where this had all come from. It was his mother.

'I was just passing and I thought I'd pop in with some good news.' She paused and looked between the two of them. 'Am I interrupting something?'

Charlotte looked as if she was about to burst into tears. He had to say something. 'No, mum. Charlotte's not feeling great.'

'Really?' She frowned. 'What's wrong?'

Charlotte shot him a look that had a thousand sharp words behind it. 'Nothing. I'm fine.'

Again, his mother looked between the two of them. He needed to do something. 'Why don't you come into the sitting room? Charlotte will come through when she'd finished her... er... dinner.'

His mother cast a disparaging eye over the thick slice of chocolate spread on toast in Charlotte's hand. But she followed him out of the kitchen.

He closed the door to the sitting room behind them just in time before his mother hissed at him. 'I'm not stupid, Freddie. What's going on here? Have you two had an argument?'

Was it his imagination or did she look hopeful? It made him distinctly uncomfortable. 'No, she's just been to her mother's house. It's difficult. And she's not feeling great.'

His mother's lips were tight. 'Look, I know you don't want my opinion, but I really think you've rushed into all this, Freddie. It's too much for you both. She's just lost her father and you're both only just starting out in life. You've rushed into this and maybe you need to slow down a bit.'

He hadn't drunk five pints of beer in one go for quite a few months; he was feeling a little unwell himself. Definitely not in the mood for his mother to give him a lecture on his relationship. 'I know you mean well. But that's not the issue.'

She took a deep breath and lowered her voice. 'She's different from us, Freddie. I can see why you were attracted to her. She's a lovely girl, but that doesn't take away the fact that—'

'She's pregnant.'

The words were a reaction to stop her from speaking. But the instant they were out, he wanted to shove them back in. His mother's mouth was a circle of shock and, in the now-open doorway, Charlotte looked furious.

THIRTY-FOUR

On Friday, Joanna finally got to meet Eliza's social worker.

She'd been in to ITU early again, enjoying the quiet before the other parents arrived. It was better to be here than sitting at home alone.

Sally had called this morning to see how things were going. Joanna had recounted Annabelle's threats after Charlotte's funeral and Sally's anger had matched her own. Today, after three attempts, she'd got her to open up about how things were going at her end, too.

'Apparently, without me there for the last few days, Harry managed to make an omelette for his breakfast, take the dog out for a walk on his own and make his own way to the shop at the corner – with a list – to buy bread and cheese and a sack load of chocolate that is more than I'd allow him in a month.'

She couldn't discern from Sally's tone how she felt about that. 'Well, that's good, isn't it?'

She'd practically growled before responding. 'It's good for Graham. More evidence for his campaign to move Harry out of the house.'

Her anger made it sound like he was dumping the boy on

the side of the motorway. 'Oh, Sally. It's not like that, is it? Graham loves Harry. He wants the best for you. For all of you.'

'It doesn't feel like that. It feels like he's made up his mind, persuaded Harry that living on his own will be the biggest adventure yet and I'm the bad guy because I just want us to take a breath and think about this before we go steaming ahead.'

'Oh, love. I know it's hard, but we don't get to hold on to them forever.'

'I'm not asking for forever. I know that he needs independence but... oh, it doesn't matter.'

'What? Don't tiptoe around me for goodness' sake. We're best friends, Sally. It doesn't matter what's going on with me, I want to be there for you. Like you always are for me.'

'I know that, but it's beyond tactless for me to be talking about this when you've just lost Charlotte.'

'Just tell me how you're feeling.'

She sighed. 'Okay. I know that we have to let our children go at some point. But it's so much more complicated when they have special needs. The fear is... well, it's paralysing. The world isn't a kind place to the vulnerable.'

They'd been friends since before their children were born. Joanna knew the hurdles and obstacles Sally and Graham had had to overcome on Harry's behalf. 'I know it's been tough.'

'And I know that Graham is a great dad. He is. But he's on the train to London at seven in the morning and not home until seven at night. That's not his fault but it means that it's been me who's had to be Harry's voice for so long. I've had to fight the system, fight for school places, fight for his right to have what other people take for granted. I don't know how to step back. I don't know how to let him try it on his own.'

'But he won't be on his own. You'll still be there. You'll still be his safety net and he knows that.'

'I'm really scared, Jo.'

Sally was always so strong, so competent. Sometimes they

were the people who needed support the most. 'Of course you are. But you're not doing this on your own.'

There were several sniffs at the other end of the line before Sally replied. 'Thank you. And you're not on your own, either. Me and Graham are here. Whatever you need.'

Knowing that Sally was there was a huge support, but she couldn't ask her to come right now when she had so much going on herself. Sally needed time to come around to the idea of trusting Harry with himself. And that was hard for any parent.

She'd had a lesson in trust that morning herself. She'd just got back from five minutes with a coffee in the parent room when the machine above Eliza's bed started beeping. Loudly. The number on the screen, which showed her oxygen sats, started to drop from 96 to 95. 94. 93. And still the beep continued. Joanna whirled around to see Jenny glance over at the monitor but continue to give medication to the baby in the far corner.

There was always at least one nurse present on the ward – it was mandatory – but Joanna knew there were other nurses in the vicinity. Why was no one coming? The monitor dropped to 92. 'Jenny? You have to come. Something's wrong. Can't you hear the beeps?'

Jenny finished what she was doing and strolled over, but she merely watched Eliza. 'Are you okay, precious?'

Why wasn't she doing anything? The beep from the machine was drilling a hole in Joanna's brain. 'Can't you help her?'

And then, all of sudden, the machine climbed back up – 93. 94. 95. 96.

Jenny smiled. 'There you go, clever girl.'

Joanna's lungs were on fire. She wasn't sure if she'd actually breathed for the last few moments. 'How did you know she was going to be okay?'

'You need to look at the baby, not the monitor. She needs a

chance to sort these things out for herself. Look at her. She did it. Just trust her. If she needs help, we'll know. You can leave that to us.'

She smiled and returned to the other baby. Joanna slid her hand into the crib and stroked Eliza's arm. 'Please don't scare me like that again.'

Trusting your child – or your grandchild – was easier said than done.

She'd barely recovered from her worry when the social worker arrived to speak to the nurse on the ward. When she came over to meet Eliza, Joanna introduced herself. 'Hello, I'm Joanna. I'm Charlotte's mum. Eliza's grandmother.'

The social worker was around Joanna's age and wearing navy trousers and a floral top that could do with an iron. When she smiled, the corners of her eyes turned downwards with the weight of the lines around them. Joanna felt tired just looking at her. But her smile was warm. 'Nice to meet you. I'm Pippa Downes. I'm the case worker assigned to your grandaughter.'

Joanna tried not to flinch at the term 'case worker' with its associations of neglect. 'I've been with the baby every day since she was born. I want to look after her. I want her to come to live with me as soon as she's well.'

Pippa rubbed at her right eye. 'Unfortunately, it's not as straightforward as that. Once I've spoken to the staff here, shall we sit in the parents' room for ten minutes and I can explain it all to you?'

Joanna wanted to stay with Eliza after her scare, but she needed to keep her eye on the bigger picture. 'Yes. That would be great, thank you.'

The parents' room was pretty bare and functional. Six wooden armchairs arranged around a low coffee table and a mini kitchen, which was really just a kettle, a sink and a random assortment of mugs. Joanna hadn't spent much time in here, but Pippa seemed to be at home. Joanna didn't want to think of all the reasons she would've had to visit premature babies here.

Joanna felt like she should offer her something. 'Do you want a coffee or tea?'

Pippa grimaced. 'No thanks. I'd rather drink my own bathwater than that stuff. I'll treat myself to a Costa when I leave later. How much do you already know about how this all works?'

Pippa explained everything clearly, but it was effectively a repeat of what she'd been told by her solicitor. In the absence of anyone with parental responsibility for the child, she would have to speak to all those who wished to apply for special guardianship and then write a report with her recommendations.

Joanna really only had one question. What did she have to do to make sure that Eliza didn't end up in care? 'What kind of things will you be looking at? How will you decide? How long does it take?'

Pippa held up her hands. 'It won't just be me that decides. Anyone who wants to look after the child will need to have a report made on them. Police checks take the longest.'

Police checks? 'What will they be?'

'Well, we'll need to make sure you don't have a criminal record.'

She smiled at Joanna as if that was outside the realms of belief. She knew she was clean in that department, but she wasn't so sure about Freddie or Annabelle. 'So that would definitely rule someone out of it?'

The social worker faltered for a moment. 'Like I say, it would all form part of a report.'

Joanna fished her phone from her bag and opened the notes app to keep a list of these. 'What else?'

'Finances.'

That was more of a worry. She thought about the calls from the bank. 'What level of... income would you need?'

'That's not a question I can answer. But in all these areas, we just need to make sure that baby is being looked after in the best possible environment.' Pippa softened her voice. 'She's already lost her mother. We need to make sure that she is with a family who can provide everything she needs.'

A family. That made it sound as if they were already considering sending her away. 'But I'm her family. I'm her grandmother.'

Pippa stood to get back to the ward. 'It's still very early days. This will be a long process. At the moment, I'm just here to check on her. We need to get the birth registered.' Her voice softened. 'Do you know if your daughter had a name picked out for her?'

Joanna got up, too, seeing again Freddie's face in that room at the crematorium. 'Eliza. She wanted to call her Eliza.'

'Then that's what we'll go with for now. I'll be checking in regularly to see how Eliza is doing. Obviously, we'll need to know the level of care she'll need, too.'

Joanna frowned. 'What do you mean, level of care?'

Pippa glanced at her watch. 'Well, she's a very premature baby. Sometimes there are complications later on. We'll need to make sure she's placed with someone who can best look after her.'

Complications? Placed? Joanna's mouth was so dry, it was difficult to swallow. She should've made a cup of that dishwater coffee. 'But the doctors have said that Eliza is fine. That she just needs time to grow.'

Pippa's smile was that of a professional who just wanted to leave and get to their next case. 'That's great. Hopefully, it'll stay that way. As I'm sure you know, there are other parties who may apply for guardianship, but I'll keep you notified and speak to you soon.'

Once Pippa had gone, Joanna sank back down onto the chair, thankful that no one else needed to be in here right now. Grief for the past and worry for the future were competing for room in her head. Even though her solicitor had warned her that there was no guarantee she would be chosen as Eliza's guardian, she had hoped that – once she met the social worker – they would see that she was the obvious choice. In the absence of a mother or father, who better to look after a child than her maternal grandmother?

But there were no guarantees in any of this. DC Lineham couldn't guarantee that Freddie would be prosecuted for Charlotte's death, or that he'd even done it. Joanna couldn't guarantee that she would be found financially stable enough to look after Eliza. And, from the look on the social worker's face and her scare with Eliza this afternoon, her continued health wasn't even a guarantee.

She needed to think. What did she have to do?

There were three phone calls that she needed to make.

One. To her solicitor to make sure that she was ready to apply for Eliza's guardianship.

Two. To an estate agent to put the house on the market and sell it. Her history, her memories there were totally unimportant – all she needed was a house good enough for the baby.

And three. To Rachael to ask if she or Lucy had any idea where to find this friend of Freddie's. The elusive Dominic. She had a scratch of a suspicion that he might be the key to finding out whether Freddie had hurt Charlotte or not. And the answer to that question was the key to all the others.

THIRTY-FIVE

The Bullseye was a bar by day and a club by night. It'd been a very long time since Joanna had been in a place like this. The darkness took a while to get used to and the loud thump of the music prevented her from hearing anyone in there. Bodies were packed together and she had to shuffle sideways after the two girls, trying to find somewhere to stand. Rachael leaned in close and shouted in her ear. 'What do you want to drink?'

She had no idea what to ask for. She was pretty sure that they wouldn't be serving the kind of wine she liked to drink. 'A beer?'

The girls had been brilliant. When she called them yesterday, they'd both wanted to know all about Eliza and how she was doing. Without questioning it, they'd cancelled their plans to bring her here, the bar where they thought Dominic was most likely to be. It may have been easier – and less shot-in-the-dark – to ask Annabelle to arrange for her to meet him, but she wanted to leave that as a last resort.

Rachael nodded at her choice of drink and veered off in the direction of the bar. Lucy reached out for Joanna's hand and pulled her towards the far wall. It was less busy here and she could hear herself think. 'Is he here?'

Lucy craned her neck to see over the heads nearest to them but shook her head. 'I can't see him. But it's still early.'

Early? It was almost ten o'clock. She'd been hoping to speak to him straight away and then head home. This place was so far outside her comfort zone, she needed another passport. Everyone was under twenty-five and brimming with the beauty of youth. Scanning the crowd herself, she could imagine Charlotte here. Laughing and joking and nodding her head to the music. How many times had she dropped her somewhere like this, or collected her at the end of the night when she and her friends were buzzing with excitement about the night they'd just had? There was so much life in this room. She turned to Lucy. 'Did Charlotte like it here?'

She smiled. 'Yeah, it was one of her favourite bars. She said you could always be yourself here. No judgement.'

How must that have felt? She had to ask. 'Unlike at home?'

Lucy looked surprised. 'What makes you say that?'

Quicker than she'd anticipated, Rachael was back with the drinks. 'I may have agreed to go on a date with the barman to make sure we got served quicker.'

Lucy shook her head. 'You are unbelievable.'

It was so odd seeing them without Charlotte here. Even in the hospital, she'd been there in body if not in spirit. It was like seeing only two sides of a triangle. 'You girls had some adventures over the years.'

They looked at each other with the kind of love only life-long girlfriends share. Like she and Sally shared. 'Yeah.' Lucy nodded. 'Usually Rachael would start the trouble, Charlotte would join in and then I would have to dig them both out of it.'

'Excuse *me*.' Rachael placed a hand on her hip in mock indignation, then let it fall. 'Yeah, okay, that's pretty accurate.'

Lucy laughed. 'Do you remember the night when we went

to that bar Dominic's uncle owned after the gig at The Garage? When Freddie persuaded the barman to do a lock-in and we were so high on our performance that we did the whole gig again a cappella?'

Their smiles were infectious. 'I'd loved to have seen that.'

Each of their memories had a sting in the tail because she could remember the times she and Charlotte had rowed because she didn't want Charlotte going to places like this. It all seemed so unimportant now.

The flashing lights showed the glisten of tears in Rachael's eyes. 'She was so talented. Our clever friend.'

Lucy reached out and rubbed Rachael's back. 'She really was. And we'll make sure that Eliza knows it, too. Always.'

Joanna pressed her hand to her chest at this subtle promise that they'd both be in Charlotte's daughter's life. But another element of their story struck her. 'You both saw quite a lot of Freddie, then? You liked him?'

Rachael glanced at Lucy, who nodded her support. 'We did. Obviously, we were a little cool with him when they first got back together, but he literally begged for her forgiveness. And once she'd forgiven him, we kind of had to. They were really good together. To be honest, we just can't believe that he's guilty. I mean, it's awful. And he loved her. Like, really loved her.'

Lucy's smile was tentative. 'And when you told us about the baby it made even less sense. I mean, I know it could've been an accident. But that would still have needed him to push her and we just can't see that happening.'

She could tell by the way they looked at each other that they'd discussed this at length. Joanna rubbed at her temples. It was so hard to think straight with that music pounding in the background. Before she could reply, or ask another question, Lucy looked up and nodded her head in the direction of the door. 'Dominic has just walked in.'

Joanna followed the two girls as they threaded their way through the crowd towards Dominic. Aside from the lights around the bar, and the strobes coming from the DJ corner, the whole place was in darkness. Even so, Joanna could see the boy's eyes smile as much as his mouth when he saw Lucy and Rachael walking towards him. He seemed less certain when Joanna materialised between them.

'Hello Dominic.'

He glanced back and forth at the two girls before frowning at her in confusion. 'Sorry, do I know you?'

Dominic was a well-built young man, with clothes that looked expensive and a tan that'd probably been caught on a jet ski somewhere exclusive. He was just like the boys she'd known at school: Jacob's friends. He had that aura of a life with well-oiled wheels.

'I'm Joanna. Charlotte's mother.'

His eyes widened. 'Freddie's Charlotte?'

Much as she didn't like that description, she nodded. 'Can I talk to you for a minute?' She glanced at the other two men he was with. 'In private?'

He looked even more confused. 'Er, yeah. Okay.'

He looked around him as if searching for one of the thread-bare benches to be free for them to sit, but the music was getting louder and she wasn't going to be able to hear him soon. 'Shall we go outside?'

At the back of the bar, there was a garden with damp picnic benches on a patio between the door and the car park. Joanna chose the one furthest away from the waft of marijuana coming from the trio of men just outside the back door.

Dominic had the decency to pay his respects as soon as they sat down. 'I'm really sorry to hear what happened to Charlotte. I liked her a lot. It's terrible, what's happened.'

He wasn't going to get any argument from her on any of

that. 'Thank you. That's what I wanted to talk to you about, actually.'

He twitched. 'What do you mean?'

'I'm trying to find out what happened that night. Freddie says it wasn't him and I want to see if he's telling the truth.'

Elbow on the table, Dominic leaned to one side in that easy way boys of his age – with their endless limbs – always seemed to sit. 'Freddie wouldn't have hurt Charlotte. He worshipped her.'

Each time she heard this, another seed of doubt grew in Joanna's mind. 'That's what I keep hearing. But the police have arrested him on suspicion of her murder. So something doesn't add up here. There was another man seen arriving at the flat that day. Did you know that?'

He frowned. 'No. Why would I know that?'

'And he was described as having the same build as Freddie.' She paused and really looked at him. 'Which would be the same as you, too.'

Dominic pulled himself up straight. 'I wasn't there.'

At least she was getting a reaction out of him now. 'Someone saw a man arrive. Park outside the house and go in.'

He held out his hands. 'Well, then it can't have been me. My car has been off the road for the last three months. My dad is refusing to buy me another one.' He looked sheepish. 'To be fair, I've had a bit of a history with cars.'

That threw her. 'Are you sure about that?'

He laughed. 'A hundred per cent. You can ask those two guys in there. They haven't stopped mugging me off about it.'

'And you definitely weren't there at any point on that Sunday?'

He shook his head. 'Definitely not. I was away that weekend. A messy one in Brighton with mates. Freddie was invited but he didn't want to be away from Charlotte. I didn't even hear what'd happened 'til I got back on the Monday.'

Joanna's shoulders slumped. She'd pinned a lot of hope on Dominic being able to tell her something.

He looked as if he felt sorry for her. 'You've got to understand, I don't want Freddie inside any more than you do. If I knew something, I'd tell you. What kind of car was this man driving?'

She wanted to be careful that she didn't reveal her source. She was pretty sure that the neighbour wouldn't want a solicitor from the Knight-Crossley camp knocking on his door. 'I don't know the make. But someone said it was white.'

Surprise, then dread flashed across Dominic's face. Then he leaned towards her, more in apprehension than threat. 'You need to talk to Freddie. You need to tell him what you've just told me.'

'What is it?'

He shook his head and got up. 'I'm saying nothing. If you want to know more, you need to talk to Freddie. I need to get back to my friends. Can I buy you a drink?'

Her head was banging, and not just because of the music. 'No. I'm not going back in. Can you tell the girls I'm here?'

'Sure thing.' He extricated his legs from under the bench. 'Go and see Freddie. Talk to him. Give him a chance.'

THIRTY-SIX

Joanna hadn't had the first idea how to arrange a visit to Freddie in prison. Her solicitor had explained that he would only have one visiting order a week and they were both surprised that he was keen to send it to her.

The prison was a vast grey building made even more depressing by the drizzle in the mid-afternoon air. She had to show her driving licence and a copy of the visiting order at a reception desk, then wait for her number to be called. She found a seat in the corner and pulled her coat around her.

After about twenty minutes, she was called with another group and walked across a courtyard to another waiting room. This one looked like the security gate at a rundown airport. Everyone was scanned and checked for contraband. Then made to line up as sniffer dogs were led past them. It was hard not to feel under suspicion for something she hadn't done.

All the while, she cast furtive looks at the people around her – almost all of the visitors were women. She was surprised how young many of them were; how beautiful they were. Their hair and make-up as perfect as if they were about to go out on a date. In some way, she supposed, they were.

She was also surprised how relaxed everyone seemed with the situation. There was some chatter – even laughter – from some of the women. Her surprise must've shown on her face. A woman beside her raised a manicured eyebrow. 'First time, hon?'

She swallowed, tried not to look like a rabbit in the headlights. 'Yes.'

The woman tilted her head, wrinkled her nose. 'Ah, it gets easier. Make sure you get to the shop before your one comes out. Otherwise, you waste your visiting time.'

She might as well have been speaking French for all the sense that Joanna could make from her words. 'Sorry?'

'There's a little shop. Tea, coffee, chocolate, biscuits, crisps —' she counted off the list on her fingers, which had long oval nails painted the most delicate shade of pink '—you know, snack stuff. You can buy what you want for you and your...'

She was obviously waiting for Joanna to fill in the blank. She had to say something. 'Daughter's boyfriend.'

Both eyebrows came up together this time. 'For your *daughter's* boyfriend? Wow. I won't ask. Anyway, it's nice to get some treats for them, even if they have to eat them there and can't take them away. But it's best if you get it before they bring the lads in, otherwise you waste some of your hour in the queue for a Snickers.'

The last thing she wanted to do was pass the time with Freddie over a hot drink and biscuit, but this woman was only being kind. 'Thank you.'

'No problem, hon. We all had to do it for the first time once. I'm Kelly. Might see you in here again.'

She forced a smile in return. 'I'm Joanna.'

When they finally got to the room where the visit would take place, she was amazed how big it was. Like the size of a school hall. Maybe even bigger. There were rows and rows of tables and chairs and the visitors were each directed towards one. It wasn't until she tried to move a chair to sit down that Joanna noticed that both they and the tables were bolted to the floor.

Just as Kelly had described, there was a kind of tuck shop in the corner, which already had an eager line of women and children. It broke her heart to see how young some of them were. Several were pregnant, one was holding a very young baby. This was no way to start a life.

Without warning, she felt the air in the room change as faces turned towards the other end of the hall. When the door opened and the prisoners filed in, she saw a full range of human expression: searching, grinning, blushing, winking, sadness, guilt, joy, they were all there. Just behind a man whose biceps were as thick as her waist, she saw Freddie loping towards her.

He slid into the seat opposite and, for the briefest second, she saw the charm in him. The smile, the blue eyes, everything that must've pulled Charlotte in.

'I'm really glad you've come to see me. I've been desperate to know how Eliza's doing.'

She was surprised he didn't know. 'Hasn't your mother been keeping you informed?'

He looked a little better than he had at the funeral, although still thin and pale. He stared down at his fingers, picking at the skin around his thumbnail. 'She said that you've been the one who's been with her. That she hasn't been allowed to get in to see her.'

It was very surprising that Annabelle still hadn't been in to see Eliza. After their conversation in the toilets after Charlotte's funeral, she'd assumed that she would be marching up to the nurses and demanding her right to get in. But she hadn't been to the hospital at all the last few days. 'I'm sure that'll change soon enough.'

He kept picking at his nail. 'No. I told her not to make a

scene. I said she needs to give you some space until Eliza is stronger.'

She was surprised that he'd said this. Even more surprised that Annabelle had listened. 'Thank you.'

He looked up then. And, for a moment, she saw him not as the man who'd stolen her daughter from her, but a young man who was as heartbroken as she was. 'No, thank you. For looking after Eliza. I know that she'll be safe with you.'

Every word from his mouth just confused her more. 'I don't understand, Freddie. Everyone I speak to wants to tell me that you loved Charlotte and wouldn't have hurt her. *You've* told me that you loved her and that you wouldn't hurt her. But this would hurt her. You going to prison? For something you've said time and again you didn't do? If you are telling the truth about this, you're leaving your daughter out in the world with no parent at all. If you know *anything*, you have to tell the police.'

He slumped back in his chair. 'It's not as simple as that.'

If she could've leaned across the table and shaken him without incurring the wrath of the guard on the far wall, she would have. 'Of course it is! How much time are they wasting in finding the real culprit while you're locked up?'

Freddie sighed. The scratch of his finger as he rubbed the bristles on his cheek was the only thing to cut the silence between them. Whatever was going through his head, the wrong thoughts won. 'The police will believe whatever they want. It doesn't matter what I say.'

Frustration made her want to scream. 'You sound like a stroppy teenager! Charlotte wanted me to believe that you were more than a spoiled rich boy and yet you're sounding just like one. And your daughter will grow up to sound the same if Eliza's guardianship goes to your mother.'

His head flicked up. 'What do you mean?'

'Did your solicitor not tell you? As soon as she was born, Eliza had a social worker assigned to her. Because you and

Charlotte weren't married, you don't have parental rights. And your mother is intending to apply for guardianship. You must know this? She has some hotshot lawyer arguing that, because it's accidental death, you'll be trying for guardianship when you get out. But, from what I can understand from the social worker, it's just as likely than none of us will get to keep her. She could be taken into care. Or adopted. Surely someone has told you all of this?'

Freddie's eyes widened. 'But she's my daughter. I should have custody of her. When I get out of here, she needs to live with me. There're other people in here who've done much worse than they're accusing me of doing. They get to keep their children.'

He didn't seem a stupid man but she couldn't believe he hadn't thought this through. 'And where do you think she's going to live before you get out?'

He looked like a small boy. 'I thought she'd stay with you. That she'd be safe with you.'

There was a sliver of hope for her in his words. Would the social worker take into consideration the wishes of Eliza's father when it came to deciding where she should live? Or would they disregard the viewpoint of a committed criminal when it came to deciding custody for his child?

'That's what I want too. I want her with me. But I don't know what the courts are going to decide. Your mother's lawyer is trying to prove that I was estranged from Charlotte.'

Her voice broke. It was impossible. Those two weeks they hadn't spoken had been the longest of her life. Not seeing Charlotte had been like losing the use of a limb; everything she did, she felt it.

Across the table, Freddie blinked as the things she'd told him were flicking across his eyes like ticker tape. 'I don't want her to live with my mother.'

She stared for a moment. Didn't he and his mother get on

well? If that wasn't the case, it might definitely help. 'Then you need to do something. You need to tell the police what you know. You need to get out and make sure you protect your daughter better than I did mine.'

Her heart ached with guilt and loss and, now, with absolute fear that she might lose the baby, too. Anything she could do to persuade Freddie to help her, she was willing to do.

'I want to, but it's not that easy.'

She had to squeeze her fists closed to prevent herself from shaking him. 'Why isn't it?'

'Because I know who did it.'

She froze, looked into his eyes as he watched her. The clock on the wall ticked once, twice, three times. 'What?'

He didn't blink. 'It was my mother.'

THIRTY-SEVEN

FREDDIE

Freddie had popped out to the shop to get some milk and, when he saw his mother's car parked in a visitor bay outside the apartment block, his heart sank. Ever since their conversation a few days ago – when he'd merely floated the idea that he and Charlotte might want to live further away at some point – she'd given him the cold shoulder. He could only imagine what she was saying to Charlotte right now.

But not in his wildest nightmares could he have imagined what he saw when he opened that front door.

Firstly, his mother ran into the hall. 'She's not getting up.'

'What?'

She reached out and grabbed his arm. 'I think she hit her head. She'd not getting up.'

In three strides, he was in the sitting room. The scene there would be etched onto his brain for the rest of his life.

Charlotte was on her back. Her head bent forwards by the corner of the metal cabinet on their far wall. Beneath her, blood was pooling around her shoulders.

He was next to her in less than a second. 'Charlotte. Baby,

can you hear me?' He turned back to his mother. 'Have you called an ambulance?'

She didn't move, maybe in shock. 'I didn't mean to—'

'Have you called an ambulance?' He screamed at her this time. Couldn't she see how serious this was?

'No. I—'

He didn't wait for her to finish. He snatched up Charlotte's phone on the table, realised it was dead, then fumbled in his jacket pocket for his own. 'Ambulance please. It's urgent. My girlfriend is unconscious. Bleeding.'

He listened to the instructions on the other end of the phone, reported back to the call handler who promised him that an ambulance would be with him soon. Yes she was breathing. No she wasn't conscious. Yes he could roll up his jacket and try to staunch the blood.

While they waited the longest twenty minutes of his life for an ambulance, he tried to get his mother to tell him what had happened. She wasn't making a huge amount of sense. 'I was just talking to her. She was so angry.'

Cold realisation trickled down his spine. 'Did you push her? Did you push Charlotte?'

His mother's eyes were wild. 'She was shouting at me. Told me I wasn't going to control her child's life like I controlled yours. I just wanted to stop her shouting.'

Freddie was cradling Charlotte's head, trying not to move her neck. The blood had stopped but she still wasn't responding to him calling her name. He screamed at his mother. 'What have you done?'

Something clicked in her then. 'I have to go. You tell them it was an accident. I can't be here. You have to protect me, Freddie. Don't tell them I was here.'

She was gone before the police and then ambulance arrived. She wasn't there when the police asked him to come with them.

At the police station, he'd called the family lawyer to be with him while he was being interviewed.

At no point did he mention his mother.

THIRTY-EIGHT

Sometimes the truth is so obvious that your brain can't take it in. Joanna heard what he'd said, but she still couldn't make sense of it. 'What did you say?'

Freddie lowered his voice still further. 'It was my mother. She was the one who did it.'

That didn't add up. 'But the neighbour said it was another man who'd visited. A man who looked like you?'

Even as she said it, she realised that she, too, had mistaken Annabelle for a young man when she first saw her. The clothes she wore, the way she held herself. She could see how that might've happened.

Freddie frowned. 'I don't know anything about that. But my mum was definitely there that night. She didn't mean to hurt Charlotte, I think she just wanted to scare her, or she just lost control with the push. But she caused the accident.'

Was he defending her? 'It was hardly an accident. The police said there was evidence of an attack. And she didn't just push her; she shoved her hard enough to make her lose her balance.'

He winced. 'I know.'

'Why? Why would she do that?'

His shoulders slumped. Secret out, he seemed to deflate in front of her eyes. 'She was angry. She thought – she always thought – that Charlotte was trying to take me away from her. Away from the family.'

That was ridiculous, wasn't it? Like an episode from a third-rate soap opera. 'What happened?'

'There was an argument. A few days before we'd told her that we were expecting a baby. Well, I'd told her. Charlotte wanted to keep it a secret until we'd told you.'

Joanna's hand went to her chest to press against the pain piercing her heart. 'She wanted to tell me first?'

He looked surprised that she'd ask. 'Of course. You were everything to her, Joanna. She told me that she wanted to be just like you as a mother.'

Tears filled Joanna's eyes. Had she really said that? If only she'd been better. 'I still don't understand why she'd push her.'

He sighed. 'My mother can be... pretty physical. Even when I was growing up. And there've been issues before with Charlotte, when she'd grabbed her arm.'

The bruises. The 'evidence' she'd believed had been a result of Freddie's temper. It was her all the time? 'Why didn't you stick up for her?'

'I did. I told my mother that if she touched Charlotte again we were done. But that day, there was a huge row. I don't know how it started, but it ended with Charlotte telling her that she wasn't going to control her child's life like she tried to control mine.'

She could imagine Charlotte saying that. A surge of pride in her daughter's strength almost distracted her from the real questions she had to ask. 'You're saying that your mother shoves your pregnant girlfriend, she hits her head and is left in a coma and you tell the police nothing?'

He dropped his chin to his chest, shame hanging over him

like a dark cloud. 'It's complicated. You don't know what it's like.'

She certainly didn't. 'Then tell me.'

'It's just been me and my mum since I was ten. My dad was only ill for a short while, but he made it clear to me that I was to look after her. Everyone did. *You're the man of the house now, Frederick.*'

She could understand that to a point, but this was another level. 'You shouldn't have to take the fall for her though!'

Freddie sighed, looking far older than his twenty-three years. 'She was strong for me, when she had to bring me up on her own. There's a family accountancy firm and she took my father's place on the board, kept the seat warm for me, as it were. I owe her so much. And it's not just that—' he paused and rubbed his face '—she's my mother. And she wouldn't survive a minute in prison if she got convicted. Even if she didn't. Her reputation would be in ruins. The business... well, it could ruin everything for us. Everything my father worked for.'

The way he spoke, she could imagine that this was exactly the way Annabelle had put it to him. 'But you have to do it, Freddie. You have to do what's right.'

He shook his head. 'If I thought it would bring Charlotte back, I would do it in a heartbeat. But what difference will it make? It was an accident. And my mum might go to prison for a couple of years and then be out and I'd have lost my whole family.'

'Not your whole family, Freddie. What about Eliza?' His logic was baffling but another question ran through Joanna's mind. 'How can your mother do this to you? How can she let you go to prison instead of her?'

It went against every instinct she had as a mother. Even when she'd got it very wrong, her instinct had been to protect Charlotte. Always. It was impossible to understand that

Annabelle wouldn't feel the same. Freddie merely shrugged. 'You'd have to ask her that.'

Though she'd never expected to feel sympathy for Freddie Knight-Crossley, that's exactly what was happening. All the things that Charlotte had tried to tell her – *he's different from his family, he's a good man, you just need to get to know him* – flooded her mind. Charlotte had wanted him to come away from them, to start a new life with her, with their baby. And she'd paid a terrible price.

But Eliza wasn't going to pay the same price. She'd lost one parent. If the other one needed Joanna's help and support – the same help and support that Charlotte had tried to provide – then she was going to give it to him. 'Eliza needs you, Freddie. She needs her dad.'

Pain creased his face. 'God, I need her, I would give anything to see her, too. I've been trying to get permission to come.'

Joanna's face was hot with the shame that she'd tried to do all she could to persuade the police to prevent that from happening. 'I don't just mean for a visit. You need to get out of here. You need to be there for her. You have to go to the police about your mum. Or I will.'

'No.' His voice was firm. 'I know you don't understand why, Joanna. Charlotte couldn't understand why things were the way they were, either. I thought for a while, when we found out that she was pregnant, I thought I could... but she's gone now. I'm not going to the police and, if you do, I will just confess and the case will be done.'

A bell rang like it was the end of school and a guard called 'Time'. All around them, bags rustled and goodbyes were said. She had to think of something to make Freddie change his mind. But her own mind was blank. She rose to go.

'Joanna?'

She turned to see his eyes – the same clear blue eyes that

Charlotte had fallen in love with – beseeching her. 'Look after Eliza, Joanna, please. Make sure she stays with you.'

She left the prison in a fog. Heavy drops of rain sank into her hair as she walked across the tarmac to her car, still reeling in disbelief. Like a montage in a Saturday afternoon film, she replayed all her conversations with Annabelle: the way she'd let her in, almost warmed to her, seen her as another mother in pain. Instead of kicking herself, she booted the front tyre of her car. Hard.

There was no confusion about what to do this time, though. Whatever Freddie did or didn't want to say, there was no way she was letting that evil woman get away with what she'd done. She might've been wrong about Freddie, but she hadn't been wrong about needing to keep Eliza away from that family.

By the time she got in her car, her hands were trembling. She fumbled in her bag to find her mobile to call DC Lineham. But, as she was scrolling for her number, the phone rang in her hand, it was the hospital.

Her heart fell through her to the car seat. 'Hello?'

'Hello? Joanna? It's Jenny. You need to come to the hospital. Can you come now?'

How she got to the hospital without crashing her car she would never know. Running down the corridor gave her the most horrific déjà vu. *Not again. Not again. Not again.*

When she got to ITU and pressed the buzzer, the wait for someone to answer was interminable. When it opened, she practically pushed them out of the way to get to Eliza.

A young doctor she'd never met before was at the end of her crib, speaking to Jenny. Joanna's legs felt as if they were moving through treacle. She was terrified about what she was going to find out.

Two of the babies on the ward had needed less care in the

last couple of days and had graduated to the High Dependency ward. Of the two other babies still on the ward, there was only one other mother in the room. In her peripheral vision, Joanna saw the nurse who'd opened the door, speak to her quietly and ask her to leave the room. It was all she could do not to fall on the floor.

Jenny smiled at her as she approached. 'Dr James. This is Joanna, Eliza's grandmother.'

Dr James held out his hand for her to shake, his hand felt cool against hers. 'Thanks for coming in.'

Inside her cot, Eliza was sleeping. Nothing was beeping and her little chest was rising and falling as normal. An initial relief swept through Joanna. 'What's going on?'

The doctor was a lot younger than the ones she'd seen before. He looked nervous as he cleared his throat. 'It's the first time I've met Eliza today and I noticed that one of her eyes takes a little longer to open. We've just done a scan and seen a spot on the brain, which concerns me a little. I'm going to refer it to my colleague, but Jenny wanted to call you, just in case you came in and she wasn't here.'

A mark on her brain? Her eye not opening? She hadn't noticed that. Had she not been looking close enough? She lay her hand on the top of Eliza's crib. Had she let her down? Had she let Charlotte down? Again.

Jenny reached across the crib and lay her hand on Joanna's. Ignoring the doctor, she had her eyes firmly on Joanna. 'I'm finishing my shift soon and I wanted to be here with you when the doctor explained all of this. I hope you didn't mind me calling you?'

Mind? She was beyond grateful. 'Of course not. Thank you. I want to be here. What happens now?'

'When my colleague comes, we can scan again and she'll be able to talk you through the next steps. It may just be a wait and see situation.'

Wait and see? 'Surely if it's her brain, it'll be urgent?'

Jenny squeezed her hand. 'Let's see what the consultant says before you worry.'

That was asking the impossible. Sometimes it was only her worry that kept her alive. 'Can I be here with Eliza when she's having the scan?'

The doctor shook his head. 'No. We'll ask you to stay outside. Or, if you want to go home, we can call you?'

She almost laughed. 'No, I'll be right here. Can I hold her until the other doctor arrives?'

Jenny opened her mouth to speak, but the doctor answered. 'She'll be here any minute.'

Jenny smiled at Joanna. 'You can open the side of the crib and hold her hand, though.'

Joanna took her usual seat and reached in to Eliza's crib. Nothing else mattered than making sure she was okay. Jenny tactfully drew the doctor's attention away for a moment and Joanna brought her face close to the crib. 'I've been to see your daddy today, Eliza. You need to get big and strong so that you can meet him. He's going to love you so much, I just know it.'

Freddie's revelation about his mother had coloured this picture very differently. She hadn't listened to Charlotte when she'd tried to tell her about him. Hadn't believed her. Hadn't trusted her. But she was listening now and she would do whatever she had to do to make this right.

As soon as the second doctor arrived, Joanna had to leave the room. Her first thought was to call Sally and tell her what was going on. Her second was to call DC Lineham and tell her what had really happened to Charlotte.

But when she was buzzed out of the ward, she was shocked to find there was someone looking for her.

'Hi Joanna. I was hoping to find you here.'

THIRTY-NINE

Joanna had never been violent, but the sight of Annabelle outside the ward made her want to tear her apart. Violence wouldn't even begin to repay Annabelle for what she'd done, though. Evidence would. If she could get Annabelle to confess – and record it – she wouldn't have to rely on Freddie to make her accusations stand up in court.

This wasn't a spur-of-the moment decision. Between worrying about Eliza, and absorbing the shock of Freddie's revelations, she'd scrolled through solutions in her brain and this had been one of them. She just hadn't expected to get the opportunity so soon.

Annabelle's face wasn't giving anything away. 'I thought we could get a coffee?'

Joanna fought to keep her voice calm. 'Good idea.'

Now all she had to do was work out how to start recording without Annabelle noticing.

On the walk from the ITU, she noticed anew how Annabelle dressed and walked in a very similar way to her son. In her jeans and sweatshirt, with her close-cropped hair, from a distance, she could easily have been one of his friends. All the time she'd been wondering who the mystery man was, she hadn't once made the connection. She didn't need to check to know that Annabelle must drive a white car.

Their walking conversation was brief. Annabelle's mobile rang almost immediately and she'd spent most of the journey talking to someone else. That helped. Having not expected to see her so soon, Joanna needed that time to collect her thoughts, decide what to say. Did Annabelle know that she'd been to see Freddie? Did she know that she knew what'd happened that afternoon?

Was she stupid to spend time with her like this without calling the police first? Was she putting herself in danger? What was she going to say? Anxiety prickled deep in her stomach. And scalding anger. Not only at Annabelle, but at herself. How had she started to trust this woman? To think that she was just a caring mother like her? They were nothing alike. Nothing.

The canteen was empty apart from a few scattered hospital staff in different colour tabards. In the prison visiting hall, the inmates had had different colour vests. It'd reminded her of the netball vests Charlotte used to wear at school. The roles children play in life are sometimes chosen, sometimes assigned. Like the family you're born into. It's all a lottery.

Annabelle pointed to the far corner of the canteen. 'You go and find us a seat and I'll get drinks. Coffee for you? Or is it too late for caffeine?'

While Annabelle bought drinks, she could set up her phone to record their conversation. 'Coffee is fine.'

Joanna found a seat by the window, which looked out onto a desolate group of grey buildings, trying to imagine why Annabelle wanted to speak to her. Could she contain herself long enough to find out? It took only a moment to set up the phone to record their conversation and then she placed it onto the chair next to her, face down.

'There you go. I got you a latte.' The cups rattled on the tray as Annabelle slid it onto the table.

It was so difficult to contain her rage, but Joanna smiled tightly. 'Thank you. What did you want to talk to me about?'

'Give me a minute to sit down.'

How could Annabelle look so calm, smile so innocently when – all the time – she knew that she was the reason they were in this hospital at all?

'I've been speaking to my solicitor and he tells me you've been in to visit Freddie.'

How did she know that already? She must want to know whether Freddie had told Joanna everything. Outside the window, clouds of steam billowed from a thick metal chimney. Joanna couldn't keep it in any longer. 'I know what happened, Annabelle.'

Annabelle had taken the lid from her takeaway cup and was blowing heat from the top of the black liquid. 'Pardon me?'

'I know what you did.'

If Annabelle had any inkling that she'd been found out, it didn't show on her face. 'You're not making any sense, Joanna. Are you okay?'

She couldn't hold it in any longer. Leaning forward, she hissed the words at Annabelle. 'You killed her. You killed my daughter.'

For the merest second, something flashed across Annabelle's face, before it became inscrutable again. 'I don't know what you're talking about.'

She'd started now, she wasn't going to back down. 'Don't lie. I've been to see Freddie in prison. I got it out of him. He told me everything.'

The blank expression on Annabelle's face curled into something dark and unpleasant. 'Did he, now?'

Even thought they were in public, fear crept over Joanna at facing this woman. For almost a year, she'd made her childhood hell. But Joanna was an adult now and she wasn't backing down. 'Why, Annabelle? Why did you do it? Why did you attack her?'

Annabelle blew on the drink once more before replacing the plastic lid. 'Those are your words, Joanna, not mine. I think you'll find your daughter had an accident. If you try to accuse me of anything other than that, you might be hearing from my solicitor.'

Joanna had never been violent to anyone, but right now she wanted to slap that smug expression from Annabelle's face. 'How could you be so vile? How could you hurt her? She was so lovely. So kind. How could you do it?'

Annabelle's eyes were as hard and dark as wet gravel. 'Of course, you think she's perfect. But she's not in the same league as my son. Do you really think I wanted him with her? I know you think you're as good as us, but you were always just a scholarship girl and the daughter of a criminal.'

Joanna flinched. 'How dare you.'

'No.' Annabelle sneered at her, the expression a perfect copy of that which had haunted Joanna's early school days. 'How dare *you*. And how dare your daughter try to take my son away from me. Filling his head with ideas of moving away. Travelling the world. Living like some kind of hobo. That might be alright for families like yours, but it is not the way we do things. Not the plans that my husband and I had for our only son.'

This was the real Annabelle.

'Do you have no remorse for what you've done?'

'Of course I do. I didn't mean for that to happen. But I'm not about to go to prison for it either.'

She couldn't believe what she was hearing. 'How can you let your son take the blame for what you've done? How can you let him go to prison for something he didn't do?'

Annabelle sipped at her coffee as if they were discussing

where to go on holiday. 'He won't go in for long. It was an accident. He doesn't have a record. My solicitor says that the CPS will throw it out on their flimsy evidence anyway. Chances are, he'll end up knowing the judge.'

Joanna felt sick. 'That's what you think, isn't it? You think that you and your family are better than everyone else and can behave however you want with no consequences. But there will be consequences this time, and you won't get anywhere near your grandaughter!'

'Really?'

The mocking smile on Annabelle's face made Joanna want to throw the coffee over her. 'Yes. Really. You're not going to get away with this.'

'If you're so sure about it, why haven't you gone to the police?'

'I will be going to the police. But I'm giving you an opportunity to turn yourself in.'

Annabelle leaned across the table. 'That won't be happening and you need to think very carefully before you do anything silly. Freddie will not testify against me and there's no evidence to put me near the crime. All you're going to do is make yourself look crazy to the people who will make a decision about Eliza's future. Add that to your financial problems and the fact that Charlotte wasn't even speaking to you.' She held out her hands as if this was an obvious assumption.

Joanna could picture the social worker's face: *'we have to make a decision based on what's best for the child'*. Would this list of her failings prevent her from having Eliza in her life? 'Freddie wants me to look after her.'

'Freddie doesn't know what he wants. He's a twenty-three-year-old boy. Your daughter turned his head. It happens. But he knows now that he has to do the right thing. I'll get guardianship of his daughter and we'll move on. I've always done the best for my son.'

She could tell from her face that she meant that. Annabelle really believed that she was doing the right thing. But she was so wrong. 'No. You are doing what you want to do to control your son. I'm not going to let you get away with this!'

Annabelle wanted to control Freddie's life. Joanna recognised it straight away, because wasn't that what she'd done to Charlotte? Tried to keep her on the path that she'd thought was best. Refused to engage with the life she wanted to make for herself. But she'd done that out of love.

Annabelle's eyes flashed. 'Just think about what will happen if none of us get guardianship of Eliza. It doesn't matter what you think of me. Think about her. Do you really want her going to a foster family goodness knows where? Because if social services see us fighting like this, that's probably what they'll do. Just think about it.'

And, with that, she pushed herself away from the table and walked out of the canteen.

As soon as she'd gone, Joanna plucked the phone from the seat next to her and checked the recording. Except there was no recording. Just a photo of the plastic seat: she'd pressed the wrong button. She put her head down on her arms and sobbed.

It took almost ten minutes for her to stop trembling enough to dial DC Lineham's number. It went straight to voicemail.

'Hi Abbie. It's Joanna Woodley. I need to speak to you. Can you call me as soon as you can?'

She pushed the rest of her coffee away and glanced at her watch. How much longer before she could go back to Eliza? She checked her email. There was one from her solicitor outlining the process for applying for guardianship with attachments of the forms she needed to complete. She emphasised how long this process could take and urged Joanna to get started as soon as possible. There was also an email from the estate agent suggesting an open house that weekend for potential buyers. Did she want to be there or just drop off the keys?

The weight of all of these decisions and tasks was pushing her under. She needed Steve. She needed her husband to hold her up and tell her that it'd all be okay. Steve, who could fix anything, make everything work. She lowered her head onto the table and sobbed, no longer caring who could see her or what they might think.

The table vibrated as her mobile rang on the table beside her; a hospital number.

Eliza.

FORTY

Joanna was already out of her seat and walking back to ITU as she picked up the call. 'Hello?'

'Hi Joanna, it's Jenny. Just wanted to let you know that the consultant has been called away to an emergency, so the follow-up scan is going to be rescheduled for two days' time.'

Two days? She couldn't wait that long to know that Eliza was going to be okay. 'Is there no one else who can do it?'

She was out of breath, her heart racing, and she forced herself to slow her pace. Sending her own blood pressure through the roof wasn't going to help anyone.

Jenny's voice was calm and kind. 'She's the top consultant we have. She's the one you want looking after your baby. Also—' she paused, lowering her voice '—I thought you might want to know that Eliza's other grandmother is here.'

Joanna almost dropped her mobile on the hard blue floor. 'I'm on my way.'

At the door to ITU, Joanna shifted from one foot to the other, desperate to be buzzed in. What the heck was Annabelle doing there? She hadn't mentioned a word about visiting Eliza when she left the canteen.

It was Jenny's voice on the intercom, confirming it was Joanna, and she was waiting for her on the other side. 'I hope you didn't mind me mentioning it. We didn't know who Annabelle was, but there was a call from admin to say she should be allowed in for a visit.'

Joanna could just imagine. Annabelle would've had her expensive lawyer ensure that she was admitted. In retrospect, it was surprising that it'd taken her so long.

Approaching her from behind, Joanna noticed again how easy it would've been for Charlotte's neighbour to assume she was a young man. All this time, she'd been looking for a mystery man and it was this woman. She wanted to throw her to the ground and rain down her anger on her. But here, among the fragile babies and their anxious parents, was not the place.

'You didn't mention you were coming here.'

Annabelle didn't even turn her head. 'She's tiny.'

Joanna followed her gaze to where Eliza lay, arms like little wings about to flap, her chest rising and falling. To her, Eliza was growing and changing each day. 'You've seen her before. I showed you a photograph.'

'I know, but...'

She wasn't taking her eyes from the incubator, but it didn't seem as if she was transfixed by the baby. She looked more... scared?

Jenny touched Joanna on the elbow. 'Just wanted to confirm that the brain scan is all booked in for the day after tomorrow.'

Joanna breathed a sigh of relief. At least they'd get answers soon. 'Thanks for letting me know.'

Annabelle turned her head at that. 'A brain scan?'

She didn't want to tell her anything, but her solicitor would only get the information anyway. 'There's concern about a shadow on Eliza's brain.'

Annabelle paled. 'Her brain? What does that mean? Is she... I mean, is she going to be okay?'

It was difficult to read her reaction. 'I hope so. But she's a premature baby. There's always going to be risks.'

She'd been living with this since the moment of Eliza's entrance to the world. Every time there was a beep from the machine, or she took extra time between breaths, or the eye doctor or audiologist would frown when they were checking her sight and hearing, she'd think: *This is it. This is the thing. This is the issue we'll have to deal with.*

'What kind of risks. I mean, could she be brain damaged? Could she be disabled?'

Joanna herself had had concerns and worries and asked questions of the nurses. But the look on Annabelle's face made her angry and defensive. Sitting in this room, watching Eliza – watching the other parents with their tiny miracles – she'd known that she would cope with anything she had to, as long as she had to, in order for Eliza to be well enough to come home. 'She seems absolutely fine. But this scan is a worry. We just have to hope and pray.'

She stepped forwards and opened the hatch at the side of the incubator, reaching out for Eliza's hand to hold. Annabelle watched her in silence. With her thumb, Joanna stroked the back of Eliza's tiny hand, her veins like threads of silk. Annabelle coughed. 'When will you know? If she's... if she's *normal*?'

There was no longer any confusion about her tone and what she meant. Joanna turned to look at her. 'Are you saying you're not interested if she turns out to have complex needs?'

Annabelle met her eye with steel in her own. 'I'm not sure I'd be equipped.'

Despite her anger, Joanna had to laugh. She lowered her voice so as not to offend anyone nearby. 'I don't think any of these parents are equipped. You love your child and you do what needs to be done to make their life as easy as possible. If Eliza needs extra help, I'm here for her. Are you?'

Annabelle pursed her lips. For a moment, she looked as if she might say something. Then she turned on her heel and left the room.

Joanna stayed for another hour, but she was desperate to get hold of DC Lineham. On the way back to the car, she called again and left another voicemail. Once she'd slid herself behind the steering wheel, she called Sally, who picked up straight away as always.

'Hello. I was hoping to hear from you but I didn't want to call if you were on the ward. How's Eliza?'

'She seems okay. I have to wait to speak to the consultant. In two days' time.'

'Flipping heck. I know how scary this must be, Jo. Waiting for results is the worst part.'

Sally had been in this position many times with Harry over the years. This is parenting, she'd wanted to say to Annabelle. Being there for all of it.

'Yes. But I've got so much more to tell you. I know that Freddie didn't do it. He didn't push Charlotte.'

'What? How do you know? Who was it?'

As quickly as she could, Joanna told Sally about her visit to the prison and her conversation with Annabelle. When she was done, there was silence at the other end. 'Are you still there?'

'Yes. Sorry.' Sally let out a deep breath. 'It's just quite a shock. How can she walk around knowing what she's done? And letting her own son stay in prison for it?'

'I can't understand it either. I'm waiting for the police to get back to me. But what if Freddie doesn't back me up?'

'You can't worry about that. Just tell the police what you know and let them do their job.'

There was more to tell. 'And Annabelle came to see Eliza for the first time today. Her reaction was weird, but she said earlier that she's going for guardianship. She threatened me, Sally. She knows about me not being able to pay the mortgage and she says she'll tell the social worker that Charlotte and I weren't speaking. And about my father being in prison. I'm scared. She has this powerful solicitor and all that money on her side. What if they listen to her? And oh God, even if she decides not to apply for guardianship, if she tells them everything, they might put Eliza up for adoption instead!' With each new possibility, her stomach clenched tighter.

As if she were reaching a calm arm around her, Sally's voice was firm. 'We're not going to let that happen. Go home. Get some rest. I'll meet you at the hospital in the morning after Harry has left for college and we can talk it all through. I can come back with you tomorrow night if you like and help you fill out those forms for your solicitor so that they're done. I can also drop off a spare key to your estate agent and they can do their open house thingy at the weekend.'

The relief of a problem shared was palpable. 'But what about Graham and Harry and all the stuff you've got going on?'

'It's all okay here. I'll tell you about that when I see you. But get some rest, Jo. You're no good to anyone if you make yourself ill.'

As soon as she ended the call to Sally, Joanna's mobile pinged with a voicemail from DC Lineham.

'Hi Joanna. Tried to call a couple of times. I'm going home now, but I have some good news. Freddie has confessed. His solicitor has changed his plea to guilty. I've got an early start tomorrow with another case, but I will call you as soon as I can tomorrow.'

Joanna let her mobile fall into her lap and brought her hands to her face. Confessed? His mother can't have spoken to him this soon. She must've rattled him during her visit earlier. But she couldn't let him take the blame for this. If he wasn't going to stand up to his mother, she would have to. But how?

FORTY-ONE

The following morning, Joanna had been with Eliza for a couple of hours and had just popped out to check whether DC Lineham had left a message when she got a call from Sally. 'Come and meet me on the bench outside the main entrance.'

The sun had strengthened since Joanna had arrived early that morning and it burned the back of her neck as she made her way to the bench where Sally was waiting. When she got closer, she could see that she'd laid out some kind of breakfast picnic for the two of them.

'I knew you wouldn't have much time to eat, so I brought pastries and all the good stuff. How's our baby girl this morning?'

The sun gave Sally's smile an even warmer glow. It was so good to see her. 'She's doing well. But I don't know what to do with myself. Waiting for the consultant's visit tomorrow is almost painful.'

Sally nodded. 'I know. Time goes backwards, doesn't it? Has Annabelle been in again?'

Thankfully, she hadn't shown her face today. 'No. And I don't think I can control myself if I see her, Sally. I really think I might do something to her. I want to hurt her like she hurt Charlotte.'

Yesterday, she'd been in some kind of shock. Between Freddie's revelation, the news about the scan, and Annabelle's threats, she hadn't known which way was up. With a night spent tossing and turning through the scenario in which Annabelle had pushed her beautiful daughter, had caused her catastrophic injuries, had lied about it to everyone, her anger had grown and grown until the need for violent retribution threatened to overtake her.

Sally didn't look shocked, but she shook her head. 'I understand. But that isn't going to help anybody. Eliza is your priority now. You have to go about this the right way. Have you spoken to the police?'

'I don't know who to call aside from DC Lineham. I've left her a message again, but she did say that she's on a case this morning. If I just ring the police station, they're going to think I'm crazy. And I'm worried about what she'll do.'

Sally tilted her head and frowned. 'DC Lineham?'

'No. Annabelle. If she knows that I've gone to the police, she'll tell the social worker all those things about me. That I might lose the house and that Charlotte and I argued. She could spin it however she wants. And I'm so worried that, with all this going on, the social worker will just decide that Eliza is better off without any of us. It's such a mess.'

Sally reached across and squeezed her arm. 'Breathe. Just take it one step at a time. First thing is finding out about this scan for Eliza. Then we'll make sure that nasty piece of work gets what's coming.'

Joanna placed her hand over Sally's. 'You're right. The consultant is coming tomorrow morning. I'm trying not to think about it too hard. Tell me something else. What's happening with you and Graham? Have you talked about how you're feeling?'

'Yes. We have. I was honest with him about how scared I feel and he understood. But he still thinks that it's the best thing for Harry. He said it was much better for him to start learning how to live on his own in one of those places while we're still here and young enough to support him. I think there was a huge subtext of "we won't be around forever", which was a bitter pill to swallow.'

'I can imagine.'

'He's right, though, isn't he? I do need to let him try this. He's actually pretty excited about it. Harry, I mean. I think I was expecting him to say he wanted to stay with me, but the little rat was quite happy to wave me goodbye when we went to look at the place.'

She laughed to show she was joking, but there were tears in her eyes. Joanna really felt for her. 'You've been to visit?'

She nodded. 'Yes. And it's very nice and feels very safe and supportive. Although, when I asked if they'd be checking whether he'd heated his dinner properly, they did look at me as if I were a crazy lady.'

'Which of course, you are. But that's another subject. I'm proud of you. I know it's not easy.'

'Thank you.' She breathed out and gave a little shrug. 'Now, back to you. How are things progressing with the solicitor?'

'I completed the last of the forms she sent me last night. I know you were going to help, but I just wanted to get things moving.'

Sally passed her a pain au chocolat and a napkin. 'Well done. What's next?'

That was the million-dollar question. 'I don't know. I'm waiting for DC Lineham to call me so I can tell her about Annabelle. I suppose I'll be guided by her.'

'The only problem is, if Freddie has confessed, they might want to leave well alone.'

That worried her, too. 'It's so strange. I've spent days

wanting him to pay the worst penalty possible, and now I find myself fighting his corner.'

'You weren't to know, Jo.'

'I could have listened to Charlotte.'

'Give yourself a break. A year ago, you lost Steve. You weren't thinking straight for months after that. You did the best you could.'

She was right. There were days and days after Steve's funeral that she didn't even want to get out of bed. Sally was perhaps the only person in the world she could confess her feelings to. 'I was so angry, Sally. So angry at Steve for leaving us.'

Sally reached out for her. 'Of course you were. Grief is so complicated. You need to be kind to yourself.'

'I have to make sure that Freddie gets to look after his daughter. I have to find a way to fix this. For Charlotte. And for Eliza.'

Sally nodded. 'Good. What do we need to do?'

Joanna appreciated the 'we' but this one was on her. 'I need to go and see him again. I need to persuade him to tell the truth.'

She had to find a way to make him understand. He might think that what he was doing was the best thing for his family. But she knew better than anyone how easy it was to get that wrong.

'What do you think you can say to persuade him?'

She thought about Eliza. And Charlotte. And what he'd said to her as she left the prison visit. *Look after Eliza, Joanna. Please.*

She wrapped the last of the pastry in a napkin as a plan started to unfurl in her mind. 'I think I've got an idea.'

FORTY-TWO

Familiarity made things easier to bear. The second time she arrived at the prison wasn't such a shock. Freddie had been surprised that she'd applied for another visiting order so quickly. In turn, she was surprised that he hadn't any family members or friends who would've already planned to come.

In the waiting area, she thought of her own mother and her refusal to go anywhere near the prison that held her father. When she'd asked why they weren't visiting, she'd been given a story about how horrible the men were in the prison with her father. 'It's not a place for people like us.'

Seated at the nailed down table in the visiting hall, she fought to keep her nerves under control. If she couldn't persuade Freddie to retract his confession, if Annabelle got away with killing her daughter, if she lost Charlotte's baby... The metal door banged open in the corner to interrupt the downward spiral of catastrophe that'd kept her awake into the small hours. She counted seventeen prisoners before she spotted Freddie. When he reached the table, she could see he was even thinner than her last visit; his blue eyes more full of concern. 'My solicitor sent me a message. Said that Eliza needs a brain scan. Is she okay? Is it serious?'

His face begged her for news, but she had none to give him. 'I'm seeing the consultant tomorrow. I'll know more then.'

His face creased in pain. 'She's so tiny. Hasn't she been through enough? I thought she was going to be okay. They said she just needed to grow.'

For the first time, Joanna truly considered what it must've been like for him. Trapped in here, not able to see his daughter. 'Has the hospital been giving you regular updates?'

He nodded. 'My solicitor passes them on. We've been trying to get permission for me to come and see her, but it's taking so long. If she needs extra help, I want to make sure she gets the best treatment possible. We have plenty of money, we can get her whatever she needs. The best doctors, the best treatment, anything. Can you make sure they know that, Joanna? I can't lose her, too.'

Her heart squeezed at the agony in his voice, she needed a moment to compose herself. 'I know. I know.'

He pushed himself back into his chair. 'I'm so desperate to see her. Have you held her?'

He'd already missed so much. Would miss even more if he pled guilty in court and went to prison for a crime he hadn't committed. She needed to get through to him. 'Yes, I've held her. She's beautiful.'

A strangled sob escaped from him. 'I knew she would be.'

The clock on the wall behind him was ticking down the minutes of the visit. She needed to do what she'd come here for. 'I don't think I'm going to get guardianship, Freddie.'

He stared at her as if she had two heads. 'Are you serious? Why?'

'Your mother came to see me yesterday. She was pretty... brutal. She wants Eliza and she has the resources to get her.'

He frowned. 'And you're just going to let her do that?'

Of course she wasn't, but she wanted him to think she might. 'The thing is, I have some money issues. And – as your mother so kindly pointed out – she doesn't. Plus, she's going to tell them that Charlotte and I were estranged.'

Freddie looked terrified. 'But that's not true. I mean, I know you'd had an argument but... no, it's not true.'

She looked him in the eye. 'It doesn't matter what's true, does it?'

The irony wasn't lost on him. His face darkened. 'I don't want Eliza with my mother. And that can't be what you want, either.' He lowered his voice. 'You know what she did.'

She looked him dead in the eye. 'And so do you.'

He rubbed at his chin with his palm, the scratch of his stubble filled the space between them. Again, he shook his head, as if there were flies buzzing in his ears. 'No. No, Joanna. You can't mean this. My mother can't have the baby. Think about Charlotte. She wouldn't have wanted that at all. She wanted...'

She looked at him, heart thumping. 'What did she want, Freddie?'

His eyes, his cheeks, his whole face twitched as he tried not to cry. 'She wanted us to move away. For me to leave my job and do something different. To raise the baby the way we wanted.'

Annabelle had been right. Charlotte had wanted to rescue Freddie and let him live his life away from his family. Emotion wobbled her voice. 'She wanted you to go away?'

He nodded; head bowed. 'Yes. The only person she was worried about was you. She thought... She hoped that if she could get us to know one another, you might come with us. Start again somewhere new.'

Charlotte had wanted her to go with them? 'You can do that, Freddie. We can still do that. But you have to tell the police. You have to withdraw your confession. And you have to tell them who really hurt Charlotte.'

Freddie stared at his fingers. There were flecks of blood

around his thumb where he'd picked at his own skin. Shoulders hunched, he looked more like a schoolboy in detention than a man on a manslaughter charge. 'She used to talk about you a lot you know. Charlotte. Particularly after we found out she was pregnant.'

Joanna pressed her hand to her breastbone, where the pain was coming from. 'Did she?'

He nodded but didn't raise his head. 'All these stories about what it was like when she was young. All the things you did together. The three of you.'

During the long hours at the hospital, Joanna had been remembering those days herself. Memories that had been too painful to unwrap since Steve had passed away had assailed her as soon as she got in bed each night. Like beautiful bullets. 'I'm not sure I always got it right. I wanted... I wanted her to have a good life. To have everything she needed. To protect her from getting hurt. But I'm beginning to realise I went about it the wrong way.'

The more she'd pored over the memories of Charlotte's childhood, the more she'd realised that she'd tried to push her into the things that *she'd* wanted or needed. Not the things Charlotte wanted. If only she could go back twenty years and shake herself, take her own face and point it in the direction of what mattered.

Now Freddie looked up. 'That's not the way she saw it.'

Joanna sucked her bottom lip hard, trying not to cry. 'No? She didn't tell you about all the times I forced her into piano lessons, or extra tuition or made her take the eleven plus because I wanted her to go to the grammar school?'

He shook his head. 'She said that she knew that you only ever wanted the best for her.'

Joanna felt her face crumple. 'But I was so controlling.'

He smiled a watery smile. 'Yeah, she said that too.'

Joanna coughed a laugh. 'I can imagine.'

'But she also said that she was grateful.'

'Grateful?'

'Yes. And that she always knew that she was loved.'

Joanna couldn't stop the tears that spilled onto her cheeks. Isn't this what she'd always wanted to hear? Hadn't she said it enough times to Steve? *One day she'll thank me.* But not like this. Not like this. 'I wish I'd been different.'

Now Freddie's eyes were misted by memory. 'She told me about your holidays. That her dad would take her on all the water slides and buy the ice creams and play in the pool for hours on end.'

Steve had always been the fun parent. She remembered watching them in the pool, while she stayed guard on the sunbeds, piled up with the towels and hats and sun cream. 'He was a great dad.'

'And then she said you'd be the one who would find the best places to eat, who'd bring colouring books and pens so that she didn't get bored at dinner. And you'd be the one to arrange play-dates and take her to her friends' parties and invite them over for sleepovers. She kept saying that to me. We have to be a team, Freddie. When this baby comes, we have to be a team like my mum and dad were.'

This was almost too much to bear, but she was so hungry to hear it, like food for her starving soul. 'She really said that?'

He nodded. 'And she also said that I wasn't to leave all the discipline to her. That it wasn't fair on you that you always had to be bad cop. She knew that you got a rough deal.'

In all these years, she hadn't realised that Charlotte had known that. Had thought that Steve was her idol. 'She loved her dad so much.'

His laugh was more like a cough. 'I know. Believe me, I knew when she told me she was pregnant what massive shoes I'd have to fill. But she also said how much she loved you. She said that she wanted to be as good a mum as you were.'

That broke her. She covered her face with her hands. Wave after wave of grief poured over her. For all that she'd lost when her precious daughter was taken from her. Her clever, beautiful, kind and funny child. 'Oh, Charlotte. My poor girl.'

Once she regained herself, she reached across the table and placed her hand over Freddie's to stop him picking at his thumbnail, taking it back immediately when she realised the guard was looking over. 'I'm sorry that I didn't get to know you when she was alive.'

He swallowed. 'I could've tried harder, too. I just didn't want to push myself where I wasn't wanted.'

She could understand that. 'I know that you loved her.'

Another sob escaped from under the hand across his mouth. It seemed to come from deep within him. 'I really did.'

Whatever he'd just told her, however much she didn't want to cause either of them any further pain, she needed to keep pushing. 'And I know that you love Eliza.'

'I do.'

'She might need extra help, Freddie. Extra support. We don't know what this brain scan is going to show, but even if it's okay this time, there's no guarantees—'

'Whatever she needs. I can't be as good as Charlotte would've been, but I will do everything I can. Until I get out of here, I want her to be with you, Joanna. I want you to tell her all about Charlotte. About when she was little and when she grew up. How clever she was, how funny, how wonderful.'

It was impossible to keep the tears from falling. 'I want to tell her those things too.'

'Then apply for the guardianship. Please, Joanna. Not for me. For Charlotte. For Eliza.'

There wasn't a doubt in her mind that she would fight with her last breath to protect that little girl. But she needed more than that. 'I can only do it with your help. You need to get out of prison, Freddie. And the only way to do that is to tell the truth about what happened. You need to tell the police the truth.'

'If I do that, my mother will never forgive me. My whole family will cut me out.'

'Eliza is your family. And I will be your family, too. Think about her. Think about what Charlotte wanted for you both.'

His whole face was an open conflict. 'I want to do the right thing.'

She wiped her tears away with the back of her hand. 'The truth is the right thing. Being there for your daughter is the right thing. Do it for her.'

Relief shook through her as he nodded. If only she could throw her arms around him.

But there was still one problem. 'What about evidence? I'm worried that it'll just be your word against hers.'

For three ticks of the clock behind him on the wall, Freddie looked at her. He seemed to come to a decision. 'I might have something that will help.'

FORTY-THREE

When Joanna arrived at the ward the next morning, two doctors were waiting for her beside Eliza's bed: the young doctor she'd seen the other day and a woman, with long dark hair and a professional smile who looked to be in her early forties and must be the consultant. Joanna tried to read their faces. 'What is it? Is she okay?'

The consultant held out her hand to shake Joanna's. 'Dr Daniela. Pleased to meet you. I've reviewed the results from both the first and second set of scans and I can't see anything of concern. We'll obviously keep an eye on things, but I've just given Eliza a thorough check and she's making great progress.'

Joanna couldn't quite believe what she was hearing. Surely it couldn't be that easy? 'What about this mark on her brain? What is it?'

Dr James blushed. 'I'm afraid that was me. I misread it. I'm very sorry to have caused you alarm.'

She didn't know whether to shout at him or kiss him. He was so young. Learning a job like this – holding the lives of babies in your hands – must be so incredibly hard. The look on the face of the older doctor spoke volumes about the words they'd said: she didn't want to make it worse for him. 'Well, I'd rather you were over cautious than cavalier.'

He looked so relieved. In the culture of blame that everyone lived through he was probably expecting a very different response. He smiled at her gratefully. 'I'm really glad she's okay.'

Once the doctors were gone, Jenny appeared by the side of the crib, a broad smile on her face. Joanna frowned at her. 'I thought you were on the night shift last night? How come you're still here?'

'I was on the night shift, but I wanted to see what happened with little Eliza. Are you okay?'

Kindness never failed to decimate a brave face and Joanna dissolved into tears. Jenny rubbed her back. 'Come on, let's get your precious girl out for a cuddle. She'll make everything better.'

Jenny was right. Holding Eliza did make things feel better. She was all that mattered. 'Hey baby girl. You gave your granny a scare.'

Jenny stroked Eliza's arm as she rearranged the oxygen tube. 'Would you like me to lift her mask a little so that you see her properly?'

This was the first time anyone had even suggested that. It would be so wonderful to see her face. 'Is it safe?'

Jenny raised an eyebrow. 'I wouldn't suggest it if it wasn't. We're planning to move her from the mask to a nasal tube shortly. The doctor confirmed it today. I know you've had a scare just now, but she's doing well, Joanna. If she copes with the transition to a nasal tube, we might move her to the High Dependency Unit as soon as tomorrow.'

It had already been explained to Joanna that the High Dependency Unit – HDU – would be the next stage in Eliza's progress. 'That's great. Will you come with her?'

Jenny's laugh was surprisingly light and girlish. 'No. I

belong here. But I'll tell them to take special care of her. And you.'

She reached over and lifted Eliza's oxygen mask just a little. Still holding it close enough that Eliza would be getting the good of it, it meant that – for the first time – Joanna could see her whole face at once. Her tiny perfect nose, twitching pink mouth, soft cheeks with the smallest suggestion of a dimple, a little chin with the exact same shape as Charlotte's. For a moment, the sight of Eliza's face took her breath away. 'She looks so much like my daughter.'

Jenny tilted her head to see Eliza's face the right way up. 'And a little like her granny, I think.'

Joanna couldn't take her eyes from her. Having had only one child, she'd thought the depth of love she'd had for Charlotte would never be replicated. Her own emotions had always been tied so tightly to those of her daughter. Any of Charlotte's bubbles of excitement, crushing disappointments, searing joys, Joanna felt them right alongside her. The love of a mother for a child was the only perfect love in the world.

But now, as she looked at her tiny yet absolutely perfect granddaughter, she felt a rush of such overwhelming love that she didn't know how to contain it. A fierce need to protect and love this child consumed her with a power that she'd never known. More like worship than love, she knew that she would never ever let anything happen to her as long as she had breath in her body.

Jenny took Joanna's free hand and showed her how to hold the mask near to Eliza's face. 'I'll give you a few minutes.'

Eliza's eyes were screwed tightly shut until, as Joanna silently adored her, the hint of eyelashes flickered and opened, showing her grandmother the most beautiful translucent blue eyes. Tears formed in Joanna's own eyes at the very sight. 'Hello, beautiful.'

. . .

Until lunchtime, Joanna spent her time between Eliza's cot and the corridor outside the ward checking her phone for a response from DC Lineham. At midday, she'd just left the ward to get herself a cup of coffee when her mobile rang in her pocket. DC Lineham's name on the call display. She held her breath as she answered the phone. 'Hello?'

'Hi Joanna, it's Abbie. How's Eliza?'

It was kind of her to always ask about the baby first, but Joanna was desperate to find out what was happening with Freddie. Had he retracted his confession? Had he told them about his mother? Had they believed him? 'She's doing really well. Is there any news about the case?'

'Yes. That's why I'm calling. Would you rather we met and spoke in person?'

'No. It's fine. You can just tell me.'

'Okay. Mr Knight-Crossley has retracted his confession. He was in possession of evidence of another person being involved and that information is now forming part of our investigation.'

'Evidence? What evidence?'

'I'm afraid I can't be specific about that at present. But we will obviously keep you informed of any developments. I hope that this has not come as too much of a shock.'

Joanna had spent too long with DC Lineham to lie to her. 'No. It's not. That was why I left you those messages. Freddie told me yesterday. I know it's his mother. Will she be arrested? Can she get bail?'

There was a pause at the other end. Was that the sound of a door closing? Abbie's voice was lowered. 'I can tell you that someone has been arrested. But I probably shouldn't tell you that the same someone was packing a bag containing their passport, so the likelihood of them getting bail is rather small.'

Joanna felt almost sick with relief. 'She's going to prison? She's not going to get away with it?'

'I can't say too much to you, Joanna, in case it compromises the investigation. But the evidence we have is quite compelling.'

'What will happen to Freddie? Will he be released?'

'Yes. As soon as the paperwork can be processed. We may need to speak to him again, but he will likely be released tomorrow morning. He may be cautioned for wasting police time, but the coercion from his mother will be taken into consideration. Are you okay? I can imagine that all of this is a lot to process.'

With her heart threatening to thump its way out of her chest, it was difficult to answer. 'Yes. I'll be fine. I just want to know that the right person has been arrested for the crime.'

'Yes. So do we. I'll speak to you again when I have more information.'

Joanna held her mobile to her chest and waited for her breathing to go back to normal. What was this evidence that Freddie had? And would it be enough?

There was also the fact that Freddie himself was going to be out in the world again. Of course, he would want to come and see his daughter. How was that going to affect the social worker's decision about guardianship? Would his claim be stronger than Joanna's? And would it now be wrong of her to even try?

FORTY-FOUR

Within twenty-four hours, Freddie was released from prison and the first thing he did was come to the hospital. As Jenny had predicted, Eliza had been moved to HDU that morning and Joanna met him just outside the ward.

'Come and meet your daughter.'

Joanna hadn't realised how comfortable she'd become around all the medical paraphernalia, and how used to Eliza's size, until she saw Freddie holding her like she was made of the finest bone china. 'She's so tiny.'

She smiled at the amazement in his voice. Though he'd been sent photographs of the baby, they couldn't convey just how fragile she looked. She resisted the temptation to tell him that she looked far more robust now than when she was born. He didn't need to be reminded of what he'd missed. 'Can you see Charlotte in her?'

He dragged his face away from a moment to look at Joanna, before being pulled back to look at Eliza as if mesmerised. 'She does. I'm almost expecting her to tell me to change my shirt because this one makes me look like a banker.'

He knew Charlotte so well. This was an unexpected, and

wonderful, bonus to sharing these moments with him. Someone who would help to keep the memory of her wonderful daughter alive. 'She was a bossy boots.'

'No, Joanna.' He held up a finger and made a comical face at her. 'She just had high standards.'

His smiled wobbled at the edges and he returned his eyes to his daughter. Joanna could almost feel the vacuum where Charlotte should be standing beside him. Still, hearing him repeat the 'high standards' phrase that she'd heard Charlotte say so many times made her smile through inevitable tears. 'Oh, Eliza. Your mummy was a one off. Are you going to be bossing us around like she did in years to come?'

Freddie's voice was thick as he gazed at the precious bundle in his arms. 'I hope so. I really do.'

Watching him with his daughter shifted something in Joanna. This whole time, she'd seen him as her enemy, as Charlotte's mistake, as somehow incidental to the relationship she had with her grandaughter. For the first time, she was forced to see him for what he was: Eliza's father. But there was so much more to that than sharing the same beautiful blue eyes.

Would he be the kind of father that Steve had been for Charlotte? Would he be the one who told her she was his favourite girl in the world, teach her to ride a bike, to tie her shoelaces, wield a saw or a drill? Would he be there the first time she grazed her knee, failed an exam, broke her heart?

Though every inch of her wanted to be that for Eliza, seeing the way Freddie looked at his daughter – how much care he took to hold her exactly the way he'd been shown, his awe at her beauty and fragility – she had to accept that this was not her place to take. She'd spent the whole of Charlotte's life believing that she knew what was best for her. But now she had to accept – however hard it was – that Charlotte had known what was best for herself and would've known what would be best for her own child.

And that was the man in front of her. That was Freddie.

Fear crept over her at the very thought of this. She'd done nothing to make this man warm to her in the entire time he and Charlotte were together. If he were the one to be granted guardianship of Eliza – which, as her father, would surely be the only right decision – would he be inclined to give her any access to her grandaughter at all?

One of the nurses who she hadn't seen since the first couple of days on the ward broke into her thoughts. 'She's doing so well.'

A swell of pride made Joanna's chest ache. 'She's like her mother. As soon as you tell her she can't do something, she'll do whatever it takes to prove to you that she can.'

Freddie nodded at her with a smile and the nurse laughed. 'At the rate Eliza's going, she'll fly through HDU and be discharged early.'

Joanna froze for a moment. 'Early? I thought the babies stayed in until their due date?'

The nurse felt along the tube feeding oxygen into Eliza's tiny nose, checking for kinks or creases. 'It's usually about then. But sometimes babies take a bit longer and sometimes they are ready to go home earlier.'

She'd grinned at Joanna who was forced to respond in kind. Although her heart was thumping in her chest.

It was good news – wonderful news – that Eliza was doing so well. But if she was ready to be discharged before the social workers had run all their checks, neither she nor Freddie would have any hope of being awarded guardianship in time. Would that mean that Eliza was taken into care? She couldn't bear to think of her with strangers, however kind they were. She belonged with family.

She belonged with her father.

FORTY-FIVE

Joanna offered Freddie a lift home from the hospital and took the opportunity to find out more about Annabelle. 'The police told me that they've arrested your mother. Apparently, the evidence they have is much stronger. What is it?'

Freddie ran his hands through his hair. 'Charlotte's phone. Just before my mother came to the house, Charlotte had been using her phone to try and video her stomach. She'd been convinced that she could see the baby moving in her belly. But every time she tried to show me, she said the baby stopped doing it. I'd been teasing her, telling her that the pregnancy hormones were making her mind play tricks on her. When my mother arrived, Charlotte must've left the phone on the side. There's no video of what happened, but the audio is as clear as day. Their argument and then... what happened and even when I arrived.'

Joanna blinked a few times, trying to remove the image that appeared there. 'So how come the police couldn't find her phone?'

He flushed. 'I took it. When I called for an ambulance, I grabbed her phone first. The battery had died by then – she never remembered to charge it every night no matter how much I told her to – and I must've put it in my pocket when I took out mine to call the ambulance. When my solicitor met me at the police station, before they'd formally arrested me, I gave it to him and asked him to find out what was on it. I've handed it in to the police.'

She knew how much it must've cost him to do this. How alone he must feel right now. 'You did the right thing, Freddie.'

When she drew up outside the apartment building, he just stared out of the window at his former home. 'I can't face it.'

She followed his gaze to the smart block, watched a man in running clothes jog up to the door and let himself in. 'It looks okay in there. There's nothing that shows what happened.'

When he turned to face her, his face was pale. 'I don't want to be there without her. It's too... I know it's stupid, but the whole time I was in prison I could kind of pretend that she was still here.'

Joanna squeezed the steering wheel tightly, knowing exactly how that felt. Even now she'd sometimes look at the clock around 6 p.m. and expect Steve to walk through the door, a treat from the garage shop in his hand. Maybe it was that memory which made her offer. 'You could stay at my house tonight?'

She hadn't actually expected him to say yes, but the relief on his face was instant. 'Could I? Thank you.'

In her hallway, Freddie shuffled from foot to foot. 'You have a lovely home.'

His perfect manners made her smile. In her ear, Charlotte's voice said *I told you he was nice.* 'Well, I suppose anywhere would feel lovely after your last digs.'

He mirrored her smile. 'That's a good point. Where shall I put my bag?'

'Guest room. Upstairs, first door after the bathroom.'

As soon as he was out of sight, she called Sally to tell her he was here.

Sally's reaction surprised her. 'I think that's great.'

'Really?'

'Yes. It'll give you time to get to know him. He's the father of your grandaughter. He's in your life forever, Joanna.'

She hadn't thought about it quite like that. 'I suppose you're right. I've got to go. I can hear him coming down the stairs.'

'Okay. Call me later. And I was thinking I could pop over tomorrow night? I've had an idea I want to run by you.'

Freddie was hovering at the entrance to the sitting room so she smiled at him. 'Come in. Sit down and make yourself at home.'

'Thanks.'

On his way to the sofa, he paused at the mantelpiece and the pictures of Charlotte at various ages: gap-toothed school photo, ballet recital, graduation gown. He stared at one of a days-old Charlotte in Steve's arms with Joanna hovering at his elbow, her eyes on her precious newborn. She'd always loved Steve's face in this photograph, the mixture of pride and amazement at his good fortune.

'I'm not sure that I can do this, Joanna.'

She tore her eyes from the photograph and faced him. He'd looked so content – so right – holding Eliza that afternoon. But it was one thing holding a baby, another thing bringing one up day after day. Would he be able to do this on his own?

The same thoughts must've been crossing his mind. 'I don't know what to do with a baby. How am I going to raise her?'

Of course he was overwhelmed, having just been discharged from prison and met his daughter for the first time. Her heart broke for him, this sweet, lost man who her daughter had loved. 'She's going to be in hospital for a while yet, you've got plenty of time to learn how to change a nappy and feed her.'

He ran his hands through his dark hair. 'They're not the

things I'm worried about. It's everything else. The things you can't just learn from someone showing you a couple of times. You'd be so much better at this than me. Maybe she should live with you. Maybe you should still apply for the guardianship.'

Joanna would like that more than anything else in the world. But that didn't make it right. 'You're her father, Freddie.'

Keeping his eyes on that photograph of Steve holding Charlotte, he shook his head. 'Biologically, yes. But not in the eyes of the law. My solicitor says that I may still be charged with perverting the course of justice. Either way, it's not going to look good on my record when social services are making a decision about whether I get guardianship.'

It was still mind-boggling that Freddie didn't automatically get parental rights. In this day and age, with the ease of DNA tests, it seemed positively archaic to be punishing him because he and Charlotte hadn't been married. 'You need to speak to Eliza's social worker.'

'Or maybe you should still try for guardianship and I can help?'

He was making this difficult to fight. 'Is that what you want?'

He turned to her with tears in his eyes. 'No. What I want is for me and Charlotte to raise Eliza together. To move up to Norfolk like we'd planned and buy a small house with a garden. Live in a village with a nice little school for Eliza and a country pub where Charlotte can persuade them to have music nights once a month so that she can still sing and play. And we would invite our friends to come and play too and they would sleep on the floor of our lounge and tell us how lucky we are to have created such a perfect life.'

None of this was coming from the top of his head. She could imagine him and Charlotte concocting this dream between the two of them. Just as she and Steve had done when she was pregnant with Charlotte and she'd laid on the sofa with her head in his lap, dreaming of their future lives together.

'Oh, Freddie. I know it's hard. But you can do this. And I'll be there to help you. Charlotte believed in you. She tried to tell me so many times how wonderful you were. She wouldn't have planned that future with you if she didn't believe you could do it.'

'But what if I can't? What if I get it wrong?'

She took a deep breath. 'We all get it wrong. I know that better than anyone. But the most important thing is that we try our best to do it right.'

They stood like that for a while, in quiet. She almost jumped when he spoke again. His voice was soft. 'Will you help me? Can we do this together?'

If Joanna's solicitor was surprised that she wished to change her application so that Eliza's guardianship was to be held jointly with Freddie, she didn't show it.

Five days later, Freddie attended the meeting at the solicitor's office and, between them, they explained the plan.

Pen poised, Louise scanned the notes she'd taken while they spoke. 'Just so that I have this correctly. Joanna is selling her house, Freddie is moving out of his uncle's apartment and you are pooling your resources and moving together?'

'Yes.' Joanna nodded. 'Just not together in the same house.'

They'd talked about it at length. Since that first night, Freddie had stayed on in Joanna's guest room and, after days spent with Eliza, each evening they'd tried to work out the best solution.

Joanna hadn't wanted to offend him, but they both needed to be honest. 'I think it would be strange for us to live in the same house.'

He'd agreed pretty quickly. 'You're right. But it would be

great for Eliza if you lived close by. And I'd love some help with childcare when I'm at work.'

Joanna wanted to be close enough to see Eliza whenever she could. 'I don't have a job to give up and, if I sell the house, I should be able to get something small and have enough to help you out with a deposit and keep me going for a while.'

'Well, seeing as I work for the family business, I don't think I have a job anymore, so that's my first priority.'

'Second priority,' Joanna had corrected him.

He'd smiled. 'Yes. Second priority.'

The solicitor checked her notes again. 'Two residences. Preferably close together. That sounds good. But they are going to want to see evidence of earnings, Freddie.'

Sally had come through for them on that. Her interiors business was taking off and she was always looking for painters and decorators and, though she usually used sub-contractors, she'd offered to take him on a permanent contract.

Joanna hadn't wanted to take advantage of her friend. 'Are you sure? This is your business, Sally. You can't just do this as a favour to me.'

Over FaceTime, Sally had waved away her concern. 'Of course, I'm sure. With Harry not living at home, I'm intending on taking on a lot more business to keep my mind off of whatever he's getting up to. And I'm not doing it for you, anyway. I'm doing it for Charlotte, so let's hear no more about it.'

It did mean that they were going to have to change their destination from Norfolk to Hertfordshire. But it came with the added bonus that Joanna would see more of her best friend. Lucy and Rachael had promised to visit Eliza wherever they moved to and Freddie assured her that his friends – especially Dominic – were always looking for a nice long drive for their latest car.

The solicitor ticked two entries on a list to the right of her notes. 'That means accommodation and finances are looking okay. What's the latest from the CPS?'

After a tense couple of days, it transpired that there was to be no charge of obstructing the course of justice. Joanna had no idea whether her impassioned plea to DC Lineham had been passed up the chain of command or whether someone had decided that Freddie had been punished enough. She was just grateful it meant that he had no criminal record.

The solicitor ran her pen down her notes one last time. 'Well, I think I have everything I need and you've completed the forms. I'll do my very best for you.'

The next few weeks were full of joy and fear, laughter and tears. Eliza got stronger every day and Freddie's confidence in caring for her grew alongside it. There were many good days – when she no longer needed oxygen to breathe, when Lucy and Rachael met her for the first time, when Freddie was allowed to lift her out of the crib himself as a nurse watched – which they shared in together. And there were also bad days when they would see another baby go home with their mum and dad and feel the pain of knowing again that Charlotte should be here to see her little girl.

For both of them, there were meetings with the social worker and the solicitor and more forms to complete. Each time, they hoped for news, were disappointed that they had to wait for police checks and other information to make its way through the system.

Freddie started his job with Sally when Eliza was eight weeks old, and headed up to Hertfordshire every Monday to Friday. Despite Sally offering him a bed in her third bedroom, he insisted on driving back to the hospital every night to see Eliza and read her a bedtime story before he came back to Joanna's guest room until five o'clock the next morning when he left to drive back to Hertfordshire and work. A fact that Joanna made sure the social worker knew anytime she had to speak to her.

While they were waiting to hear from the social worker, Joanna's house was on the market and having viewings. In one of her many trawls online, she'd found two houses on the same street in a pretty village only thirty minutes away from Sally.

When they finally got the news that the joint guardianship had been approved, they both wept. One week later, Eliza came home.

FORTY-SIX

Freddie drove home from the hospital so slowly that Joanna was seriously concerned that they might get pulled over by the police for causing a traffic jam.

In the back with Eliza, so tiny that she was only just big enough for her car seat, Joanna couldn't believe that she was finally coming home.

'Is she okay, back there?' Freddie called over his shoulder. 'That was quite a big speed bump.'

'She's absolutely fine.'

At the house, she waited for Freddie to slide the car seat out before getting out the other side, not wanting to let Eliza out of her sight for a moment. Then she let them both into the house.

It'd been impossible to get the house sold before Eliza came out of hospital, but now she was glad that they had a few more weeks here. It felt right that Eliza should see the home that Charlotte grew up in. She followed Freddie through to the lounge where he placed the car seat in the middle of the carpet and looked at her, then at Joanna.

'What do we do now?'

She had to laugh. 'Get her out of her seat and show her around.'

Memories assailed her of the day she'd brought Charlotte home from hospital. Steve carrying her from room to room, introducing her to every ornament and picture frame.

Freddie crouched down beside his daughter and clicked her harness open, reaching to lift her out of the seat as if she were made of bone china. 'Are you waking up, little Eliza?'

Her fingers itched to reach for the baby, but this was his moment; she was grateful that she got to share in it. He'd let her indulge herself in choosing an outfit for Eliza to travel home in. Knowing Charlotte had never liked pastel colours she'd chosen a navy blue striped sleepsuit, with feet that looked like little blue boots. 'Shall we start upstairs?'

Freddie climbed the stairs so gradually that it took them twice as long to get to the top. If only Charlotte could see the care he was taking with their daughter, how precious she was to him, how much he wanted to get it right. Touring her around the landing, the bathroom, and stopping to show her the picture of the seaside in the hall.

Her smile turned down at the edges when they entered Charlotte's bedroom. Freddie had been staying in the guest room, so it was still unchanged from when Charlotte had slept here every night.

'This was your mummy's room.'

The tremble in Freddie's voice made her heart ache. She'd learned just how much he'd loved Charlotte over the last few weeks. He'd told her all about how they met and how – he devoutly believed – he'd fallen in love with her at first sight. She'd told him stories from Charlotte's childhood and he'd lapped them up like an eager puppy. He was still so young. They'd both been so young. It was difficult not to torture herself with thoughts of what might've been if she hadn't been so stubborn about getting to know him when Charlotte had wanted her to.

She stepped forwards and slipped her finger into Eliza's little hand. 'If these walls could talk, they'd tell you all about your mummy and the things she got up to.'

Freddie wiped away a tear with the back of his free hand. 'I wish she could be here. I wish she could be bringing her home with me.'

They would both be wishing that forever. Every milestone, every celebration, every ordinary day. It would never go away. 'We'll make sure that Eliza knows all about her. She'll know how wonderful her mum was and how much she would've loved her.'

Freddie's watery smile squeezed her heart. 'She did love her. From the moment we knew she was pregnant.'

'And that's what we'll tell Eliza.'

Freddie nodded, then turned and left the room to go downstairs again, Joanna lingered, her hand pressed to her chest. Soft enough that Freddie wouldn't hear her on his way back down, she whispered into the air,

'I've got them, my darling Charlotte. I'll make sure they're okay.'

EPILOGUE

Joanna pulled a couple of leaves from the bottom of the rose bush. 'This yellow rose bush is your mummy's because it's called the Charlotte Rose and it has the most beautiful scent.'

She pulled a bloom closer to Eliza's nose. This week, she'd learned to sit up completely unaided, just in time for her first birthday party this afternoon. On a blanket, she was content to listen to Joanna's commentary on the garden while running her left hand through the grass.

'And this red one is called Grandpa's Rose, but I like to call it Grandpa Steve, because that was *your* grandpa's name.'

Joanna sat back on her heels and watched Eliza pulling at the grass. 'Your grandpa would've loved you, Eliza Charlotte Knight-Crossley. He would have told you crazy stories and built you dens and taken you paddling in the sea.'

Some days she still felt very sad. Eliza brought so much joy to her life, but she would find herself wanting to tell Steve about each new thing she was doing each day. The doctors had told them not to expect Eliza to hit the milestones at the same age as her peers because she was effectively three months younger in her development. But she continued to grow and thrive and charm everyone she met with her big blue eyes and easily won laugh.

The back door opened and Freddie appeared carrying a large white box. 'I've picked up the cake. Thanks for having the party here. There're toys all over the place at ours. Should we put her new dress on? They'll be here soon.'

Joanna lived four houses down from Freddie and Eliza, close enough that they would eat together each night when Freddie collected Eliza after work, but they still had their own space. She was conscious that this might not last forever – one day he was going to meet someone and make a new family – but Joanna had decided to enjoy it while it lasted. She scooped Eliza up into her arms. 'Let's get you ready to receive your guests.'

Sally, Graham and Harry were the first to arrive.

'Hi Harry. So lovely to see you.'

Harry seemed to grow another inch every time she saw him which, now they lived in Hertfordshire, was a lot more often. He flicked his long fringe from his eyes, gave Joanna his usual high five and then made a beeline for Eliza, who patted the grass either side of her in delight at his appearance. How was it that children – even babies as young as Eliza – had an instinct for the people they could trust? Harry's mere presence made her face light up.

Sally hugged her. 'You're lucky he made an appearance. Apparently he now has a girlfriend in his block. It's very difficult to get him to come out with his boring parents.' She sounded equal parts sad and proud.

Graham kissed Joanna on the cheek, then winked at her. 'He's a charmer, like his father.'

Five minutes later, she opened the front door to Rachael and Lucy bearing a gift each. 'But they're both from the two of us,' Lucy told Joanna.

After kissing Freddie hello, and a high five each from Harry, they sat in front of Eliza on the grass and Rachael held out her parcel. 'Which one do you want to open first, perfect goddaughter?'

Eliza scrunched at the wrapping with her pudgy little hand, blinking at the noise it made, and Rachael helped her to open it to reveal a huge yellow teddy bear almost twice the size of Eliza. Rachael made Eliza laugh by tickling her nose with the bear's soft paw. 'I wanted to get you a pink one, baby girl, but I knew that your mummy would've been very cross with me.'

Charlotte hated pink. It was so precious that Eliza would be surrounded by people that could tell her everything about her mother, keep her alive.

'And speaking of your mummy, we made you this.' Lucy tore a hole into the front of the second gift, putting the end of the paper into Eliza's hand and helping her tear it. It looked to be a frame of some kind.

When she turned it around, Joanna gasped. A collage of pictures of Rachael, Lucy and Charlotte. In school uniform, on a night out, playing in their band. Three beautiful girls, not a care in the world, living and loving life and each other. She'd give everything she had to see the three of them laughing like that again. 'Oh, girls. That's such a wonderful thing to do.'

Freddie had to clear his throat twice before he could thank them. 'It's amazing. I'll put it up in her room tonight.'

Rachael had tears in her eyes, too. 'We want Eliza to know how special her mum was.'

Yes. There were already photographs of Charlotte in every room, but this one would be extra special. 'I'd like to take a photo of it, too.'

Lucy smiled up at her. 'We also made you one. It's in the car.'

These girls. She hoped their mothers knew how wonderful they were.

Charlotte had left a hole in her life that would never be

filled. Joanna had learned to live with the ache, not expect it to go. Long conversations with Freddie had healed a lot of the guilt she felt about her failings as a mother. Many of the boundaries that Charlotte had railed against, were the self-same things that she'd quoted to Freddie as evidence of her mother's love. This time around, as a grandmother, she had a different perspective. 'As long as she's happy,' she would tell Freddie, 'you're doing a good job.'

Freddie clapped his hands. 'Right then, it is time for birthday cake. Can you bring the birthday girl, Jo?'

Joanna scooped Eliza up from the blanket and tickled her neck with her nose; her giggle always made her heart happy. Before leaving the garden, she glanced back at the yellow Charlotte Rose and, as she always did, blew her beautiful daughter a kiss.

A LETTER FROM EMMA

Thank you for choosing to read this, my fourteenth book! I hope you've enjoyed getting to know Joanna, Charlotte and Freddie as much as I enjoyed writing their story.

If you did enjoy it and want to keep up to date with all my latest releases, just sign up at the following link. Your email address will never be shared and you can unsubscribe at any time.

www.bookouture.com/emma-robinson

I doubt there is anything more terrifying to a parent than losing a child, so some of these scenes were really difficult to write. My children know when I'm writing sad scenes because I randomly appear in their rooms and hug them tightly. I usually write about mothers of younger children, so it has been interesting to explore what it's like to be the mother of an adult daughter. As my own children get older, I'm realising how difficult it is to let them make their own decisions – and mistakes – so I do sympathise with Joanna and her fears for Charlotte.

Although there is tragedy in this book, there is also – as in all my books – hope for the future. In my mind, Joanna and Freddie will spend the rest of their lives making sure that Eliza knows just how much her mother would've loved her.

Emma

KEEP IN TOUCH WITH EMMA

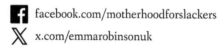 facebook.com/motherhoodforslackers
x.com/emmarobinsonuk

ACKNOWLEDGEMENTS

As always, thank you to my wonderful editor Susannah Hamilton for knowing exactly what the plot needs! I've really loved working with you and learning from you and wish you all the very best in your exciting new role.

Thank you to Sarah Hardy and the rest of the PR team and to everyone at Bookouture. You are all amazing to work with and I feel very lucky to be here.

For helping me to avoid any embarrassing errors and typos, thank you to Donna Hillyer and Deborah Blake for your attention to detail and to my good friend Carrie Harvey for checking the final proofs when I can't even read my own name any longer. Thank you Alice Moore for this brilliant cover.

This book required a lot of research and I want to say a HUGE thank you to Louise Margiotta, Nina Barnard, Daniela Rader and Brendan Ryan for sharing your time, experience and knowledge with me. Any mistakes are mine.

Being a writer means always learning and honing your craft. While working on this book, I've been part of a brilliant online writing group taught by Anstey Harris and some of the sections of this book were written as part of that. Thank you for your great teaching, Anstey and thanks to all the members of the group from whom I've learned so much.

The book is dedicated to my great friend Sarah Stonehouse. Who always reminds me of how far I've come when I most need to hear it. Thank you for being my friend and a wonderful godmother to my now not-so-little babies.

Lastly, as always, to my family. I love you.

PUBLISHING TEAM

Turning a manuscript into a book requires the efforts of many people. The publishing team at Bookouture would like to acknowledge everyone who contributed to this publication.

Audio
Alba Proko
Sinead O'Connor
Melissa Tran

Commercial
Lauren Morrissette
Hannah Richmond
Imogen Allport

Cover design
Alice Moore

Data and analysis
Mark Alder
Mohamed Bussuri

Editorial
Susannah Hamilton
Nadia Michael